Aylen Isle

by

Aud Supplee

Winnie and the "Wizard", Book Three

Cover Art by *Kristian Norris*

The Wild Rose Press, Inc.
PO Box 708
Adams Basin, NY 14410-0708
Visit us at www.thewildrosepress.com

Publishing History
First Edition, 2024
Trade Paperback ISBN 978-1-5092-5595-5
Digital ISBN 978-1-5092-5596-2

Winnie and the "Wizard", Book Three
Published in the United States of America

Dedication

To Brian for accepting my process. To Gretchen for relating to my process. To Antigone for laughing with me through the process. And to Jo, editor extraordinaire, for bringing order to my process and helping me eradicate dangling modifiers.

Prologue

Magic fluctuated whenever the Guardians of Time, known as the Sisters Three, congregated. When the news reached them that a Watcher had placed an unauthorized time-hold between the alternate worlds of Earth and Hutra, the trio believed their reunion worth the risk.

The sisters sat around a small table at a nondescript café outside of time. They had barely voiced their concerns about the Watcher when an unexpected pop and sizzle inside their cloaks sent them leaping from their chairs. Each shoved her hand into her respective pocket. They simultaneously withdrew three-inch-long sticks. They matched the size and width of the palm-sized telescope-shaped objects previously stored there. The missing devices, called Frama-scopes, allowed the possessor to journey between alternate worlds, not that Guardians of Time needed them. They kept the scopes only to safeguard them from misuse. They never expected to lose them all at once.

Bayla, the middle sister, gasped. "What sorcery is this?"

Ava, the eldest, gazed from one sister to the other. "This takes priority. We must find the thief and retrieve our Frama-scopes before they fall into the wrong hands."

They settled back into their chairs. Ava turned to Catrell, the youngest. "Have you brought the conjuring bowl, Sister?"

The ruddy-cheeked woman beamed. "It's in my bag of wonderment."

Bayla let out an indignant sniff. "Bag with no end, more like. We'll be here all the week whilst you rummage through it."

"Hush, dear," Ava said gently.

Catrell hefted the magical bag onto her lap. She plunged a chubby hand inside and retrieved a golden candlestick. She grinned apologetically and placed it on the café table. Next, she removed three brass doorknobs.

Bayla let out an exasperated puff of air and shifted in her seat.

After adding a second candlestick, a wooden ladle, and a black knit shawl to the growing pile, she finally uncovered a battered copper bowl and set it on the table.

"Use my wand," Bayla said. "We haven't the time for you to go riffling for yours."

Catrell accepted it with a serene smile. "So kind of you, dear." She dipped the wand into the empty bowl and stirred once to the left, then twice to the right. Pale smoke rose from the bowl, revealing the image of a teenaged boy with sun-yellow locks. He bent forward and laid three short sticks on the ground. The lad's brow furrowed in determination. His thin lips moved, suggesting a murmured incantation. Instantly, the sticks transformed into three Frama-scopes.

"Our meeting is creating a magic vortex!" Bayla cried out.

Ava nodded. "So we mustn't tarry. Let's trust that the Watcher is no threat to the timeline. At least for now, the lad appears unaware that he's gained additional magic over what he already had. I'll have a word with him. And while I'm out and about, I'll retrieve our scopes. Catrell, you can—" She paused. Her younger sister's attention seemed unduly focused on the bottom of her conjuring bowl. "Something wrong, Cat?"

She looked up. "Didn't we assign a special Watcher to the one called Krell? He's poised to start a conflict between two territories in a world classified as Frama-7."

"We never should have allowed him free rein," Bayla muttered.

"While I understand your dismay," Ava said, "we cannot discount the good he's done in spite of himself."

"From the looks of it," Catrell added, "he's got Bayla's Frama-scope."

"Mine?" Bayla peered into the bowl.

"Sisters," Ava announced, "we must separate before Krell catches wind of our vortex."

Bayla muttered an incantation and disappeared.

Ava sighed. "She's left without an assignment, but I'm sure she has a plan. Cat, you know what needs to be done on your end."

The younger sister's body pulsed with eagerness. "I do indeed. I'll create a prophecy on Frama-7. And I know just the young female general who must fulfill it."

Ava smiled. "Off we go, then."

Both sisters vanished with a poof.

Chapter 1

After a much-needed shower and a change into fresh jeans, a T-shirt, and pink hoodie, fourteen-year-old Winnie Harris poked her head through the open doorway to the screened porch of her family's beach house. Her friend and fellow time-tear traveler, Kip, and her little stepbrother, Mikey, hadn't moved since she left them fifteen minutes ago. Both reclined on matching lounge chairs, their eyes closed.

She guessed their latest adventure to the alternate world of Hutra had exhausted them as much as it had her. Even Mikey's newest companion, Stompy, a toad he'd brought back from that other world, hadn't moved from the boy's shoulder. Eager for her own rest, Winnie strode to her room and flopped on the bedspread. She didn't even bother to brush off the sandy footprints Mikey had left behind at the start of their last adventure.

Sleep came immediately. The dream came later. How much later, she couldn't tell, but it had to be a dream. How else could she explain the appearance of an unfamiliar girl, barely in her teens, admiring herself in the mirror above Winnie's bureau? The stranger wore a white brocaded gown with puffy sleeves. Even without a crown, the outfit screamed "princess." Winnie propped up on her elbows and studied the girl.

Her thick black hair pulled into a tight bun exposed flawless beige skin. Long lashes framed eyes so vibrantly green they reminded Winnie of early summer leaves. The girl's expressive black eyebrows, perfectly shaped nose, and full lips made her the most beautiful girl Winnie had ever seen.

The girl turned, facing Winnie. "Oh good, we can talk now. My name is Princess Gwenevieve deEste of Aylen Isle. Your brother promised me you'd help."

Winnie sat up all the way. "Ha! I knew you were a princess."

The girl clasped her hands together. "General Windemere, I've come to beg an immense favor of you."

Winnie's inner warrior beamed with pride. If a princess needed a general, how could she resist? "I'm at your service, Your Highness. What do you need?"

The princess offered a gracious nod. "Thank you. Despite General Takka's assurances you'd help, I worried he might have overstated. He appears to be currently trapped within the form of a small child."

Winnie nodded in understanding. She'd barely believed it when she learned an adult general from an alternate world called Frama-12 lived inside her stepbrother's six-year-old body.

"I too," said the princess, "find myself housed within a form not of my choosing."

"Sorry to contradict, Your Highness, but Mikey, or General Takka, chose the body he's in right now. But let's stay on topic. Did you say you're in a different form?"

"What you see before you is my original shape. Outside of this dream, I've fallen under an enchantment. I need to go home for help to change back. If you would be kind enough to transport me to my world, Frama-7, all should go well."

5

"My world, Earth, is also known as Frama-11. I have a scope that opens time tears so we can travel through Framas, but if your home world is Frama-7, I'm not sure how to get there. Alternate worlds stand side by side. I think that means I can only visit worlds beside this one. That would be Framas twelve and ten."

"I'm surprised General Takka never mentioned the scope's ability to Frama-hop through multiple worlds. You just need a jump point, and I know where one is."

Winnie cocked her head. "No disrespect, but if you're from Frama-7, how do you even know Mikey? I mean General Takka. Through dream messages like this one? As far as I know, he's never traveled to your world."

Princess Gwenevieve sighed deeply. "He rescued me while you were at Frama-10 and brought me back to your world."

Winnie's mouth dropped open. "You're Stompy?"

The princess grimaced. "That's what the general named me. I didn't have the heart to correct him."

"Now you mention it, I think Mikey did say you, or rather Stompy, wanted to go to Frama-7. Kip and I thought he made that up. I don't know if you know this, and no offense, Your Highness, but Mikey thinks you're a dude."

The girl's lips curled into a sad smile. "I didn't want to jeopardize our friendship by contradicting him. I thought we could wait to tell him after we've located Argamel."

Winnie had already encountered her share of crazies in the two alternate worlds she visited. But a fairy-tale world? The possibility sounded too nutty to pass up. "Is Argamel the prince who can unlock your enchantment?"

Princess Gwenevieve bristled. "Who needs a prince at a time like this? Argamel happens to be my father's conjurer. He's sure to have a spell to change me back."

"In my world, there's a story about a princess who kisses an enchanted frog, and he turns back into a prince."

The girl folded her arms. "That has got to be the most ridiculous thing I have ever heard."

"More ridiculous than being stuck inside a toad right now?"

She slumped against the bureau. "You're right. I'm in a most ridiculous situation."

"Probably not the most ridiculous. I've seen some weird things traveling through time tears. Frama-12 has a giant toad for a queen." An idea suddenly struck her. "Mikey's originally from there. And he's a prince! General Takka was a toad prince before his essence traveled through a time tear and landed in Mikey's body. Are you sure a kiss won't work? Mikey would probably do it. He cares about you."

"I'm sorry, but kisses are not the answer. We're running out of time. Before you wake from this dream message, I must show you a few things about the jump point."

In an eyeblink, the pair faced the shrub on the right side of Winnie's beach house.

"If you point your Frama-scope toward that bush, you should find a time tear. You might need to expand it to fit through."

Winnie's scope hung from a ribbon she kept hidden inside her shirt. She pulled it out and peered through the miniature telescope-like device. A robin-egg-blue bubble, visible only through the scope, hovered three inches above the ground. She twisted the scope's central ring, enlarging the bubble.

Both stepped through the opening and into the lush backyard of an alternate world. A dozen trees, covered in bright-green leaves, shaded the sunny area. A two-story house, hidden mainly by fir trees, stood on a small incline. The princess, now dressed in a brown tunic and beige britches, pointed to a bush fifty yards away. Its thin leafy branches cascaded to the ground. "That's the entry point."

They strode across the lawn to the bush. The princess separated the willow-like branches and crawled inside.

Winnie followed her into the shadowy interior. A break at the back of the bush revealed dazzling white light. They passed through the brightness to another world with a sandy beach and calm turquoise ocean.

"Wow! I didn't see this coming!"

The princess spread her arms. "Welcome to my world and my father's kingdom. This is Aylen Isle."

Winnie grinned and nodded. "I like it."

"When you wake and come to the jump point, the season might—"

An unexpected rat-a-tat drowned out the princess's voice. Winnie turned toward the sound. "Did you hear that?"

"I didn't hear anything. Maybe it was a bird. Pay it no mind. I've a sister—"

The urgent rapping pulled Winnie's attention from the other girl's directions. Did all the birds in this world make jackhammer noises?

Winnie jumped awake in bed, alone in her room. The loud knocking persisted from her closed window.

She rolled toward the sound. A big ugly beak battered the glass.

"Bird!" She sprang out of bed and waved at it.

The alien creature, with its black swan neck, hawk's beak, and buzzard's body, had followed her through the time tear when she left Hutra, also classified as Frama-10.

"Stop! You'll break it! I'm coming out."

She jammed bare feet into her sneakers and dashed from her room, past the sleeping boys, to the outside. Around the corner, the oversized black bird barely had room to perch on her windowsill. In her rush to stop him, she almost collided with a stout woman whose head barely reached Winnie's shoulders. A pair of rectangular glasses rested on the tip of the older lady's little pink nose. Ordinarily, a stranger hovering by her beach house would have bothered her. Still, the woman's twinkling, fairy-godmother eyes put her at ease.

Bird fluttered from the window and strutted to Winnie.

The fairy godmother nodded. "I see the azzinfin is with you, then?"

"You know his name? We've been calling him Bird."

"Azzinfin is the bird's breed. I've never known of his kind to interact with humans, but he seems quite fond of you."

Bird preened himself at Winnie's side.

"When we first met in Frama-10, I worried about him, but he helped us out."

"He's not from that world," the woman said. "I'm guessing he got caught in the Esten Winds and landed there. You've probably gathered that he wishes to go home. Unfortunately, his internal radar got scrambled. He'll need help to find his way."

"And we're happy to do it. I think that's why he came through the time tear with us." But who was this lady who knew about Bird and Framas? She leaned her weight from one foot to the other, unsure how to ask. "Um…so…"

The woman flashed an affectionate smile. "I'm so terribly sorry, General Windemere. I was so focused on our avian friend that I forgot to introduce myself properly." She held out her hand. "I'm Sister Ava of the Sisters Three. We're the Guardians of Time."

Winnie shook the woman's hand, bewildered. How could a guardian of anything know her off-Earth title?

Sister Ava let out a trill of a laugh. "I can see by your eyes I've quite surprised you. My sisters and I have that effect on people. Nevertheless, I am pleased that you'll help Bird. He lives on a special diet found only in his world."

"He seems to like our fish."

"Fish probably don't offer enough of the proper nutrients. He can't stay away much longer."

"How much time does he have?"

"His feathers are still black, so it's not quite crucial yet. When the tips turn gray, you'll know it's time to help him home. So you mustn't linger over your other quest."

Winnie blinked in surprise. "I have another quest?"

"Your dear brother brought a friend through the time tear after your last visit. This friend is under an unfortunate curse."

"Princess Gwen DeeSomething?"

Sister Ava beamed at her. "Princess Gwenevieve deEste. Exactly so!"

"I just had a dream message from her asking us to take her to Frama-7 so she can get turned back into her normal shape."

"And you've agreed?"

"Like you said, she's my brother's friend. I couldn't say no."

"How splendid! Now we must call the rest of your merry band."

The bird let out a screech as if calling to Kip and Mikey.

Chapter 2

Kip jumped awake with a start, his pulse thudding in his ears. His surroundings hadn't changed since he first settled onto the lounge chair on Winnie's screened porch. The calming whoosh of the surf sounded from outside. He must have imagined the alien shriek.

He shifted his gaze to the right where Mikey blissfully slept on the lounger beside his. The silly toad seated on the boy's left shoulder stared at him a bit too intently for his comfort.

He sat up and scowled at the toad. "What?"

Mikey yawned and blinked awake. "Huh?"

A second screech sounded. Kip shot to his feet. "Bird's in trouble."

Mikey also rose but with less urgency. "He's just calling us."

Unconvinced, Kip dashed off the porch in the direction of the sound. Winnie and Bird stood together, perfectly safe. A short, round, gray-haired woman faced them. Her gentle smile reminded him of a cookie-baking gran.

He took a deep breath to settle his nerves. *What is wrong with me?*

Mikey joined the group and bowed low. "Guardian."

The woman bowed in return. "Greetings, General. And hello to you, young wizard. I am Sister Ava, a time guardian. Now that we're together, perhaps one of you can help me." Sister Ava removed a three-inch-long stick from her cloak. "Does anyone recognize this?"

Kip couldn't be one hundred percent cert, but it resembled one of the small sticks he'd used to fashion three fake Frama-scopes during their last adventure. He bit his lip, unsure how to reply.

Winnie answered first. "A little stick? I mean, I recognize it came off a tree."

Sister Ava stared kindly at Winnie. "It also happens to be the same length and thickness of a Frama-scope. If I'm not mistaken, the scope hanging from the ribbon around your neck belongs to me."

How did she know they had scopes? He instinctively touched the front of his T-shirt. Underneath the material, another Frama-scope hung around his neck. He'd attached it to a long shoelace.

Winnie produced hers from inside her pink hoodie. "I earned this one. Plus, I saw it glow pink, which means it belongs to a girl. I'm the girl."

"You are quite correct that ownership can be proven by the color that radiates from a Frama-scope. Your personal scope, though, glows orange. Mine exudes a pink light."

"Orange? That can't be right."

Kip shifted from one foot to the other. He'd known all along the scope in Winnie's possession was supposed to be a decoy. Since it worked, he never felt the need to tell her it wasn't hers.

"I'll grant you," said the woman, "you might not have noticed the glow. There's another way to prove ownership. I believe your scope is unmarked. Mine is engraved."

Winnie turned the device over. Kip leaned toward it.

Unintelligible markings decorated the shiny gold tube.

"It's not written in English, of course," the guardian said. "Roughly translated, it reads, 'From the loft to the lea.' "

Winnie frowned. "How did I get your scope? We've never met."

Sister Ava stared directly at Kip. His heart thumped to an uneasy beat. *She knows.*

Now Winnie faced him. "This isn't my scope?"

Kip shrugged. Nothing since he'd woken made sense. Where had this strange woman come from? And why would she claim a scope he'd created through magic belonged to her?

Winnie hesitated, then returned the scope to its alleged owner. "Does that mean my scope was the one that broke on the rocky platform in Hutra?"

"Quite possibly. If you've brought it back with you, I can easily repair it."

"I have the two scopes that broke when we were in that world." Mikey removed one from each of his front pockets.

One damaged scope belonged to Winnie. The other belonged to their nemesis, Thaddeus Krell. Mikey had given Krell one of Kip's fake scopes. At least Kip had thought they were fake when he created them from the short sticks he'd found in the forest. He'd been just as surprised as the others when Krell successfully opened a time tear with one of Kip's scopes and vanished into another world.

Winnie examined the scopes in Mikey's open palms. She looked up. "They're almost the same color."

"Of course they are," Kip said. "They're all made of gold."

Winnie shook her head. "I meant the way they glow."

Kip squinted at them. "I don't see a glow."

"Mercy me," Sister Ava said. "As a rule, the average eye can't see the glow. General Windemere, you've got the sight. Well done!"

Winnie grinned, looking pleased with herself.

"The glow from these scopes is similar," Sister Ava said, "because they came from the same region in Frama-12. Of course, Krell came into possession of the one that glows dark orange through theft. You, dear General, received the yellow-orange scope as a reward for valor in combat."

The girl blushed. "I don't know if what I did counted as valor."

Sister Ava pocketed one scope and waved a hand over the other. "That should have repaired it." She aimed the scope at a nearby bush. "Yes, there we are. Back working again." She returned it to Winnie. "You'll do well to retie it to your ribbon, General, so as not to lose it."

Winnie focused the scope on the same bush. She must have seen something because she retied the repaired scope to her ribbon and hung it around her neck. "Thank you."

"Now that you have your Frama-scope back, you can help the azzinfin return to his home world."

"We don't even know what that is," Kip said.

"She's referring to Bird," Winnie replied. "Sister Ava, where does he live?"

"Frama-22."

"What?" Kip blurted. "How many bloody Framas are there?"

"More than you'd care to count, dear."

"But first, we need to go to Frama-7," Mikey announced.

"We're in eleven right now," Kip said. "I thought we could only visit ten and twelve."

"I've got that covered," Winnie said. "I had another dream message, and now I know how to go there."

"Dream message," Kip retorted. "Lah-dee-dah."

"Jealous much?" Winnie snapped back.

"Come on, guys," Mikey said.

"Friends, please," said Sister Ava. "You've got multiple tasks to complete. It would behoove you to get along with one another."

Mikey slid between Winnie and Kip. "Guys, we can do this."

"Spoken like a true adventurer," Sister Ava said. "Now, if you'll excuse us, Generals, I'd like to speak briefly with the young wizard."

The pair returned to the beach house, leaving Kip with the woman.

She held out her hand. "Might I see the Frama-scope in your possession?"

He reluctantly pulled his shoelace necklace free, exposing a Frama-scope identical to Winnie's. He passed it to her.

She magically released the knot and returned the shoelace. She pocketed the Frama-scope. "My sister will be pleased to know you took good care of this. I, on the other hand, am disappointed in you." Her loving-gran expression morphed into an annoyed-librarian stare. "You stole our Frama-scopes."

He gasped at the accusation. "That's not how it happened."

"Nevertheless, your actions led to the same result. Theft."

"All I meant to do was create false Frama-scopes. I'm so sorry. If I'd known other people's scopes would come to me, I never would've done it."

Her gaze softened. "I believe you, but you were inadvertently caught up in a magical vortex that has increased your powers. For that reason, you must consider all potential consequences before casting any future spells. Magic is serious business. If you don't treat it as such, I can and will strip you of those powers. Is that clearly understood?"

His insides bounced from confusion to despair to certainty. If his powers had increased, he'd do whatever it took to keep them. "Sister, I believed I *had* considered everything. I'd envisioned duplicating the scopes' outsides only. I never intended for them to work."

"That is your burden to bear, young wizard. Before you speak your next incantation, be certain to consider all potential negative outcomes first."

"I don't think negatively. I've only done magic for good." He chose not to mention the time on Frama-12 when he'd threatened to kill the oracle's sister. But he'd been under Krell's power, so it wasn't totally his fault. He'd also come to his senses and hadn't harmed her.

"The rogue wizard, Krell, is now traveling through time tears using the Frama-scope you misappropriated from one of my sisters. Do you consider that *good*?"

He ducked his head. "How can I make up for that?"

"A worthy plea." She pulled from her pocket the second scope she had accepted from Mikey. "We can begin to put things right with one small enchantment."

She closed her eyes and held a hand over the scope

in her other palm. The hush of the surf and an occasional seagull cry drowned out her soft murmurings. Bird lifted his head, telescoping his neck as if for a better view of her magic.

Sister Ava opened her eyes and offered the Frama-scope to Kip. "You may tie this to your interesting necklace for safekeeping with the caution that you must never use it. No matter what time tear the user activates, he will reach only one destination. Thaddeus Krell's home in Cambridge, England. Your task is to replace this enchanted scope with the one currently in Krell's possession."

He gasped. "That's impossible. Krell's magic is stronger than mine."

She frowned back. "Didn't you just ask how to compensate for your previous miscalculation? This must be done."

"I don't even know where he is right now."

"Your increased powers will help you."

The air crackled, and with a poof, the guardian vanished.

Her sudden disappearance didn't faze him. Two unsettling thoughts troubled him more. What if he couldn't find Krell? And if he did, what if Sister Ava had lied about his extra power?

Chapter 3

Winnie opened and closed cabinets, searching for snacks. "I'll get the food. What else should we take?"

"The canteens, definitely." Mikey opened a kitchen drawer and pulled out two, still in their casings with long straps.

"We're taking a day pack this time. No more baggies tied to belt loops. Plus, we can bring more food." She laid a bag of pretzels and a box of granola bars on the table beside the canteens. She added a loaf of bread and a jar of peanut butter. "I wonder if we should bring our bathing suits. Frama-7 looks like the Caribbean."

"What's the Caribbean?"

Because he knew so many otherworldly things, she often expected him to know everything about his adopted world. "It's a place with pretty blue water. Lots of it."

"I don't like lots of water."

She hugged him. "I'll keep you safe."

Unexpectedly, her ears popped.

Mikey must have felt it too. "Sister Ava just vanished."

She nodded, guessing the same thing. Whenever anything or anyone magically disappeared, it caused a vacuum. A moment later, Kip stepped inside, eyes wide.

"What happened? What did she say?"

He smiled, but it looked forced. "It's fine. We're fine."

He helped fill the day pack and even volunteered to carry it.

Outside, Mikey jumped to the lead. He stepped up to the bush Winnie had seen in her dream message. "Stompy says this is the opening to the Frama jump."

Kip turned to Winnie. "The Frama what?"

She shrugged. "It's a way to pass through multiple worlds."

Mikey nodded. "The jump point is in Frama-10."

"Blimey, we're going back there again? With those mechanical sentries?"

"I don't think it's in the Reserve. The person in my dream message took me to a backyard. We found the opening to Stompy's world through a bush with drooping branches like a willow. Ready?"

They formed a line with Mikey on her left and Kip on her right. She aimed her Frama-scope. A blue time bubble hovered above the ground where the princess had shown her. "Everybody move closer to me. The tear's straight ahead. I'll widen it."

Mikey tugged her arm. "Windy, wait."

She released the scope, letting it hang by the ribbon around her neck. "Bathroom?"

He lifted the toad off his shoulder. "Stompy might fall when we go through. He almost did last time. Can you keep him in your sweatshirt pocket?"

She carefully positioned the princess toad inside her left pocket. She lifted the scope to her eye again and twisted its central ring. She took a deep breath. "Stay close. Here we go."

Mikey clasped the edge of her sweatshirt from her left, and Kip pressed against her right side. Even though they entered together into the foggy nether-space between worlds, she immediately lost physical contact with them. She had barely acknowledged the loss when she stumbled forward into a white world. Needle-like sleet pelted her in the face. She slid a protective hand into her pocket, cradling the toad, thankfully still there. Kip tumbled into her from behind, causing her to fall to her knees into four inches of frigid, fluffy snow. "Careful."

Kip helped her up. "Where are we?" He had to shout over the howling wind.

Mikey, back at Winnie's side again, clasped her arm. "Is Stompy okay?"

"Yes, but…it should be summer."

"Are we in the wrong place?" Kip called out.

She bent closer to Mikey. "Ask Stompy if this is right."

"He says it is. He also says he tried to tell you the seasons could change, but you stopped paying attention."

Still cradling Stompy in her left hand, she shaded her eyes with her right. A building, barely visible through the blinding ice crystals, stood straight ahead. Could that be the house from her dream message? If so, they should find the leafy bush on their right. "This way."

Bird, little more than a flying black lump in the blizzard, shrieked and soared past them. She'd forgotten all about him. "He knows. Follow him." She hoped he knew.

The boys flanked her and marched toward a tangle of thin, bare branches, swaying in the wind. "I think that's it."

Kip squeezed her right shoulder. "There's a building the other way."

A series of fierce barks sounded from the house.

Kip let go. "Never mind."

The trio charged in the direction Bird had flown.

Winnie reached the bush first and spread the branches apart. "In here!" The boys burst through the opening. She followed, relieved to recognize the inside of the umbrella bush. "Toward the back."

Bird waddled ahead of them and slipped into a bright opening. They crawled after him and onto a sandy beach. Balmy air gently rolled over them, melting the thin layer of snow covering them. They sat in the sand, puffing for breath.

"The Frama jump worked," Mikey announced. "This is Stompy's world."

Winnie eased the princess toad from her pocket and handed her to Mikey.

A long stretch of sandy beach and a blue-green sea replaced the opening they'd traveled through. "Uh-oh. I'm not sure how we're getting back home."

Mikey frowned. "Stompy says don't worry about that. We need to hide first and then have some water."

A pine forest stood ten yards from the beach. They ducked behind the first row of trees to a spot that still gave them a view of the calm ocean. Once adequately hidden, Kip slid the day pack off his back and plopped it on the ground. He rummaged briefly, producing one of the canteens. He handed it to Mikey, who took a drink, then poured some on the ground and set the toad in the middle of the puddle. Mikey passed the canteen to Winnie.

She took a long swallow and offered it to Kip. "Has anybody seen Bird?"

Kip chuckled. "I'm sure we'll hear him in a bit." Less than a minute later, a shriek sounded in the distance.

"There he is."

"Guys, Stompy's afraid he's losing himself to his new form."

Winnie waited, but Kip didn't volunteer his magic expertise. "Don't you have an incantation floating around in your head that can help?"

He looked away.

"Don't tell me you lost your magic when we Frama-jumped."

"It's not that." He took a deep breath. "It's…well, Sister Ava said magic can cause unexpected consequences. If I misuse it, I could lose it forever."

"I don't think it counts as a misuse of powers if you save an enchanted toad from turning into a real one."

"I don't know. Let me think." He sprang to his feet and stomped onto the beach.

"I thought we were supposed to hide," Mikey mumbled.

"Is he acting weird, or am I just imagining it?"

He only shrugged.

Kip stood in the open, hands on his hips. He stared out to sea, gazed at the sky, then peered at his feet. He pushed the sand aside with his sneaker and picked up a shell. He slid it into his pocket, strode a hundred yards down the beach, and then returned to them. He sat on his knees facing them, his jaw set in grim determination. "Right. For good or ill, I've got an incantation that should prevent Stompy from losing his true identity."

He closed his eyes, took a few slow breaths, and waved a hand over the toad. He chanted in a language Winnie didn't recognize. He repeated three incomprehensible sentences twice and opened his eyes. "How does he feel now?"

After a pause, Mikey nodded. "Better, but still afraid. He needs to go to the castle now."

"Wait. Kip, how'd you know to say all that?" Winnie asked.

"Not sure." He rose. "Lead the way, Stompy. With Mikey translating, of course."

Horse hooves shushed across the sand, nearing their hiding place. Kip ducked. Winnie crouched behind a bush and parted the branches. Two dozen horsemen, riding in pairs, strutted along the beach. They wore red uniforms and silver helmets with dark-red plumes. The saddle pads and bridles matched the plumes.

After the last pair walked beyond their line of sight, Mikey whispered, "Stompy says that's the king's outer patrol, heading back to the castle."

Winnie stood and dusted the sand off the back of her jeans. "Good. That's where we want to go. As long as we stay out of sight, we can follow."

Mikey lifted Stompy from the puddle and rose. "No. He wants you to take him through the path in the woods. Me and Kip have to wait here."

"We do?" Kip asked.

"Stompy does?" asked Winnie. "But I can't hear what she, I mean, he's saying."

Mikey offered her the toad. "If you quiet your mind, you'll hear."

She reluctantly set the enchanted princess on her left shoulder.

"Winnie keeping quiet?" Kip teased. "That I've got to see."

"Har, har." She poked him with her elbow. "I can be quiet."

He smiled. "Just larking."

Winnie peered at Stompy from the corners of her eyes. "Are we sure about this?"

"One last thing." Kip scooped an orange pebble from the ground and handed it to her. "Magical communication shouldn't break any rules. If you need me, just say my name into that pebble. I'll be on the other end with this." He pulled a seashell from his jeans pocket.

"Thanks." His magic, nature-based cell phones had helped in the past. Just knowing she had it raised her confidence.

"You'll need this too." Mikey offered Winnie the second canteen from the day pack.

She slid the strap over her right shoulder so the canteen dangled against her left hip. "How far are we from the castle?"

When Stompy didn't answer, she turned to her brother.

He stood silently for a moment. "About twenty minutes through the woods. Thirty minutes tops. There's a path fifteen paces behind us. If you go straight, you'll reach it. Turn left and follow it to a T. Then turn right."

She resented the enchanted princess for telling Mikey and not her. She also hated verbal directions. "I'm not going to remember all that."

"You'll be okay. Stompy can tell you."

Kip settled onto a nearby stump. "We'll wait for you here. If you need us, give us a ring."

"Keep your cell shell nearby. If I get lost, and I will, you'll hear from me."

She trudged into the forest and pushed between two bushes. Their willowy branches gently grazed her arms. Fifteen paces later, she reached an open forest carpeted with yellow-brown pine needles.

"I don't know why you won't talk to me, Princess. You have no problem letting Mikey know what's going on. Why isn't he taking you to the castle?" Even as she said it, she knew she'd never let a six-year-old hike through the woods by himself.

A dozen yards later, she found a sandy path that ran left to right. She followed it to the left. "What am I even supposed to do when I reach the castle? Who's going to recognize you in your toad shape? They'll think I'm insane if I go in there and say, 'Hey, here's your princess.' "

No response. Winnie stomped her foot.

A familiar squawk overhead pulled her from her negative commentary. Bird lit and waddled beside her, murmuring contentedly.

"I'm glad you're here. The princess isn't speaking to me, apparently."

He muttered, which she interpreted as a shared annoyance.

For ten minutes, girl, bird, and toad hiked along the sandy trail. When the path narrowed to fit between a pair of elephant-sized boulders, Bird toddled to the lead. Past the boulders, the trail broadened, and he moved to her side again. The path wound around a batch of smaller boulders and curved sharply to the left.

She hesitated. "I don't remember Mikey mentioning this." Did that mean she'd accidentally passed the crossroad, or did it mean she hadn't reached it yet? "What do you think, Bird? Do we keep going?"

He made a quacking sound.

"Hey, you're bilingual." Her comment earned a laughter-like response. "I like you, Bird."

He quacked again.

The curve finally straightened. Another boulder, twice her height, stood in the center of the path. A person straddled the boulder, facing away. Long black hair, twisted into multiple, tight braids, hung down his back. His? She skidded to a stop.

Two internal emotions warred with each other—alarm and recognition. The first made sense. What if he had a weapon? What if... She recognized him? How would she know a tree sprite from behind? Tree sprite? Where did that thought come from? What was a tree sprite?

Bird, apparently misinterpreting her indecisiveness as fear, let out a fierce screech and flew at the figure. The boy let out a yelp and jumped behind a berry bush.

"Bird, wait! He's not a threat." The moment she said it, she knew the statement to be true. She hurried to the boulder, ready to pull the bird away, but he snapped his beak shut and strutted to her side again.

"Sorry about that. Bird can be overprotective at times. He's…" An idea struck her, so she said it out loud. "My guardian."

A brown face peered from between the branches. Even from several feet away, his amber eyes captivated her. The shade reminded her of leaves underfoot on an autumn day. A memory of that crisp scent put her at ease.

"It's okay," she promised.

The boy, about her age, hesitantly stepped into the open. "I'm Eggar."

"Edgar? Do you go by Ed for short?"

"Eggar," he repeated.

Weird name. Not that she'd admit it out loud. A second thought blasted through her consciousness that

Eggar was a perfectly fine name for a tree sprite. She never would have thought of that term on her own. Had Stompy given it to her? To test her theory, she asked, "Are you a tree sprite?"

He gave a half nod. "And you must be General Windem."

She stumbled back a step. "Whoa! That is so close. My name is Windemere, but how did you know?"

His eyes sparkled with good humor. "My truth stones foresaw your appearance on this path. Although I expected you to come from the other direction." He flashed a smile filled with joy. "And, of course, I recognized you from the prophecy."

She cocked her head. "What prophecy?"

"The one about the young female warrior who will save Aylen Isle from an invasion. An elder first spoke of it ten years ago."

"Then it can't mean me. Ten years ago, I used to hide behind furniture and jump out at company to scare them."

"It wasn't just foretold. My truth stones provided me with the same answer. And"—he nodded at her hoodie— "it was foretold that our champion would come to us clad in pink armor."

"This?" She tugged at the material. "It's a cotton blend. It won't even protect me from a water balloon. Sorry to tell you this, but your elder's prophecy totally meant somebody else. I'm just here for directions to the castle."

He graced her with another dazzling smile. "I've been waiting here to do that very thing."

"Perfect. Then I'll follow you."

They walked in silence for the first few minutes.

Curiosity prompted her to ask, "Did your truth stones tell you why I needed directions to the castle?"

"I didn't ask but assumed you'd wish to meet with the king."

Based on her past less-than-stellar experience with a monarch, she hoped to delay that meeting. A sudden sense of urgency splashed over her. "I have to meet someone else. No offense to the king," she quickly added. She knew how touchy royalty could be.

"Wishing no disrespect, but if not the king, who do you wish to see? The queen?"

She needed to see the king's wizard, but her mouth said, "Princess Abbidrelle."

Eggar stopped with a jerk. "The princess? With a threat on the horizon?"

"Again. I'm not the warrior. I didn't mean to say the princess. I actually meant the princess." Winnie shook her head, but every time she tried to say "wizard," the word "princess" came out. "Wait a minute. Is that how you communicate?" she asked the toad.

"Are you quite all right?" asked Eggar. "We've been communicating all along."

"Just thinking out loud." If she admitted the truth, he'd think she was bonkers.

They resumed their hike. In the silence, she tried to communicate with the toad. *Is this how you talk to Mikey? By putting words in his mouth?*

She received no reply. At least nothing obvious came through.

Since I can answer myself, how will I know if we're having a conversation or if I'm just making up stuff?

Her head throbbed. Either her question gave her a headache, or Stompy did. She forced a blank mind as she plodded forward with her head down. She didn't lift it until the dimness of the forest lightened. She and Eggar had reached the edge of the woods.

The terrain opened into a grassy field. Beyond several hundred yards of rolling hills lay a dirt road that led to an immense stone castle. Hundreds of people, some pulling carts, tramped down the road toward it.

"Look at that crowd! It'll take a year to reach the front."

"It's market day, but don't worry. I can direct you to the princess for a brief visit, but you really must see the king afterward."

An unexpected suggestion popped into her head. Since it must have come from Princess Gwen, she spoke it. "Princess Abbidrelle likes animals, right?"

"She does, indeed."

"That's why I wanted to see her. I brought her this toad. As a gift."

Eggar paused to inspect the toad princess. "It looks rather ordinary."

"It does tricks." This time she distinctly sensed the princess's disapproval. *What? You can't do a little tap dance to show him you're special?*

Chapter 4

Kip regretted sending Winnie on her own. If she didn't trust her sense of direction, maybe he shouldn't either. Minutes passed, though, and she didn't call. He and Mikey shared a granola bar. They tossed pinecones at a rock to kill time. He even taught Mikey the trick behind making a quarter disappear. He'd used up all his entertainment ideas and still hadn't heard from Winnie.

Mikey, growing restless, peered through the brush at the beach. "This water looks different. I think I could stand in this sea and not be afraid."

He gave the little lad an encouraging smile. "Want to try it? I could hold your hand to keep you steady."

They rolled up their pant legs and stepped out of hiding. Mikey clasped Kip's hand and set the pace. At the water's edge, he took a tentative first step. He grinned, revealing the gap where his front baby teeth used to be. "It's so warm."

Kip smiled in agreement. The tepid temperature belonged in a sunny tide pool more than in an ocean. A ripple of a wave rolled over their bare feet. Mikey giggled and entered the ocean in a pause-step-pause-step fashion until he stood shin deep in the crystal, blue-green water.

The little lad's joy at conquering his fear of the ocean filled Kip with so much pride he forgot to pay attention to their surroundings. The water nearly reached the little boy's knees when shushing horse hooves in the sand sounded from behind them.

Kip clasped Mikey's hand tighter and turned with him toward the beach.

Two guards on horseback, wearing shiny armor and helmets, halted at the water's edge. "Hoy!" a guard shouted. "What have we here?"

"Too young to be spies," said the other, "but old enough to know they don't belong in a restricted area."

Kip instinctively mumbled a convincement spell at the guards to let them go.

"Come on, then," said the first guard. "Out of the water with you."

"You'll be coming with us, so you will," ordered the other guard.

Kip sighed and slogged through the water with Mikey at his side.

One guard hoisted the little boy onto his saddle. The other pulled Kip onto his horse, causing his muscles to tense. If only he could overcome his fear of horses as quickly as Mikey mastered his fear of the ocean.

They rode down the beach to a break in the woods that revealed a sand-covered path. When the horses sped to a gallop, Kip clenched his eyes shut and held tighter to the rider. He tried to distract himself from the hurtling beast with thoughts of Winnie. Had her mission succeeded? What would she think of him and her little stepbrother riding into town as prisoners if she spotted them? Why hadn't his convincement spell worked? And why would anyone think he and Mikey posed a threat? What harm had they caused by having a bit of a wade in the ocean?

He hoped they'd fare better once they met the blokes

in charge. As long as Winnie didn't ring him on his shell phone at an inopportune moment, his polite nature should save them from punishment. He'd performed enough magic shows at birthday parties to know how to please an unsympathetic crowd. Elder siblings rarely foiled his tricks, allowing his young audiences to enjoy a show clearly designed for them.

In time, their mounts brought them to a clearing that exposed a formidable stone fortress. Kip gulped. Even if he'd packed his magic props, he doubted his sleight of hand would impress a human monarch.

A pair of guards in metal armor met them at a side entrance and raised the portcullis. The horses trotted into a sandy courtyard. Four other guards, dressed in leather armor but wearing the same silver helmets, helped Kip and Mikey from the horses. The four guards, two in front and two behind, escorted them inside and guided them through a dark corridor. Little Mikey had to jog to keep up with their brisk gait.

After too many turns to count, the guards directed them into a bright room with barely enough space to hold a table and three chairs. The guards led them deeper into the confined area. A heavy hand clamped over Kip's right shoulder and pressed him into a chair. Mikey, treated more gently, eased into the one on Kip's left.

The guards stepped aside, allowing a grim-faced man in a metal-gray uniform to enter. Two pointy-eared women dressed in similar uniforms crammed inside and shut the door behind them. *Elves?*

Kip, who preferred a window when confined to tight spaces, glanced from the women to the solid walls. He peered upward, hoping to at least find a skylight. The light source, a collection of fist-sized orbs attached to the ceiling, glowed down on them.

The grim-faced man dropped into the chair on the opposite side of the table. "You lot were discovered in a restricted area." The man must be the interrogator. "Who are you, and what were you doing there?"

Knowing Mikey's tendency to blurt the truth at inopportune times, Kip leaned toward him and whispered, "Don't say you're a general."

"Here then!" the interrogator blurted. "Enough of that."

Kip straightened in his chair. "I'm his solicitor."

The interrogator turned his frown on Mikey. "What did he say to you earlier?"

"He said don't tell you I'm a general."

Kip smacked himself on the forehead. Why did he bother telling Mikey anything?

"Are you a general?" one of the guards asked with a grin. Several chortled.

Mikey nodded, which caused an uproar of laughter from the men and gentle smiles from the ladies.

"See?" Kip muttered out of the corner of his mouth.

Mikey blinked innocently back with his big brown eyes. "Can I go to the bathroom?"

Everyone's hardened expressions relaxed.

"Of course," the interrogator said gently.

One of the women removed a white marble from her pocket and mumbled into it. Instantly, another pointy-eared woman entered and smiled encouragingly at Mikey. She held out her hand. "I can show you."

Mikey, who should've known better than to obey strangers, followed her out.

Kip leaped up. "I promised his sister I'd protect him. He can't leave me."

"He will be well taken care of," said the interrogator.

"Where are you taking him?"

"To a much more welcoming room than this one. He is a general, after all," the interrogator said with a grin.

When the group relaxed their stances, Kip tried his convincement spell again.

"Magic!" an elf shouted. She and her companion bolted to Kip's side and shoved him back into his chair.

The one on his right slammed a white stone with a flat bottom on the table. She snatched his hand and slapped it on the smooth top. "Leave it there," she said through clenched teeth.

He fought the instinct to pull his hand away. To his surprise, the stone radiated a comforting warmth.

"Only the king's conjurer is authorized to use magic in this realm," the interrogator announced. "Who are you, and how did you get here?"

Good question. Should he give his full name or the one he preferred? How vague could his answer to the second question be?

"I should warn you," said the interrogator, "if you lie, the stone under your hand will sting you. For every lie, the sting's intensity will increase."

"It can also detect unlawful magic use," said the other woman.

He slowly lifted his head. "My name is Kip, and I'm a traveler."

His muscles tightened at an anticipated sting. The stone beneath his hand remained smooth and warm. He breathed easier.

"From what land?"

Kip hesitated. "Have you heard of Framas?"

"Is that a town?"

He shook his head. "It's what travelers call alternate worlds. They're lined up next to each other. The little boy and I came through a doorway called a time tear to your world."

The interrogator's eyes bulged and then narrowed. "That's not possible."

One of the guards said, "With respect, sir, it shouldn't be possible for a lad this young to have magic."

The interrogator leaned forward. "He makes a good point. Explain yourself, *Kip*." He spoke his name as if it were a curse.

So far, the stone under his palm hadn't reacted to his responses. "As I mentioned," he said, choosing his words carefully, "I'm a Frama traveler. I've picked up the odd spell or two in my travels."

"Eelan," the interrogator barked.

The woman on Kip's left jumped to attention. "Sir."

The man nodded once. She spread a folded cloth on the table, then untied a small pouch from her belt and upended it. Three flat stones dropped into her open palm. She rattled them in her closed fist and tossed them onto the cloth. She scooped them up and threw them again. And again. No matter how often she gathered and threw them, they always landed with the black stone and the blue one landing equidistant from the white one.

Kip couldn't keep his curiosity to himself. "What does that mean?"

The interrogator stared at the stones for a long moment. He slowly lifted his head. "It means you are an anomaly."

Chapter 5

Winnie hid the princess toad inside her hoodie pocket and followed Eggar past the long line at the front gate to a side entrance. Two guards immediately opened the gate. They even bowed to her. After she passed them, she leaned toward Eggar and mumbled, "Did they let us in because of the prophecy?"

He nodded. "Everyone knows about the young female warrior in pink armor."

"I'm only wearing pink because my navy one is in the laundry hamper."

He didn't slow their brisk pace. "All the more reason to believe it was meant to be. We should find the princess just through here."

They marched under a long archway to a grassy courtyard. A marble fountain stood in the center, spouting water. A mirror image of Princess Gwenevieve stood nearby. *You never told me she was your twin.*

According to the whisper of understanding in Winnie's head, Princess Abbidrelle went by the nickname Abbi. Rather than a royal gown, the girl wore a leather tunic and green tights. She leaned against a chubby tan pony with a white-blond mane and tail. He grazed on the royal lawn, attacking each blade of grass as if it had personally insulted him.

A tall man with braided black hair stood a few feet away. The name Cedric flashed into her mind. Abbi's royal bodyguard.

Eggar strode ahead. "Sir Cedric, please pardon the interruption. A special visitor from outside the realm has requested an audience with the princess."

The girl turned. Her green eyes widened in surprise. "Are you…"

"I guess you noticed my pink armor." Winnie tried not to smirk. Did everyone in this world accept her based solely on a randomly selected sweatshirt?

Eggar cleared his throat and gave Winnie a stern side glance. "Your Royal Majesty, Princess Abbidrelle, I present to you the warrior Windemere."

"Officially, it's General Windemere, but I usually go by Winnie." She leaned forward and stretched her arm to shake the other girl's hand.

The princess moved backward one step and turned toward her bodyguard. "Cedric, are all foreigners this disrespectful to royalty or just the female warriors?"

Winnie's back stiffened. "I was trying to be— begging the respectful pardon…I was—" A sudden sharp stab behind her left eyeball caught her attention. No words flooded her mind, but she understood the princess toad wanted her to use formal address on a kid younger than her. "No way," she muttered toward her hoodie pocket. "I'm not saying that." She pressed her lips together to prevent the unwanted words from escaping.

The princess looked to Eggar. "Is she not well? She seems to be speaking to herself."

Cedric stepped between Winnie and the princess and took a defensive stance.

Winnie glared at him. "I'm not talking to myself. I'm talking to the person in my pocket. Okay, that came out weird. Let me try again. Technically, I'm here about the princess's sister. I know where she is."

Eggar bowed deeply. "Your Majesty, forgive me. The warrior never mentioned that. She said she had a gift of a small pet to add to your menagerie."

"That too," Winnie said. "Princess, can we speak privately about your sister?"

Cedric sniffed indignantly. "That is ill-advised, Your Majesty."

Princess Abbi straightened her shoulders. "I'm sure we'll be fine. The warrior came to help us."

"Very well, Your Majesty," Cedric said. "I'll be standing just here, by the fountain."

The girl nodded and led Winnie to a private corner of the courtyard. "You have news of my sister? Is she well? She's been missing."

"That explains all the guards on the beach. The whole army must be looking for her."

Princess Abbi shook her head. "They don't know."

"Nobody? Not even your parents? How'd you pull that off?"

"By dressing and acting like her. We're not always seen together, even at meals with our parents, so I managed it, but it's been exhausting. Where is she?"

"Okay, brace yourself. An enchantment was involved, so she isn't exactly herself." She carefully dipped her hand into her hoodie pocket and pulled out the toad.

The princess let out an alarmed gasp.

"I know it looks bad, but if you clear your mind, she'll talk to you."

Princess Abbi accepted Stompy and lifted her for a closer look.

Winnie held her breath and waited. What if the toad princess didn't speak to her sister? She hadn't always been forthcoming with Winnie. What if this princess thought Winnie made up the enchantment story and sent her to the dungeon?

A long minute passed. The girl pressed the toad to her cheek. "How did this happen? Where did you find her?"

Winnie let out a long thankful breath. "In an alternate world called Frama-10, or Hutra, if you know the place. We brought her through a portal to our world, and now we're here. As for the 'how,' we don't know. Hopefully, now that she's home, somebody can fix this."

A tear rolled down Princess Abbi's cheek. "I know none of those places. Gwennie slipped out of our rooms three nights ago. I haven't seen her since."

"Do you have somebody who does magic here?"

The girl considered it. "Oh! You must mean Papa's conjurer, Argamel! I don't always think of what he does as magic."

"Argamel. That's the one."

She cradled her sister in her hands. "You believe Argamel can undo the spell?"

Winnie nodded. "At least your sister thinks so."

"I hope he can, but I've never seen him change one object into another." She raised the toad to eye level again. "Gwennie?" She kissed the top of the toad's head. "Can you tell me how this happened?"

After a slow count to ten, Winnie asked, "What did she say?"

The princess shook her head. "It was hard to follow. It came into my mind like a splash. The night she disappeared, she followed a stranger. I think she wants to go back to where it happened. First, hide her." She held the toad to Winnie, who immediately complied. "Cedric," she called out, "see to Ollie, please. He belongs in his stall before he destroys the yard." To Winnie, she added, "Follow me." She spun on her heel and marched toward the castle's nearest doorway.

Winnie shrugged at Eggar and hurried after the princess. They marched along a corridor to a marble staircase. The princess increased her speed, nearly scampering up two levels. Winnie, in training for distance running, easily kept up. So far, they'd met no one.

They wended through various short corridors, finally stopping at an alcove with a closed door guarded by two sentinels. Would they need a password to be let in?

The guard on the right answered her unspoken question. "Warrior, enter."

When she put on her pink hoodie, she'd never guessed it could open doors.

The princess moved to join her, but the guard held up a hand. "The warrior only."

The young royal put her hands on her hips. "You're not allowed to bar the door against me. I'm heir to the king."

The sentinel, eyes still focused forward, said, "His Majesty is in a private meeting and wishes only to be disturbed with news of the war."

Winnie gulped. "War?" Did that mean it had already started? If so, she needed a war room. She needed councilmen with information. She needed a plan.

Princess Abbi glowered at the guard. "Let me pass. I'm the one who found the warrior."

Winnie chose not to quibble over who found whom. She wouldn't have to face the king alone if the princess accompanied her. "Please let her come in with me."

The guards stepped aside. The princess opened the door and whisked through with Winnie at her heels.

A stern-faced man looked up from the papers on his shiny desk. The four men seated across from him bounded to their feet.

"Papa, send these brutes away. They're interfering with crucial business we need to discuss with you."

"Is that so?" The king's crown, a simple golden band that encircled his head at the brow, began to glow.

"I brought the female warrior from the prophecy. We need to speak with you privately."

He nodded to the men, and they quietly exited. After the last one closed the door behind him, the king laid his fountain pen on the desk. He scowled at his daughter. "Since when do you come charging into my office without a proper invitation?"

"When it's desperately important. We need the royal conjurer. Now!"

The glow from the king's crown flared to a brilliant white. He folded his arms. "You can't just come in here, ordering me about."

She clenched her fists. "Do it now, or I shall scream so loud your ears will explode."

"Before we start blowing out eardrums, maybe I should…" Winnie reached into her pocket and gently placed the toad on the king's desk.

He reared back. "What in the name of all that's holy is the meaning of this? Why would you place that creature on my royal papers?"

"Papa, it's Gwennie. If we don't change her back

soon, she'll be stuck this way forever."

"Just stop it," the king demanded. "That is not your sister. Until just now, I thought you were Gwen, playing dress-up. First, you burst in here unannounced, and now you want me to believe your sister has been enchanted. Take your pet away, Abbi. I've got work to do."

She tenderly gathered up her sister-toad. "Papa," she said tearfully, "have you ever known me to lie to you?"

"As a matter of fact, yes. I can't even count the number of times you've pretended to be your sister. There was also the incident where you blamed my horse for eating holes in the topiary garden when Ollie is the only animal that grazes there."

"All right, but only those times."

"You blamed the wash maidens for the knotted bed sheets that one of you used to climb out of your bedroom window."

"That was Gwennie's idea."

"You lied about the broken goblets, the spilled ink pot. The time you knocked over your mother's reading lamp and said a ghost did it."

If this kept up, they could be here all day. Winnie stepped forward. "Your Majesty. General Windemere Harris at your service." Since they expected someone in pink, she'd take advantage of it. "I'm the warrior from the prophecy. Did you notice my pink armor?"

The king stared at her with disdain. "You're not wearing armor."

"Thank you for being the first person to notice that. But unless somebody else comes and claims the title, I'm probably the one. I've helped armies before. I'm a Frama-traveler if you're familiar with the term."

"I am not."

"O-kay. Well, here's the thing. Somebody put a spell on your other daughter. We respectfully need you to send for the conjurer so he can undo it."

"The meeting you two just interrupted was about the conjurer. He's missing and has been for the past three days."

"But we need him to turn Gwennie back to herself." Princess Abbi lifted the toad and held her up.

He waved it away. "Take it and leave us. I wish to speak privately with the…warrior."

She cradled the toad in the crook of her left arm and exited the room, glancing back at Winnie.

Chapter 6

The interrogator blasted a laser-sharp stare at Kip. "Let's try this again. How did you come to be on the western shore of Aylen Isle? If you sailed from the mainland, where is your boat? Our guards found nothing hidden in the brush. Did someone deliver you and leave?"

Clearly, the man didn't believe the truth. Kip peered at the rounded stone beneath his cupped palm. If only he could silently speak directly with it—*she*—for a better feel for how best to respond. She? The stone's surface changed from room temperature to a comforting warmth. He sucked in a breath of air. *Can you hear my thoughts?*

Heat from the stone briefly rose again and returned to a cooler temperature. Did that mean they could communicate?

"Young man. Answer the question."

He lifted his head. "Just trying to properly organize me thoughts."

The interrogator harrumphed and folded his arms.

Do you understand Framas?

The stone reacted the same way. Warmer than cooler.

So you do. But not everybody here does, right?

He felt the same brief warmth. It cooled again.

Then how do I adequately explain where I'm from?

No temperature change.

Apparently, she could only give yes or no answers. Kip huffed in frustration. They'd be at this forever if he had to play twenty questions. *Is there any way we can actually speak?*

The interrogation room dissolved. Kip sat at a small round table outside a quaint café with a red-and-white-striped awning. A collection of antique shops and a bakery stood across the street. A young girl sat opposite him at the table. Not a typical girl, judging by her pointed ears and fine, white-blond hair.

"Are you the truth stone?"

She beamed at him with aquamarine eyes. "Are you the not-entirely-honest wizard?"

Self-conscious heat warmed his cheeks. "I'd like to think of myself as mostly honest."

She let out a trill of laughter filled with loving acceptance.

He smiled back, confidence restored. "My name is Kip. Might I ask yours?"

The girl's smooth forehead rippled. "I've never understood the need for names."

"Are you saying you haven't got one?"

She shrugged.

"But I have to call you something. What about Tee? You know, for Truth?"

After a brief consideration, she nodded. "I accept."

"Tee it is, then."

"We haven't much time. You've probably noticed Garran isn't a patient man."

"Is that the bloke asking questions back in that little room?"

"Yes, and he won't allow you much longer to 'collect your thoughts.' We'd better get started. What

46

questions do you have for me?"

He nodded. "Right. I have two. First, since Garran doesn't seem to believe I'm from an alternate world, how do I explain myself without winding him up more than he already is? And second, my friends and I aren't spies. We're travelers who visit different worlds. Not to steal or cause trouble," he quickly added.

"I accept that you are a traveler from a distant place. You needn't get any more deeply into it than that. I suspect Garran will ask for more information about your magic. He'll probably also want to know why you chose to come to our shores."

"I'm originally from a place called Earth. We don't have real magic there, but we have illusionists who do tricks that look like magic. Back home, I'm an illusionist or a magician. When I visited the world Frama-12, I learned spells and incantations that allowed me to do a bit of real magic. And I found a book called *The Power of Krell*."

Tee nodded encouragingly.

"The book strengthened me magic but came from a negative place. I thought I conquered its darkness, but sometimes I worry the darkness isn't completely gone."

Tee leaned toward him. He expected the deep stare, but then she sniffed him, which he hadn't anticipated. She settled back. "You're right. You still have some on you."

Kip slumped against his chair. "That probably explains how I accidentally stole Frama-scopes from the Sisters Three. Have you heard of them?"

She let out an endearing giggle. "I have, but don't share that story with Garran. It would only confuse him. Now, for the second half of the questioning. Why did you come here?"

"We came to help…an enchanted prince." Though Mikey had never specifically claimed his toad was a royal, why else would he ask Winnie to take Stompy to a castle?

"I know you speak the truth, but our king and queen have only two daughters, and neither is enchanted."

Could Stompy be a princess? If so, how could Tee not know about it? "I guess I could be wrong about who got enchanted, but one of your subjects definitely isn't human right now. That person needs magic to turn back."

"I believe you. But again, you probably shouldn't say that to Garran either."

"What can I say?"

Tee gazed at the leafy branches overhead that swayed in a breeze. "You didn't just arrive with the little general. You mentioned a sister."

He nodded. "Winnie, a.k.a. General Windemere."

Tee's pale eyebrows lifted. "Windemere? The warrior?"

Kip snorted. "She's a warrior the same way Mikey's a general."

"Is she by chance dressed in pink?"

"Yeah, her sweatshirt is pink, but I think her jeans are navy. She took the enchanted person to the castle for help."

"She's probably looking for the king's conjurer. Again, this isn't information Garran needs to know at this time. When we return to the interrogation room, you need only tell him you're with the Warrior Windemere."

He scowled. "Why does Winnie get all the acclaim? She isn't even a real warrior."

Tee flashed an indulgent smile. "Perhaps she is."

He rolled his eyes, but she might have missed it. The outdoor café vanished, replaced by the interrogation room.

Garran glowered at him. "You've had more than enough time to 'collect your thoughts.' "

"Yes, um, Sir Garran."

The man's eyes bulged. "How do you know my name? No one spoke it."

Kip pointed at the stone with his free hand. "She did."

The woman who'd brought out the stone started. "That's impossible. Why would she communicate with a spy?"

He turned his head toward her. "She wouldn't. But she would communicate with the person who accompanied the Warrior Windemere. I believe you're familiar with that name."

Garran jolted as if shocked. His stunned expression quickly returned to a frown. He impatiently snapped his fingers at the guard on his left. "Summon the king. We either have an innocent young man or an evil conjurer here to do the kingdom ill. Young *Kip*, His Majesty will determine your punishment if your claim about the warrior proves false."

The guard removed a white object shaped like an oversized marble and mumbled into it.

Was that how they communicated? If so, he hoped Winnie had found her way to the castle and the monarch. If not, would he land in a dungeon?

Chapter 7

Winnie waited for the king to say something. At least he nodded for her to sit at the opposite side of his desk. Sitting across from a sullen monarch reminded her of past visits to the principal's office. Speaking her mind got her into more trouble than she cared to admit.

"Can you speak the truth, or do you enjoy telling tall tales like my daughter?"

"I'm honest." *Mostly*.

"And you believe Gwen was enchanted into a…" He made a sour face. "A toad."

"I don't believe it. I know it."

He leaned back in his chair and sized her up. He shifted forward, removed his crown, and set it on the desk. "I don't know if you're aware of objects that can detect the truth."

"I'm aware of lie detectors."

"I'm sure you are."

She recognized the sarcasm in his voice.

"My crown is more than a simple adornment. It's sentient."

Winnie gulped. Sentient? Did that mean his crown knew it was alive?

"If you speak the truth, no harm will come to you. If you say anything less, you'll receive a nasty shock. If you evade the truth multiple times, the crown is within its right to kill you."

Could a simple gold circlet do that? It began to glow white.

"Is there a button battery in there?" How else could it light up on its own?

"I'll be the one asking the questions. Why do you believe my daughter was enchanted? Speak, then touch the crown."

She hesitated. He might have exaggerated about it killing her, but she didn't want to take the chance. "What if the crown doesn't believe me even when I tell the truth?"

"It'll know."

Winnie took a deep breath and gave a condensed version of her brother finding the toad in another world and Princess Gwen's dream message that she had been enchanted and believed someone named Argamel could help change her back.

The king nodded for her to touch the gold crown. She reluctantly reached out. Rather than cool metal, her fingers touched soft warmth. It vibrated under her fingertips.

The king nodded in satisfaction. "Clearly, you believe your story to be true."

"Dude!" Her grip tightened around the gold circlet. "Your enchanted daughter talked in my head. I know it was her."

The crown pulsed and made a soft sound like a melody. To hear better, Winnie lifted it to her temple. The king stared in horror as she placed the crown on her head. The crown tightened until it fit. She knew, without understanding how she knew, that the crown belonged exclusively to King Steffin. Her temptation to confirm the king's name disappeared along with his office. A bigger question crowded that one out. How did she suddenly appear on a grassy hill shaded by a leafy tree with the thickest trunk she'd ever seen?

Happy voices and laughter from her left sent her scurrying behind the tree. She peeked around the side. A younger version of the identical twin princesses gripped each other's hands and twirled in a circle. Seeing both together clued her in that she must have entered a memory. She stepped unnoticed into the open. Had the crown sent her here? And if so, why?

The barefooted pair, clad in matching pale-green sleeveless summer dresses, wore their hair in two cute little buns on the sides of their heads. A regal woman, with high cheekbones and skin the color of tree bark after a heavy rain, sat on a blue picnic blanket. Winnie had never met the queen but knew the woman had to be the girls' mother. She shared their leaf-green eyes.

The memory didn't just come with sight and sound. She smelled the queen's fresh, woodsy perfume. The term "tree sprite" finally made sense. The king hadn't married another human. He'd married a person related to trees. Winnie mouthed the word "wow."

The queen smiled and pointed. "I see Papa!"

At the bottom of the hill, half a dozen riders, including the king, dismounted.

The girls leaped in unison and rushed to him with open arms. In long, quick strides, the king met them halfway up the hill. He lifted them together and swung them in a circle. He set them down, laughing with them. A nostalgic twinge rippled through Winnie. Years ago, she used to greet her own dad the same way.

The king kissed the tops of his daughters' heads, let them go, and continued up the hill to his queen. The girls skipped along on either side of him. The one on his right said, "Papa, I'm going to see Dardin." She turned and galloped toward the horses.

"Don't braid his mane," he called after her.

She giggled and kept going.

"He's a warhorse," he said, but Winnie knew the girl didn't hear and wouldn't have obeyed if she had.

"I'll make you a daisy crown," the other said and scampered away.

The king and queen embraced at the top of the hill.

Mr. Crown or whatever, I don't need to see this part.

The crown didn't release her. At least the couple didn't get too mushy. They kissed once, then sat together on the picnic blanket.

"Where did Argamel take you this time?" The queen sounded skeptical.

"To Mistress Maven and the sacred ground."

Winnie felt his exhaustion from a three-day trek by horse through rough terrain.

"The woman brought the portent stones with her."

"And?" the queen prompted.

"For the next two years, we'll have peace and prosperity. In the third year, we'll have three uncertainties and one possibility. Maven interpreted it to mean unrest from the sea unless the female warrior appears as foretold."

The prediction sent a chill through Winnie. The enemy from her last war had also come from the sea.

"I've communed with all the Great Mothers," the queen said. "No female within childbearing age will agree to fight. Before you ask, that statement included humans as well as tree sprites."

The king stretched his legs in front of him and

leaned back on his elbows. "One could still arrive from the mainland. Although, Maven suggested she might come from another world entirely. And there's one true way to establish her identity. She will wear my crown and live."

"How is that even possible?" blurted the queen. "It killed two of your brothers, and they were heirs."

The news shocked Winnie back to the king's office. She lifted the crown off her head and slowly held it out to its rightful owner. The king stared back with unblinking eyes. He accepted it without a word and returned it to his head.

Despite the prediction, Winnie wanted to distance herself from it. She eased off her seat. "I, uh, better go."

"A moment," he said softly, motioning for her to sit again.

She slowly settled back onto the edge of her chair.

"Clearly, because you mentioned your pink 'armor,' you're aware of the prophecy that a young female warrior will save my kingdom from an unknown enemy."

Winnie flopped against the back of the chair in defeat. "Ah, crap. Not another unknown enemy. Are they spiders?"

"Unless that's the name of a secret army, most definitely not. We're still trying to figure out which kingdom would choose to attack us. We've all lived in peace for decades."

"I really hope nobody wants to attack us right now. We have to focus on turning your daughter back into a princess."

"Agreed."

"First, we have to find your conjurer." She searched

for a phone or intercom, but the king's desk only held paperwork. "How do you usually contact him? With a note attached to a pigeon's leg?"

He squinted at her. "Of course not." He withdrew a little white ball from his desk.

"A marble?"

"It's a communications orb. All I need do is hold it in my palm and think his name. When he's in range, he uses his magic to materialize in the room. Unfortunately, he's been out of range the past few days."

Winnie held out her hand. "Can I see it?"

"It can only be handled safely by its host."

"And you're its host."

He nodded. "The orb is forged from a glow stone, the same as the crown."

"The crown liked me. Maybe your orb will like me too."

The king frowned. "The crown doesn't *like* anyone, it…" He paused as if listening. "I stand corrected." He laid the orb on his desk. "Move your hand slowly toward it. If you feel heat or an electrical charge, don't touch it."

The possibility that a little white marble might shock her put a damper on her enthusiasm. She leaned forward and slowly moved her hand toward it. Several inches away, it glowed pink and let out a pleasing hum. "So far, so good," she murmured. Even though the king didn't tell her to, she rested the back of her hand on the desk. The ball rolled onto her palm. It glowed brighter and spoke to her. Not with words, more like inner thoughts.

With whom do you desire to contact?

Even though the king had no luck when he tried it, she silently asked for the conjurer. Maybe he'd moved back in range.

The one you beckon is no longer here.

The answer came with an eerie sensation that she'd just been tasked with finding and bringing him back. She rotated her hand, allowing the ball to roll back onto the desktop.

"Okay, that was weird."

The king cocked an eyebrow. "Did it communicate with you?"

"Either that or I'm going mental, which I'm not ready to rule out yet."

The king flashed a warm-hearted smile. "It has that effect on people. What did it say?"

"I think I'm supposed to bring back the conjurer."

The king looked contemplative, or maybe he was talking to his living crown. Either way, a moment later, he nodded. "We believe in you."

Winnie liked it better when people doubted her so she could prove them wrong. What if the king had misplaced his faith and she failed? *Positive thoughts or no thoughts at all.* That used to be her mom's motto.

A sudden reminder raised her spirits. "I have a friend who knows magic. If he can't find your conjurer, maybe he can help your daughter."

The king raised a royal eyebrow. "Do you mean Kip?"

Shock from his statement lifted her half an inch off her chair. "How did you know?"

"Besides discussing the missing conjurer during my meeting, I also received word an outsider named Kip tried to use unauthorized magic. He's in one of our interrogation rooms."

She chewed her lower lip. He wouldn't have been caught using unauthorized magic if he and Mikey had stayed hidden. Mikey! "Is my brother with him?"

"He's currently enjoying the rocking horse in the royal playroom. A nursemaid is keeping watch." He brought out his white marble again. "I'll have them meet you at the East Gate. Abbi can show you where that is."

She breathed relief. "Thank you."

He nodded, then called toward the closed door, "Abbi, come in."

The princess, with the toad perched on her shoulder, entered. She looked hopefully from Winnie to the king.

"Abbidrelle," he said in a stern voice, "listen carefully. I'm trusting you to lead Warrior Windemere to the south forest. That was the last place Argamel was seen."

She enthusiastically bobbed her head up and down. "Yes, Papa."

"And take…Gwen with you. If Windemere can't find the conjurer, you'll need to direct her to Oram Forest. I'm sure Maven can help. I'll send the Messenger for extra protection, should you need it."

"Thank you, Papa." She clasped Winnie's hand and pulled her to the door.

"And Abbi?"

She paused to look back. So did Winnie.

"Don't tell your mother."

"I won't." The girls burst through the door.

Chapter 8

After passing the sentries in the outer hallway, the princess returned the toad to Winnie. "Can you keep her safely in your pocket? We need to move fast."

She accepted the princess toad and lightly gripped her inside her pocket. They tore through another maze of corridors, charged up two staircases, and zigzagged through even more corridors. A maid dressed in a black uniform and white cap let out an alarmed squeak and dropped the tall stack of towels in her arms.

"Sorry," Winnie called over her shoulder.

After one final turn, they burst inside a royal bedroom. Princess Abbi banged the door shut behind them and hunched over, panting from the exertion.

Sunlight shone through three arched windows on the outer wall. One pale-green canopy bed pressed against the wall to the left of the first window. A second matching bed stood to the right of the third window. Two identical gold-trimmed nightstands beneath the center window separated the beds. A scratched and crumpled shield hung from the cream-colored wall on Winnie's left. The sky-blue wall to her right held a mural of a wide-trunked tree. Its thick, leafy branches spread outward and up.

When the princess's breathing returned to normal, she sped around Winnie to the closed double doors to the right of the room's entrance. She threw open twin doors to a walk-in closet larger than Winnie's bedroom at home. "I'll need some manner of disguise."

Only satin gowns hung inside. "Yeah, none of those are going to work."

"Don't insult me," the princess said absently. She pushed past ruffled sleeves and flowing skirts. She backed out, holding shiny black slacks and a white blouse with long, puffy sleeves. "This belonged to a visiting minstrel. Gwennie stole it from the laundry. She uses it sometimes when she sneaks out of the castle."

Winnie gave the clothes a dubious stare. "Does she cover her head with it?"

"Don't be silly." The princess ducked behind a screen to change. "Gwennie went out after dark. Since we can't wait that long, I'll wear a hat pushed low enough to obscure my face." She stepped from behind the screen in the minstrel's outfit. To Winnie, she resembled a casually dressed princess.

The princess snatched a plumed hat from the closet shelf and positioned it rakishly on her head. "Don't stare like that. Nobody's going to notice me anyway. They'll be more focused on the young female warrior in her pink armor."

Winnie tugged at the front of her hoodie. "You guys realize this isn't armor, right?"

"It's a foreign fabric. Anyone who sees it will believe it repels arrows."

"I guess that's all right as long as nobody tries to test that theory. The king said my brother and my friend would meet us at the East Gate."

"Excellent. Hardly anyone uses that one."

They scurried through more corridors. Whenever a servant or court member happened by, they ducked into alcoves or behind statues.

"Why are we hiding from everybody?" Winnie whispered. "I thought your dad said we could do this."

"He also told us not to let my mother know we're leaving."

On the ground floor, they stopped at a gated door. A lone guard snapped to attention. "Warrior Windem. It's an honor to open the gate for you."

She mumbled a distracted thanks as she glanced left to right. Where were Kip and Mikey? If they got themselves arrested again, she'd never speak to them. She turned her back on the guard and discreetly removed the orange pebble phone from her front jeans pocket. "Kip?"

"Hey, Win," his Cockney voice sounded from the stone. "I was just about to ring you. The queen isn't to know we're here, so a guard led us out the back way. We're headed to the south forest. Do you know the place?"

"That's where we were supposed to take you."

"Looks like we're going separately, then. I'll ring when Mikey and I reach it."

Winnie slid the pebble back into her pocket and turned to the princess. "You and I are going alone to the south forest."

The girl stared with wide eyes. "I've never seen a common stone do that."

Winnie pressed her lips tightly together and shook her head. She hoped the princess understood they couldn't discuss it in front of the guard. She didn't speak until they reached a deserted, tree-lined road one hundred yards from the castle. "You were right about the pebble you saw me use. It is a plain stone. Kip, the dude on the other end, used magic to turn it into a communications device."

"No wonder the guards took him to the interrogation room. Only the king's conjurer can use magic. For everyone else, it's illegal."

"How'd you know that's where Kip was?"

She grinned. "I have excellent hearing. Even through closed doors."

Winnie laughed. "Your Highness, you're my kind of princess."

The other girl smiled back. "Coming from a female warrior, I accept that as high praise. Now that we're away from the castle, you needn't bother with titles."

"The few times your sister talked in my head, she referred to you as Abbi. Earlier, I almost accidentally said your name without the title. I know there's royal protocol and all."

"You're right about the protocol, but out here, please call me Abbi."

"Thanks. And you can call me Winnie."

They entered the forest from a different path. Less sunlight filtered through the thick leaves. As they rounded a curve, black boots and black pant legs swung from a branch overhead. Winnie clutched her canteen, ready to use it as a weapon.

Abbi peered upward and smiled. "There you are. I wondered when we'd see you."

Winnie relaxed her grip. The owner of the boots and pant legs sprang from the tree. He acknowledged Abbi by raising his right eyebrow and giving a single nod.

The lanky man stood a good head and shoulders above Winnie's five-foot-ten height. Oddly, a black bandage covered his mouth.

"That's not weird at all," Winnie mumbled.

"This is the Messenger," Abbi introduced with pride. "My protector."

"Is he…" Winnie looked from the princess to the man. "Are you hurt?" She tapped her own mouth.

"He's perfectly fine. He took a vow of silence."

The Messenger nodded vigorously, rustling his spikey black hair.

How much protection could he give? Did he have to play charades every time he spotted trouble? Winnie's own protector soared through an opening between two trees and landed at her feet. He murmured softly, then preened his breast feathers. Could Mikey and Kip be nearby?

At the sight of the bird, the Messenger scuttled behind a tree. Winnie'd had a similar reaction the first time she encountered Bird. But shouldn't the guardian for a princess be braver? The Messenger slowly inched back onto the trail. Black eyeliner emphasized his worried eyes.

Abbi appeared unfazed. "What a glorious creature you are! What's his name?"

Winnie scuffed at the ground, embarrassed to admit the truth to an animal lover. "We…kind of just call him Bird."

The princess stared lovingly at him. "That will never do. You're much too noble for such a common name, aren't you?"

Even though the shiny black feathers around his eyes gave the appearance of a perpetual scowl, Bird stretched his long neck upward as if pleased by the compliment.

"I dub thee Gallant Sir Henry," Abbi announced.

Bird bowed his head low.

Winnie opened her canteen. "If I'd known you wanted a better name, I could've thought of one." She took a long drink just as an unexpected ting-a-ling sounded from her jeans pocket. She sputtered, "Gack!" and lost her grip on the canteen. Fortunately, the strap kept it from hitting the ground. Only a little water sloshed over her pant leg, but her swallow went down wrong. As she hacked and thumped her chest, the pebble phone rang again. She pulled it out and answered with a raspy voice.

"Win, are you all right?" Kip's voice blasted from the little orange rock. She must have accidentally put it on speaker.

Winnie coughed again. "Water went down the wrong pipe. Where are you?"

"Headed your way. We sent Bird ahead."

"He's here now."

Bird honked. Kip laughed through the receiving end. "Thanks, old boy!"

"Hi, Windy," Mikey's voice sounded through the pebble. "We got arrested!"

"Ignore him," Kip said. "We'll see you soon."

Winnie returned the stone to her pocket. "I think I know where I am. There should be a giant boulder around the next bend. Let's keep going and meet them."

As predicted, they came to the boulder where she'd first met Eggar. To her surprise, he sat perched on top again. He bobbed his head to the princess and grinned at Winnie.

"Did your truth stones tell you we'd be here?" Abbi asked.

Eggar leaped down from the boulder and bowed.

"They did, Your Highness. The queen asked me to keep watch for you."

"Papa said she wasn't supposed to know!"

He chuckled. "The queen knows everything."

Abbi glanced at the Messenger, who simply shrugged.

Kip and Mikey strolled around the corner and joined the small gathering. Bird let out a satisfied honk and soared upward between the trees.

"Didn't mean to send you away, mate," Kip called after him.

"He's hungry," Mikey announced.

"I'm sure he'll find something out here," Winnie said, then introduced Kip and her little brother to her new friends.

Kip bowed to the princess. "I am at your service, Your Majesty."

A twinge of jealousy rippled through Winnie. But only a twinge.

"Where's Stompy?" Mikey asked.

"He calls the toad Stompy," she explained to Abbi. "They're kind of friends. You don't mind letting Mikey take over?" As long as the princess didn't accidentally mention the toad's gender to her brother, they should be fine.

The princess smiled down at the little boy. "Not at all."

Winnie carefully removed the toad from her hoodie pocket. Mikey slid the day pack straps off his shoulders, letting it fall. He gently accepted the toad. "I missed you too," he cooed, placing her on his shoulder.

Winnie bent close to him. "Bud," she said gently, "you know we're on a quest to turn Stompy back into a person."

"I know." The loving look he gave Stompy implied he preferred his friend as a toad. They even seemed to return to their secret conversations.

"So, Your Majesty," Kip said, "what is our course of action?"

Winnie scowled at the slight. He could've asked her.

"We're hoping to find Argamel, the conjurer. He might be somewhere in these woods. If not, I'll lead you to Oram Forest."

"From there," Eggar continued, "I'll take over as guide."

Abbi pouted. "I wanted to go into the forest with you."

Eggar smiled apologetically. "Sorry. The queen's orders."

Kip nodded to the Messenger. "Vow of silence, then, eh?"

The Messenger bobbed his head vigorously. It seemed he made no subtle motions.

"Got any more of that tape?" Kip said in a playful voice. "We might need it for Winnie."

"I was just thinking that about you," Winnie teased back. She reached to push him, but he clasped her hands. They grinned at each other and had a short shoving match that ended with Winnie stumbling backward and Kip catching her in a quick hug. They laughed and looked into each other's eyes. The world stopped long enough for her to fall into the deepness of his gaze.

"We need to find Argamel," Abbi announced.

Kip jumped and let go. Winnie, also startled by the interruption, stumbled backward. She expected to bump into her little brother, who often stood too close. Only an empty trail lay behind her. "No way! Did anybody see Mikey leave?"

The Messenger made an exaggerated point of sifting through the fallen leaves on the trail as if he'd find a six-year-old and a toad hidden underneath. The princess shook her head.

"I was looking in the opposite direction," Eggar confessed.

Kip removed his magical seashell from his pocket. "I'll just contact him, shall I?"

A muffled ring sounded from the day pack Mikey had left on the ground. "Why did I bother giving him a phone?" He snatched the ringing pebble from the bag and silenced it with a decisive pinch.

Winnie fought rising panic. "He was here a second ago. Mikey!"

Kip held up his hand. "Listen."

She heard nothing over the pounding pulse in her ears. "I'm a terrible sister."

"Shh, wait," Kip whispered.

The group went still. After a moment, he pointed. "This way." He strode off the trail and into the woods.

Winnie grabbed the day pack and hurried after him. Why did she keep losing her little brother?

Chapter 9

Kip plowed through the undergrowth. The frightening yet annoying reminder that Mikey had a penchant for disappearing spurred him. What if ogres lived in this forest? The little blighter had had a caretaker when they were separated at the castle. Out here on his own, what horrors might he face?

Winnie, who must have felt the same, shot ahead of him on the right.

In time, the brightness between the trees caught his attention. He skidded to a halt just outside a clearing and called to Winnie. She jogged back to him. He nodded to his left. Ten feet away, Mikey's bright-blue T-shirt stood out against the forest's greenery. Both stepped closer. Mikey stood still with the toad on his shoulder.

"Bud, you can't just take off like that."

"Stompy wanted to show me where he got enchanted."

The princess, the Messenger, and Eggar strolled toward them. From a trail.

Kip smirked. He might have noticed the side trail that led straight to the clearing if he hadn't dashed off without thinking. Instead, he'd thrashed through leaves and briars in the overgrown terrain.

The little boy pointed into the clearing. "This is where it happened."

Kip opened his mind. Magical energy swirled

around him. He sniffed deeply. A sour scent reached his nose. Had Tee caught the same odor on him?

"What did Stompy tell you?" Winnie asked.

"Two conjurers had a battle in there."

"There's a mother tree on the other side." Princess Abbi nodded across the clearing to a tree with a trunk large enough to hide all six if they stood side by side.

"We wanted to ask the mother tree what happened," Mikey explained, "but we're not allowed to go through the clearing."

Winnie whistled. "That thing is mammoth."

"She's not a thing," Eggar said. "She's one of our ancestors."

Mikey turned toward Eggar. "You're a tree sprite, just like Stompy and the princess."

Eggar stood tall. "Yes, I am."

Didn't tree sprites have pointed ears? The princess's ears only had a hint of a taper. Eggar's ears lay hidden under his long black braids, making it difficult to determine his lineage.

Another magical pull called to Kip. "Something definitely happened here."

The Messenger licked his finger and held it out as if checking for wind direction.

"I think I can do it," Kip said, more to himself than to the others. "I'm not one hundred percent cert, but if I can set my intention, it might work."

Winnie squinted at him. "What in the world are you talking about?"

"I'm talking about showing what happened here. If everyone stays silent and still, I'll try to bring up an image. Kind of like using the clearing as a crystal ball."

She smiled. "I like it."

Her encouragement boosted his confidence. He closed his eyes and focused on the swishing sound of leaves from a gentle breeze. In the distance, Bird honked. He guessed that meant Bird hadn't left the area and could offer aid if needed.

Kip slowly inhaled and exhaled. In time, his soft breathing quickened to a tense rumbling inside. When the sensation intensified beyond his comfort, he raised his arms and pointed at the clearing. He slowly opened his eyes.

White smoke shot from his fingertips and poured into the clearing. It filled the air above the open space. As the smoke drifted toward the ground, a frozen three-dimensional image appeared.

Narrow beams of light, some orange, some green, hung suspended across the open area. Many ran parallel to each other. A few intersected, creating an ugly brown color. Multiple beams ricocheted off the trees and zigzagged in different directions. A green streak jetted from a black wand held by a bushy-haired man with a trimmed beard.

The green beam of light pointed at his opponent, ten feet away. The other man, his face hidden behind a black hooded cape, shot back with his wand, sending an orange streak toward the first man, missing him by inches.

"Right," Kip said. "The image solidified. We're allowed to speak."

Eggar peered between two trees. "That man with the beard is our king's conjurer, Argamel. Can we go inside the clearing for a better look?"

"I don't recommend it," Kip replied. "We might lose the image. But it should be all right to walk around the outer rim. I wonder who that other chap is."

He hiked along the clearing's edge toward the unknown wizard. The others followed, with Mikey at the back.

Kip stumbled to a stop now that he'd caught a better view of the other wizard. "No way!"

The princess, first to Kip's side, pointed at the image. "That's the stranger Gwen told me about. She said he was a scientist from the mainland."

Winnie hustled to Kip's other side. She turned her open-mouthed stare from the frozen image to Kip. "It's like he's following us."

"Actually, since he came here first, it's more like we're following him."

"You know him?" Princess Abbi asked.

Kip nodded. "He's from our world, and his name is Thaddeus Krell."

"Except he isn't a scientist," Winnie added. "He's a—"

"No, he really is," Mikey cut in. "He told me."

Winnie stroked the back of his head. "He also told you he was your dad, and that turned out to be a lie."

"He must also be a conjurer," the princess said.

Kip nodded. "Unfortunately, he's a conjurer with evil intentions."

Mikey crossed his arms and pushed out his lower lip. "He can't be. He's my non-dad and is always nice to me."

Winnie rested a hand on his unoccupied shoulder. "And we're glad he was, bud."

Mikey shrugged away and tramped to another view of the clearing. A moment later, he blurted, "That's Stompy's people body, and she's a girl!"

Kip and the others thundered around the rim to a

third image, partially hidden behind a tree. Stompy's human form wasn't just a girl but a duplicate of Princess Abbi. An ugly brown streak of light pierced her in the chest.

Chapter 10

Abbi crumpled to her knees and sobbed into her hands. Winnie stretched a hand toward the princess, but the Messenger sprang to the girl's side first. He wrapped his arm around her trembling shoulders with a tenderness that brought up memories of Winnie's loving father. She ached for Abbi and for herself.

Kip nudged her. "This complicates matters. See how the colors merged when they hit the princess? The curse must be a combination of spells from both wizards. I wonder if one wizard can even fix this on his own."

Winnie shuddered. "Does that mean we have to find the king's conjurer *and* Krell? He's probably ten worlds away by now."

"Let's not worry about Krell just yet. We need to find Argamel. Maybe his image can give us an idea of where he went." He strode around the circle to the right.

She hesitated. Should she ask the others to follow? Abbi and the Messenger remained on the mossy ground, probably still processing what happened to Gwen. Eggar sat in the middle of the nearby trail, rattling pebbles in his hand. He tossed them, then scooped them up again. Mikey moved to his side to watch, still carrying the princess toad on his shoulder.

Winnie left them to their respective activities and hiked along the outer rim until she caught up with Kip. He stood flanked by the mammoth mother tree and a tall pine. He faced Argamel's frozen image between a pair of pine branches, probably using them for cover from Krell's attack.

"Any ideas where Argamel went?" Winnie whispered.

"I don't believe he owned a Frama-scope, so he must still be in this world."

"They use magical white marbles to contact each other here. When I was with the king, I used it to call Argamel but couldn't get through. Maybe your shell phone can reach him."

He shrugged. "Worth a try." He pulled out his shell but only stared at it.

"Well? What's the holdup?"

"Just thinking about Sister Ava again and her warning. I don't think there should be negative consequences from releasing that image or using my shell phone, but what if there are?"

She considered it for the briefest moment. "First, if you hadn't shown us that image, we never would've known what happened. Second, trying to call Argamel on your shell is a good thing."

He nodded. "Let's make a pact that I won't use magic unless we both agree I should."

"Sounds good. And I agree you need your magic phone now."

He raised the shell to his mouth. "Argamel."

After a short delay, a faint ring sounded nearby. They frowned at each other.

"Where's it coming from?" Kip murmured.

The ringing stopped.

"Try again."

On his second attempt, the muffled ring seemed to

come from inside the pine tree nearest Argamel's image.

"That can't be right. Argamel."

The muted noise sounded again from the same place.

Winnie pointed at the tree trunk. "It's definitely coming from there."

"How is that even possible? Let me try once more."

This time when he called, they both leaned closer to the pine's trunk.

"What are you doing?" spoke a voice from behind.

Winnie let out a startled yip. She and Kip turned toward the princess. The girl's mute guardian hovered behind her.

Winnie frowned, annoyed with herself for jumping. "Give us a warning next time."

Abbi ignored her. "Can you speak with trees?"

Her breathing finally returned to normal. "We were listening."

Abbi cocked her head. "To that tree? What did he say?"

"Not the tree. This." Kip demonstrated by speaking into his shell.

The ring sounded from inside the tree again.

The Messenger bent closer, listening. So did Abbi. "Is your shell doing that?"

"Yes. He's trying to contact Argamel," Winnie explained.

The Messenger raised an eyebrow, then squinted at Kip's shell.

Abbi gently laid her hands on the ringing trunk. "I don't know how your shell knew, but Argamel is here. In stasis."

Kip scrutinized the trunk. "Are you saying he's alive

inside there?"

"Yes."

"How can you tell?" Winnie asked.

"The tree told me."

"You can speak with trees?" Kip asked.

Abbi's back stiffened. "Of course, I can. Didn't Mikey just tell you I'm a tree sprite?"

Kip, always more diplomatic than Winnie, bowed. "I do beg your pardon, Your Majesty."

Winnie rolled her eyes.

Kip smirked back, then turned to the princess. "How do we get him out, then?"

The Messenger mimed chopping down the tree.

Abbi folded her arms and scowled at the Messenger. "Don't even say that as a joke. The king's conjurer could die if any harm comes to this tree."

"Nobody wants that," Winnie said. "Could we bring him out with Kip's magic?"

"Tree magic put him in there," Abbi said. "Human magic won't get him out."

Mikey and Eggar rejoined the group. Winnie quickly caught them up on the missing conjurer's location.

"Hate to say it," Kip said, "but if we can't get Argamel out of there, we have no choice but to contact Krell and ask for his help."

"Well." Mikey drew out the word. "When I stayed with him, he never helped anybody unless they promised to give him something in return."

Winnie snorted. "We are not giving that man anything."

"Before we make any decisions," Kip said, "we have to figure out if Krell's even here."

Eggar stepped forward. "I could ask my truth stones."

"Are they anything like the one I met earlier?" Kip asked. "An elf made me lay my hand on it to tell if I was lying."

"We haven't got elves here," Abbi said, as Eggar said, "That's a different stone."

Eggar cleared the ground of dead leaves with his foot, exposing a section of brown earth. He opened the felt bag tied to his belt and withdrew three smooth, shiny, round stones. They lay in his open palm with a black stone on the right, a white stone in the middle, and a milky blue one on the left. "Mikey told me you don't have truth stones in your world."

"True, but I have seen them here," Kip said. "A woman, I guess she was a tree sprite, used them when I was in the interrogation room. She kept rolling them out and collecting them. She never told us what they said, though."

"We can either think the question or speak it out loud as we shake the stones. To gather complete information," Eggar said, "we ask multiple yes/no questions as quickly as possible. This white stone is the indicator. The answer is yes when the black stone lands nearest the indicator stone. The answer is no if the blue one lands closest to the indicator."

The process reminded Winnie of a fortune-telling game she and her friend Kimber played in third grade, but they used marbles. Still, she wanted to believe and joined the others as they gathered around Eggar.

Kip inched closer. "Can you ask if Thaddeus Krell is in this world?"

Eggar repeated the question, then let the stones go.

The blue stone landed near the edge of the cleared area. The black one stopped barely an inch from the white indicator. He gathered the stones. "He is."

Could his stones know that? She looked to Kip.

He apparently accepted Eggar's gift as real and asked, "Can you find out where he is? I mean, how close?"

Eggar nodded. "We can begin here and move our way outward." He rattled the stones in his palm as he asked, "Is Thaddeus Krell on Aylen Isle?"

When the stones rolled to a stop, the "no" stone landed closest to the indicator.

"Is Thaddeus Krell in Greater Aylen?" Eggar asked the stones. To Winnie and Kip, he said, "That's the nearest country on the mainland."

This time, the stones answered, "Yes."

"Is he in Brenna? That's the easternmost seaport on Greater Aylen."

Again, the stones answered in the affirmative.

"I'll give it a go, then, shall I?" Kip brought his shell phone to his mouth. "Thaddeus Krell." He held it out. "I've put it on speaker."

A soft purr sounded from the shell. It stopped abruptly in the middle of the third ring.

"Did he just reject the call?" Winnie wondered out loud.

Eggar asked the stones and received another "yes" in reply.

"Did he know it was me on the other end?" Kip asked.

This time, after Eggar asked the question, the blue and black stones landed the same distance from the indicator stone. He looked up. "When that happens, it usually means they're done answering for now. Sorry."

"We have another problem," Mikey announced. "Stomp—I mean Princess Gwennie is losing herself again. Can you do another spell like you did before?"

Kip's brow rippled. "I expected the first one to last longer than this."

Winnie's shoulders slumped. How could they bring the toad princess this far and not be able to help?

"I'll ask the mother tree." Abbi curtseyed in front of the mega-sized deciduous tree, then gently rested her hands on the trunk. The group stood quietly by.

Abbi spent a long moment in silent meditation. Winnie shifted from one foot to the other. Did the delay mean bad news or good?

Finally, the princess stepped away. "Mother says Argamel is being punished for allowing harm to come to my sister. He won't be released until Gwennie is restored. But he can't restore her while he's in stasis. And that's not all. Mother says the only way to prevent Gwennie from losing herself is to also send her into stasis."

Mikey shook his head and stepped backward. "Kip can help her with his magic."

"I don't like it either," Abbi said, "but we have no choice."

She gently lifted the toad off Mikey's shoulder. "Gwennie, do you understand what we need to do to help you?" She set her sister under the mother tree, and Gwen hopped toward one of the exposed roots and disappeared by melting into it.

"I don't like it," Mikey said tearfully.

Winnie pulled him into a hug. "I'm sorry," she whispered, "but we have to do what's best for her."

The others stood in respectful silence. Mikey whimpered. Winnie agreed with her brother's anguish. Sending Stompy into the tree felt too much like they'd given up. She let out a disheartened sigh.

The Messenger directed an odd pantomime at Abbi. When he finished, the princess faced the others. "He says we might as well guide you to Oram Forest. He'll take us to where the horses are waiting."

"What about Argamel?" Kip asked. "We can't just leave him inside a tree, can we? It doesn't seem right."

"I understand how you feel. I hate leaving Gwennie after finally finding her, but putting her in stasis will keep her safe. Argamel is also safe but no help to us."

Eggar bowed to her. "Your Majesty, if we can't use the conjurers, maybe my grandmère can make a special potion to restore your sister."

Abbi pressed her palms together. "Thank you. I think that's why Papa wanted you to go there if we couldn't get help from Argamel. I wish I could come too, but I'm only allowed to go as far as the edge of Oram Forest."

"We promise to update you through the communication stones."

She sighed again. "I still wish I could come along."

The group set off down a narrow path. When it expanded, the princess and the Messenger walked side by side in front, followed by a downcast Mikey. Winnie, Kip, and Eggar brought up the rear.

"I'm glad the Messenger convinced the princess not to go farther," Eggar said in a secretive voice. "It might not be safe for her to enter Oram Forest."

Winnie glanced at Mikey several paces ahead, then back to Eggar. "What about Mikey? Will he be safe?"

He nodded. "The princess's case is different. She's royalty."

"Mikey is too in his home world. He's a prince."

"That may be true, but he isn't a half-tree sprite like the princess. Oram Forest is enchanted, and not all the inhabitants are pleased that a tree sprite queen married a human. Someone might try to do her harm."

"Will any of the enchanted people mind that *we're* human?" Winnie asked.

"You should be safe if you're accompanied by a full-blooded tree sprite, which I am." He held out his hands and turned them upward, displaying a tiny green leaf that sprouted from the inside of each wrist.

"Are you guys part tree?" Winnie asked.

"Win," Kip warned, "don't be rude."

"Oh. Sorry. I didn't mean…"

"No, it's all right. For a special few of us, we can grow into a tree at the end of our lives. Obviously, only females can become mother trees, like this one." Eggar affectionately patted an oversized tree that grew at the trail's edge.

Winnie gazed in wonder at its vastness and stoic beauty.

"Years ago, the king proved worthy of entering Oram Forest without a guide. The princesses, though, haven't completed their diplomacy lessons yet. A misspoken remark can get a non-magical being expelled from the forest or worse."

Kip grinned and nudged Winnie. "Hear that? Don't misspeak."

She playfully bumped him with her shoulder. "You should've seen me with the king. I was super respectful."

"I'd like a second opinion," he teased and gripped

her hand.

She laughed with him, but his touch started an intense attack of belly flutters. The rest of her insides jittered the way they did when she hurtled down a roller coaster's first hill.

Even after he let go, the blissful sensation stayed with her all the way to the edge of the woods. Two overly tall black horses obediently waited for them. They stood beside a chubby little palomino she recognized as Abbi's pony, Ollie.

The horses each wore a double saddle. She'd never seen a saddle built for two riders. The horse on the left reminded her of a solid black Clydesdale. It had long hair from its lower legs to its hooves.

Abbi skipped to the other horse. He lowered his regal head so she could kiss his nose. She turned to her pony and hugged his neck. "I love you too, Ollie."

"They're awesome," Winnie said, still admiring the horses.

Abbi turned her smile on Winnie. "They are, aren't they?" She pointed to the black Clydesdale. "That's Bella, one of our plow horses. She's carrying your supplies in the saddlebags. The Messenger packed two canvas tarps for the trip, blankets, rope, skins with water, and flint to start a campfire. Ollie has your food. And this handsome gentleman is Dardin, Papa's war horse. I love him almost as much as I love Ollie."

"He's stunning," Winnie gushed. She didn't have to be an expert equestrian to appreciate a pretty horse. Dardin's title, though, worried her. "Has he been in many battles?"

"Not one. Aylen Isle has been a peaceful nation for over three generations."

Kip eyed the horses uneasily. "They seem rather large."

Winnie silently agreed. "Can I ride your pony? I need something close to the ground so when I fall off, which I'm sure I will, I won't have as far to fall."

Abbi's eyes widened in surprise. "Neither of you ride?"

"Oh, I ride," Winnie said. "But for some reason, horses like to stop short. Then I fly over their heads and embarrass myself."

Abbi stroked her pony's forelocks. "Ollie would never do that. He's sure-footed and will take good care of you. Won't you?" She kissed her pony's nose. To the Messenger, she said, "You were right to suggest Bella." To Kip, she added, "She plods along at a nice slow pace."

"You'll never fall either, Kip," Eggar promised. "We'll be riding two and two. I'm guessing Princess Abbi and the Messenger will be riding Dardin?"

She nodded. "Papa is expecting me and his horse to return tonight. Along with the Messenger, of course."

"Kip, you can ride with me on Bella, which leaves Winnie and Mikey on Ollie."

"Sounds like a plan," Winnie agreed, happy to ride the smaller of the three.

Abbi led her father's war horse to a stump and nimbly climbed onto the front of the double saddle. The Messenger followed, settling behind her. She steered her horse out of the way, allowing Eggar and then Kip to use the stump. Winnie hefted Mikey onto the saddle, then slid her right leg over the pony's back.

They rode east through a broad plain that stretched so far around them that Winnie felt lost in a sea of grass. Clouds skimmed across the sun, preventing them from

getting too hot in the open area. When would they reach
Oram Forest?

Chapter 11

Kip had nothing against horses personally. Still, he yearned for an alternate world where the inhabitants drove cars. For now, though, and for the second time that day, he found himself seated atop a mountain of a horse. At least this time, he shared a double saddle with Eggar and had his own pommel to grip. Bella, the draft horse they rode, ambled at the leisurely pace of a sofa on wheels rolling uphill. He relaxed into a motion so gentle he nearly fell asleep.

They rode for ages before the terrain sloped downward to a stream. Thankfully, their princess guide let them stop so the horses could drink and they could stretch their legs.

"Are we still a million miles from the forest?" Winnie asked, voicing Kip's own impatience to get their adventure started.

Princess Abbi grinned. "It only feels like we'll never get there. But we will."

They climbed back on the horses and rode on. The ground gradually sloped upward. They had ridden no more than ten minutes beyond the stream when a low rumble of thunder sounded from behind.

"Is it going to rain?" Winnie asked.

Abbi halted Dardin. The others also stopped.

Kip glanced over his shoulder at a black wave charging toward them. He faced forward, heart pounding.

Winnie also looked back but quickly twisted forward. So did the princess.

"What are they?" Kip and Winnie asked in unison.

"Mostly harmless," the princess said.

"But exceptionally stupid," Eggar added.

"Move closer," Princess Abbi said in a grave voice.

The black horses sidestepped until they almost pressed against the pony, Ollie.

Winnie wrapped a protective arm around Mikey and looked up at Kip. "I wouldn't say no to a protection spell."

"No magic," the princess barked. "Stay perfectly still. They'll mistake us for boulders."

The threatening sound grew louder.

"Hold," she ordered the horses in a tight voice. "Hold."

Kip wanted to disobey the princess and conjure a protective bubble to shield them but couldn't calm his mind enough to recall the incantation.

He clenched his eyes shut and tensed for the clash sure to come. Too soon, the racing mass reached them in a deafening din. They whooshed by in so many waves they generated their own wind. Without meaning to, his mind separated from his body. The roar in his ears dimmed. All sound vanished as his mind rose above the never-ending stampede. He hovered alone in a dark nonplace, welcoming the silence. The sound of an old-fashioned telephone broke through the stillness. Two rings, three rings, four, followed by a beep. Voicemail? A tinny-sounding voice spoke through the darkness. "Go home."

The voice belonged to Krell.

Kip jolted back to the din and his surroundings. He opened his eyes to a herd of buffalo-like creatures, no taller than German shepherds, veering around them. He might have scoffed at their size if they hadn't become such a raging river of fear. Once past, the herd charged up an incline. They cut to the right and kept running. Finally, the deluge reduced to a trickle of stragglers. Bird shrieked overhead and hurtled toward the smallest one. He clasped it in his talons, soared back into the air, and flapped away.

Princess Abbi urged the horses forward.

"What was all that?" Kip asked.

"Dindals in the wild," Eggar replied. "Early pioneers brought them from the mainland. They spook too easily to keep them in pens, so the settlers released them. Today, farmers can only safely keep a few. The meat is delicious, though."

"I'm sure Cook packed dried dindal for your trip," Princess Abbi added, "so you'll get to try some. I know you'll like it."

"Does it taste like chicken?" Winnie asked in a teasing voice.

"More like a mellower version of wild boar," Eggar replied.

Despite the genial conversation, Kip's muscles remained tense. He continually scanned the area for further threats. When minutes passed and the surrounding open land remained clear, he finally allowed himself to settle into the long, tedious ride.

At the crest of a tall hill, Oram Forest appeared far in the distance. A line of trees spread across the entire horizon. After three more hours of riding, the horses stopped in front of a tree line thick with undergrowth.

"How are we getting through there?" Kip asked.

"You aren't," Princess Abbi replied. "This is as far as I'm allowed to go, but you're in good hands with Eggar. Travel well and come back quickly."

"I won't let you down, Princess," Eggar called out.

She nodded and swung her horse around. The Messenger waved, and the war horse galloped back the way they'd come.

"What did she mean we aren't getting in?" Kip asked. "Wasn't that the point of coming?"

"Oh, we'll get in," Eggar said. "Just not through this brush. The princess only brought us to this area because it took her the least amount of time. We'll set up camp here and continue our journey tomorrow."

After all that riding, Kip appreciated the opportunity to walk again. Winnie dismounted and helped Mikey down, then she and Eggar removed bridles and saddles.

To Kip's surprise, neither horse, though free, made a move to wander away. They simply lowered their heads and grazed on the grass under the trees.

The brush grew thick at the edge of the forest but didn't conceal the darkness that lay within. A shudder of ill ease rippled through Kip. Danger lurked in there. He distracted himself from that thought by helping Eggar unpack the camping gear. The pair also tied a tarp to the overhanging branches for shelter. The four of them fit comfortably beneath it with enough overhang to protect the horse and pony from the elements.

They had barely fastened the final rope to a tree when it began to drizzle. They spread a second tarp on the ground to protect themselves from the damp grass. A few yards beyond their tarp, Eggar put up a smaller one for their "kitchen." On his direction, they gathered stones for a fire ring.

Winnie and Mikey organized the supplies. Kip moved away to help Eggar gather loose limbs. "I didn't want to worry Win and Mikey, but there's something dangerous in there." He pointed his chin toward the shadowy forest.

Eggar paused in his work. "Did something call out to you?"

He shook his head. "I sense…I'm not sure. An impenetrable blackness?"

"I've never felt that, and I live here. Although there is the Mysterious. The Myst, for short. But he's only a threat to humans with ill intent."

Neither Kip nor Winnie and Mikey harbored ill intent. Still, the name sent an unexpected shiver down the back of his neck. "Is he a wizard?"

Eggar let out an amused snort. "He's more like a roaming fog that acts as a gatekeeper, except in his mind, the gate is the entire forest. And he doesn't trust humans."

"Fog? Like the vaporous stuff that hovers over the ground early in the morning? That doesn't sound so bad."

"I heard he suffocated a human once. But that might be a rumor."

Kip gulped. "Maybe we need a new plan. I don't want anything to happen to Winnie or Mikey." *Or myself.*

"Are you planning on harming any trees or forest inhabitants?"

"Of course not. We're here to find a way to help the princess."

Eggar resumed gathering sticks. "See? Nothing to

worry about."

"If you're sure. But let's not concern Winnie about that fog thing."

They finished collecting wood, and Eggar quickly provided a blazing fire. The four sat together, drinking hot tea and snacking on thick, crusted bread, cheese, and dried dindal meat. The dindal didn't taste half bad. It reminded him of extra-spicy beef jerky.

After their meal, Eggar tended to the horses. Kip tucked the day pack under his head and closed his eyes. He tried to sleep but couldn't curb his anxiety. They were in grave danger.

Chapter 12

Winnie didn't say so out loud, but her first official meal on Aylen Isle disappointed her. She always counted on bread as a safe food choice whenever she visited alternate worlds. The Messenger ruined that trust by packing stale crusty bread. At least the cheese—she didn't dare ask what animal provided it—made the bread edible. The dried-up dindal meat that Abbi and Eggar raved about smelled too weird, so she only pretended to eat it.

After dinner, Eggar strolled away to bed the horses.

Gentle rain pattered on the tarp, which should have offered a cozy atmosphere, but the damp air had a chill to it. Kip stretched out, using their day pack as a pillow, and closed his eyes. She hoped his head didn't squish the fresh bread she'd brought from home. She'd also packed a jar of peanut butter. How could he sleep on a lumpy pack?

As night fell, a gust of wind whooshed over her. She shivered and hugged her arms. Mikey had the right idea to sit on the tarp's edge nearest the fire. She huddled closer and wrapped an arm around him for added warmth.

Mikey shook under her arm but not from the cold.

"You okay, bud?"

He slowly nodded.

"Ya know," she said gently, "generals and warriors

do cry sometimes."

He looked up tearfully. "They do?"

"When things are sad, definitely."

Apparently accepting her statement as permission, he fell against her and silently cried into her chest. She held and rocked him the way her mom used to when she was little. She even made a few sighing sounds. She used to wonder why Mom did that. Maybe to remind her to breathe. In time, he sat up, sniffled, and rubbed his nose against his T-shirt sleeve. Winnie let it go since they had no tissues in the wilderness.

He swiped the tears off his face with the back of his hand and took a deep breath. Neither spoke for the longest time. Finally, he said in a small voice, "Windy?"

She lightly squeezed his shoulders. "Yeah, bud?"

"What if…" He took another slow breath. "What if I made a mistake bringing Stompy back here?"

"Why do you think that, bud?"

He sniffed. "When we were in Frama-10, Stompy was happy to be a toad and to be my friend. It wasn't till we got back to our world that he remembered. I mean, *she* remembered the enchantment and asked to come home. See? If she stayed on Frama-10, she'd still be happy and not be sucked inside a tree."

"Well…" She disagreed with his take on the situation, but that wouldn't soothe him. In a way, didn't Mikey's alter ego, General Takka, share a similar dilemma? Did the general, whose essence had slipped between worlds and entered Mikey at birth, belong in his adopted world or in Frama-12? The possibility that he belonged in his home world sent a shudder through her. She and her family could never give up Mikey as willingly as he had given up his pet toad.

"What if she can never leave the tree?" Mikey's question pulled her from her troubled thoughts. "What if we can't help her turn back into a person?"

She let out a relieved breath. He hadn't made the connection between Stompy's situation and his own. She gently bumped against him. "Who defeated the lurkin on Frama-12?"

"You did."

"And who stopped Krell from starting a war on Frama-10 between the mountain folk and the people on the Reserve?"

He smiled. "We did."

Winnie hugged him. "That's right. So who says we can't help Stompy?"

As quickly as his joy came, it vanished again. "When Sister Ava called me General Takka, I didn't feel like a general." The boy snuggled closer. "I know I *look* little, but I'm starting to feel little."

"It'll be okay, buddy. Ya know why?"

He shook his head.

She hugged him again. "Because nobody stays little forever. You're probably taller today than you were yesterday."

His face brightened. "I am?"

"Definitely." Even as she smiled, worry still pulsed inside her. *What if he chooses Takka over Mikey?*

Eggar rejoined them, carrying two thick blankets. They settled down for the night with Eggar and Kip under one and Winnie and Mikey under the other. Rain pattered on their tarp roof, lulling her to sleep.

****

The hissing sound from Eggar dousing the dying embers from last night's fire woke her.

The rain had ended, but dampness filled the air. Low-hanging clouds covered the rising sun, making the hour seem earlier than it was. Winnie often rose early to train for long-distance running. Today, she just wanted to roll over and fall back to sleep.

"What's he doing?" Mikey asked.

Curiosity prompted her to sit up. The silhouette of a lone figure stood by a copse of trees on the nearest hilltop. "Is that Kip?"

Mikey swallowed a mouthful of jerky. "Yup. He's been like that for ages."

"Since breakfast anyway," Eggar added. "Winnie, you should eat something too. We'll be leaving soon."

Kip stood alone, seemingly frozen. She pushed back the blanket. "Maybe in a sec. Wait here, bud."

She climbed the hill, fully expecting Kip to acknowledge her before she reached the top. He stared intently into the distance.

"What's out there?"

He slowly turned, sucked in a deep breath, and let it out. "I...don't know if I should say. We need to keep our wits about us, and I don't want to alarm you."

She huffed at him. "Warriors don't get alarmed. Spit it out."

"Last night, I couldn't sleep, so I attempted a relaxation incantation."

"Let me guess. It had the opposite effect."

"Not exactly. It relaxed me so much that I heard someone calling my name. Maybe it was only a dream, but I'm afraid it means Krell knows how to invade my thoughts."

Her mouth dropped open. She quickly snapped it shut. "Maybe it was just a nightmare."

"Or maybe he *was* in my head and knows we're here. He could come after us."

"For what? We don't have anything he needs. He already has a working Frama-scope."

"Here's where it gets dicey. Remember when Sister Ava asked you and Mikey to pack for the trip and she kept me back?"

She nodded.

"She didn't just mention I've got extra magic. She also gave me a job." He pulled out the shoelace hidden under his T-shirt. A shiny Frama-scope dangled from the end.

"Isn't that the one you brought back from Frama-10?"

"Sister Ava took that one. This is Krell's original scope." He breathed out the wizard's name in a nervous whisper.

Winnie lifted it by the lace for a closer look. "Are you sure? His had a broken lens."

"Sister Ava fixed it, then put a spell on it. She asked me to secretly switch this one with the one he currently has. The next time he uses this…poof…he'll land in his laboratory on Earth. If he tries again, he'll just stay in his lab. Kind of brill when you think of it."

"That's a perfect way to keep him from messing with people in alternate worlds. Except Krell can read minds. He'll know what you're up to before you even pull that shoelace out of your shirt."

"Now you see why I didn't want to alarm you."

"No, you needed to tell me. Now I can focus on how to switch the scopes while you…focus on anything else so Krell won't know. Just think of a white bear."

"Seems oddly specific, but I'll try."

He looked away as if in thought. A second later, he nodded and faced her again. His lips curled into an endearing smile. "If we're about to face Krell, there's something I'd like to do first, but if I do it without warning, you might punch me in the neck."

Winnie laughed. "When have I ever punched anybody in the neck?"

He gave her a sheepish grin. "First time for everything, right? But what I meant was…well, last time when we came back through the time tear, you didn't come out right away, and I thought I'd lost you." He shrugged. "So I might've gotten caught up in the moment when I kissed you."

She frowned at her feet. If that kiss meant nothing to him, then maybe she should've punched him in the neck. "I almost forgot about that," she lied.

"Oh. Because now that we're about to face the enemy, I was thinking about kissing you on purpose."

Winnie sucked in a breath of air. She kept her head bowed, unwilling to let him see her stunned expression. Did he care after all? Did she?

He groaned. "You already have a boyfriend."

"No," she mumbled to the ground. "Last year, I told a guy on my track team that I liked him. He said he just wanted to be friends. I felt like a total dork. When I started liking you, it seemed better to keep that to myself."

He gasped. "You like me?"

She rolled her eyes and looked up. "Come on. You know you're cute. You probably have a ton of girlfriends back home."

"I'm cute?"

She playfully shoved him. "I notice you didn't deny

having girlfriends."

"You're forgetting I'm a magician in our world. Remember how you felt when I pulled a quarter out of your ear? My tricks rarely impress the ladies."

She flashed a relieved smile. "In that case, okay. I promise not to punch you in the neck."

He leaned toward her and gently kissed her. The ground hadn't dissolved, but a weightless sensation caught her breath. He eased away and blinked at her. She wanted to laugh. She always did when she whooshed down a steep hill on a roller coaster and her stomach stayed at the top.

"Hey, guys!" Mikey called out.

They jumped apart.

"Eggar says it's time to go."

Kip grinned. "Thanks for not punching me in the neck."

She grinned back. "Thanks for not pulling another quarter out of my ear."

They held hands back to camp but separated to clean up the campsite and to pack. Too bad neither of them had more practice with horses. They could've ridden Bella.

"How do we get in?" she asked, ready to begin the journey.

Eggar adjusted the pony's stirrups. "We'll follow to the south, beside the forest until it veers to the left. That's where we'll find the eastern entrance."

She pointed at a break in the trees. "Can't we just go in there and ride through the woods till we reach a path?"

"The underbrush is too thick for the horses," Eggar replied. "And don't forget. Humans aren't exactly welcome. The forest won't allow you in unless you prove yourselves worthy."

"Have many humans been turned back?" Kip asked.

"Not many try. Of those who do"—Eggar shrugged—"few get admitted."

"Let me guess," Winnie said. "One human did something stupid, which ruined it for everybody else."

"That's rather a good guess."

She warmed with pride.

"Long before King Steffin married the queen of the tree sprites, human settlers believed themselves more entitled to the land than the original inhabitants. They drove the majority of them into this wood. Some humans used to shoot arrows into the forest, hoping to strike them."

Kip gasped. "That's horrible."

"Yes, it was," Eggar said.

"We're not like that," Winnie promised. "And we're not even from this world. Besides, wouldn't they make an exception since we're here to help the princess? Can you ask the stones if we're allowed in?"

"I already did."

"And?" she prompted.

"We have to take the eastern entrance."

She didn't like his nonanswer but said nothing when he steadied the pony for her to climb aboard. Kip lifted Mikey onto the saddle in front of her.

Even though Kip used a flat boulder as a mounting block, he still had to stretch to get on. "She's so ruddy high up," he muttered from the saddle.

Eggar agilely climbed onto her broad back. "She might be big, but she's docile as a lamb and slow as a garden slug."

The garden slug set their plodding pace. At her speed, they'd never reach the entrance. "Can't we go faster?"

Eggar chuckled. "Told you she was a slug."

"Mind if Mikey and I jump ahead? I feel Ollie losing patience."

"Go ahead. We'll catch up when he decides to stop. And he will."

She lightly pressed her knees against the pony's sides. He immediately transitioned from a walk to a gentle trot.

Mikey laughed. "Go faster."

"Hold the saddle horn. Here we go." She squeezed Ollie's sides again. He moved at a livelier pace than she'd ever ridden. She grinned, willing to give the steady Ollie all the credit. "This guy's a dream."

They zipped so far ahead that they lost sight of Bella. When she slowed the pony to a more sedate speed, he veered closer to the tree line. He stopped completely and stretched his neck to eat leaves from a bright-green bush.

"Well, Eggar warned us he'd do that." She slid off the pony's back and helped Mikey down. "This looks like a good place to wait for the guys." That was when the urge hit her to find a private bush. She pointed up the hill. "I'm going up there for two seconds to go to the bathroom. Promise you'll stay *right* here."

"Yup."

She sprinted to a bush that stuck out farther than the others and hid behind it to relieve herself. Even though she took less than a minute, she still hated leaving her little brother alone. She finished and rushed back. Ollie continued to devour the plant life. Mikey stood on tiptoes at the pony's side, trying to reach into the saddlebag.

Winnie held her breath. If the pony bolted, Mikey

could either be trampled or dragged. She edged carefully toward them and said softly, "Whatcha doing, bud?"

"There's leftover bread in here." He struggled to undo the clasp. "I need some for my new friend. He's hungry."

Ollie ignored everything but the heart-shaped leaves he chomped. Winnie clapped him lightly on the neck and reached inside the saddlebag for Mikey. She pulled out the bread left over from last night. "Did you find a squirrel?"

"I found somebody even better. He can't run away."

Intrigued, she followed Mikey to a bush with two yellow-green human-like hands and wrists poking between the normal leaves.

She skidded to a stop. What if a hand yanked him into the brush? Or worse, what if it was this world's version of a Venus flytrap and tried to eat him?

The little boy, unfazed by the anomaly, clapped. The plant's "hands" did the same. They even accurately mimicked his elaborate handshakes. "See? Way better than a squirrel." He held up his hand to one of the plant hands for a high five.

"And he's, um, hungry?" Winnie pinched a piece from the loaf.

The yellow-green hand opened, and she carefully laid the bread on its palm. Its fingers clasped around the food and disappeared back into the bushes.

Mikey grinned. "Told you he was hungry."

Two new yellow-green hands sprouted from the bush, palms up. With a shrug, she offered half the loaf to Mikey.

Soon after the fingers clasped around the bread, they zipped back into the bushes. More waving hands appeared, replacing them. She and Mikey fed over a dozen hands by breaking the bread into smaller portions.

"Sorry, guys," Winnie said, "that's all we've got."

The hands disappeared back into the bush as if they understood. Only normal leaves covered the bush.

"I call him Handy," Mikey announced. "He likes us."

Bella's heavy footfalls clomped toward them.

"Let's keep the hand thing to ourselves," Winnie mumbled. "Nobody would ever believe us." She hardly believed it herself.

****

The forest finally swerved to the left. A stream burbled not far from an awning of leaves that provided welcome shade.

"We can keep the horses here. They won't stray." Eggar removed the saddles and bridles and hung them over a log. "From now forward, you must keep your minds neutral. We're about to encounter leaflings. They can hear thoughts."

Winnie stopped midway through sliding the day pack straps over Mikey's shoulders. "You mean they can read minds?"

Eggar considered it. "I suppose that's one way of describing it. Remember, they don't trust humans in there. Don't give them a reason to deny your entrance. If that happens, our quest is over before it begins."

"What exactly are leaflings?" Kip asked.

"No offense intended, but they're a bit difficult to explain to humans. I guess you could say they're leaf-like creatures that fly. If they choose to examine you, stay very still. And most importantly, don't display any form of aggression. Let's silently enter."

Winnie gravitated toward Kip, hoping to hold his hand, but Mikey wiggled between them. She smiled apologetically over her little brother's head.

Eggar led them to a break in the woods. The grass outside converted to a dirt path the width of a two-lane road. The entrance felt less like a forest and more like a massive leafy tunnel with an arched ceiling twenty feet above their heads. The shimmering yellow-green walls seemed to breathe.

Winnie glanced at Kip again, but his wide-eyed stare focused straight ahead. A pale-gray film put an end to the path.

Eggar stopped beside Kip. "We can't go farther without permission."

"Is that wall poisonous?" Kip whispered.

Eggar shook his head. "Just enchanted."

All four stood silently in a row.

After a long minute, Kip said in a reverent voice, "Do we knock?"

"No," Eggar replied. "We wait."

Chapter 13

Kip's sudden desire to keep Winnie safe filled him with an urgency he'd never experienced. Never mind that she'd never requested a protector. And never mind that she might punch him in the neck for even thinking she needed one. Still, he wanted to guard her from harm. He also wanted to hold her hand again. When they entered the enchanted tunnel, or whatever it was, with Winnie at his side, her blighted little brother ruined it by jumping between them. The child slid his cold little hand into Kip's.

They stood in a line, Eggar, then Kip, Mikey, and Winnie, facing an odd grayish film that blocked the entrance. The film distended in the image of a tall, lanky man as if encased in opaque plastic wrap. The elastic obstruction finally released a seven-foot-tall man with pale-gray skin, pointed ears, and piercing black eyes. The flexible wall closed behind him.

"Goblin?" Kip murmured from the corner of his mouth.

Eggar gave a barely perceptible nod.

The goblin's penetrating stare moved from Winnie to her brother. He bared his pointy teeth in a hungry grin. His leer at Mikey brought the wall to life, and thousands of tiny green creatures flew toward them. Could these be the leaflings Eggar had mentioned earlier? Kip stood stone still and closed his eyes to the swarm. Air from their beating wings cast a gentle breeze over his face. He emptied his mind and concentrated on slowing his breath. To his relief, he sensed them flying away.

"Drop it," the goblin ordered. "It can fly."

Kip opened his eyes. Drop what? Winnie carefully slid a leafling into her sweatshirt pocket just as the yellow-green cloud flew at the goblin's face.

"Bah," he spat. The leaflings hovered for another moment, then returned to the walls.

The goblin used a knobby hand to smooth his meager tufts of white hair as if the leafling encounter had mussed them. He turned to Eggar and dipped his head in what must have been a show of respect. "Tree sprite, you are, as always, welcome here. Proceed."

Eggar hesitated. "Might I wait with the others until…"

The goblin sneered. "No, you might not. Wait on the other side if you feel the need. No promises I'll let them all in, though."

"I'll be just inside." Eggar turned his back on the opaque wall and leaned into it. He melted into the film until it swallowed him whole.

Kip shuddered. Had Eggar safely made it to the other side? And what was over there?

The goblin stared critically at Kip. "I sense magical energy in and around you, boy. I never expected that kind of power from such a young who-mon."

Mikey sniggered. "He said who-mon."

The goblin's pointy ears twitched. "We'll see how amusing I am, little one." He pointed at Kip. "You may go."

With a shrug, he let go of Mikey's hand and turned back toward the way they'd come. Winnie and Mikey might be sent away too, so he'd wait with the horses until they joined him.

"No, you fool!" The goblin pointed over his shoulder.

Kip sucked in a nervous breath. "Right. Meet you on the other side, guys."

He backed into the film the way Eggar had. At first, it cradled him. He kept leaning into it until it released him with a pop. He fell over backward, bumping into Eggar. Both tumbled to the ground.

Kip leaped up first and held out his hand. "Sorry, mate."

Eggar accepted it and regained his footing. "Winnie and Mikey should join us shortly."

"That goblin fellow didn't seem too keen on them." He dusted the back of his jeans as he peered over his shoulder toward the way he'd come. Only woods surrounded them. Where had the elastic doorway gone? "That's odd, innit?"

Odder still, the birds that had twittered from the trees only moments ago went silent. An ominous shadow fell over the immediate area as if a giant cloud covered the sun, preventing the golden rays from slipping through.

Deep in the forest, a white fog, low to the ground, rushed toward them.

Eggar muttered a curse. Louder, he said, "It's the Myst. Don't move."

"Hadn't planned on it."

Eggar hissed for silence.

When the roving fog reached them, it gathered into a cylindrical shape that rose just above Kip's head. The top curled into a bend at eye level. "What isss thisss?"

Talking fog?

"He's with me," Eggar said calmly as if conversing with weather conditions happened every day. Maybe it did.

"He givesss off the ssstench of a wizzzard."

Without thinking, Kip said, "I'll have you know I washed this morning."

"Insssolence."

An invisible force froze Kip in place. Thankfully, he could still breathe.

"He didn't mean that, I'm sure." Eggar cast a disapproving stare at Kip. "Our princess Gwenevieve has been enchanted. We've come with the hope that my grandmère, Mistress Maven, can help us find a way to restore her."

The bent end of the cylinder turned from Eggar to Kip. "Outsssider. Confesss."

Even if he wanted to speak, he had no voice. An invisible flame seared into his head. His temples burned, but he couldn't lift his hands to rub them. The heat intensified, knocking the breath out of him. His body went slack, and he crumpled to the ground, blinded by unbearable pain. When the assault finally ended, he lay in the dust, blind and again unable to move but fully aware of sound and physical sensations. Eggar jostled him.

"Did you kill him?" Eggar spoke in a frightened voice.

"Not completely," the Myst replied.

"He came to help. You must have seen that."

A long silence spread between them. "Now you mention it, his intentionsss might have appeared…sssomewhat benign."

"Because they are. Myst, release him. Please."

Hadn't Eggar told him the Myst only attacked humans with ill intent? So why did Kip now lie frozen in darkness?

"There'zzz a healing willow jussst there."

"You have the ability. Why can't you simply resuscitate him?"

"Becauzzz he possessesss evil intent. I sssaw a memory of it."

Memory? If the fog had invaded his thoughts, which memory had it accessed? The time on Frama-12 when he'd accidentally released the power of Krell? He'd changed since then. The Myst had to believe in personal growth, surely.

Eggar muttered words under his breath that Kip couldn't make out.

"Cursss all you wisssh. They have no effect on me. I can either absorb them or hurl them back at you. You choozzz."

Eggar just grunted.

Normal forest sounds returned. Did that mean the Myst left? If so, why hadn't Kip's vision returned? He felt the hard ground under his back. Despite the strength of his desire, only his chest moved with his breath. The ache in his head dissipated, but the paralysis remained. He thought he felt the pressure of Eggar's fingers around his ankles. Maybe he sensed movement across the ground. He lost track of time and might have drifted off. The motion finally stopped. Where had Eggar taken him?

"Jajee," Eggar's voice said in a respectful tone. "The Myst did a truth test on my friend and scrambled something. I wondered if I could…"

"Friend?" spoke a deep rumbling voice. "You've brought a human enemy into my bole."

Jajee was a tree? That spoke?

"He means well, I promise. He might be human, but he's not from this world. May I please leave him with you for healing? I have to return to the entry point. I'm expecting two others. They won't understand if they don't see me there."

"If you choose to associate with outsiders, that's your affair, but if you leave this creature alone with me, I'll devour it. It will deteriorate my leaves for a season, but I can live with that."

Kip just got paralyzed by a fog, and now a tree wanted to kill him. Could the day get any worse?

"Please, Jajee," Eggar begged. "I need to greet the others. They won't know where we've gone if I don't."

New waves of desperation rolled through Kip's paralyzed body.

"That is not my affair. You know my feelings on the matter. If you stay, I'll see what I can do. If you go, that tells me you care as little for it as I do, and I'll vanquish it."

"Heal it, I mean *him*, please. Can't you do that while I stand outside to greet the others?"

"I choose not to. Decide what is more important to you. This creature's healing or your need to play host to more interlopers."

Kip had never felt more helpless.

"All right, you win," Eggar muttered. "I'll stay. How long will the healing take?"

"Oh, I never agreed to do the healing. Keep still. I'll call to the others."

A wave of panic splashed over Kip. *I'm trapped*

inside my own body. At least his inability to hyperventilate prevented him from losing his mind.

"Well, well, well," Jajee said. "It's your good fortune that your grandmère is esteemed by the queen mother. Alil has agreed to house and heal your human pet."

"Thank you." Eggar's voice sounded annoyed. "And will you kindly give my friend peaceful rest for transport?"

The last thing Kip heard before he lost consciousness was the grumpy tree's reluctant agreement to do so.

****

Kip, still cocooned in blackness, gradually regained consciousness. At least the throbbing in his head had vanished. Could he move again? He tested his fingers first. They wiggled under his direction. He pressed his hands against the floor and slowly pushed himself to a sitting position. A light wave of dizziness passed quickly. "Yes!" Motion and voice.

He rose in the dark and shuffled forward with arms outstretched. Three steps later, his palms touched a smooth surface smelling of wood. He slid both hands along the wall, hoping to locate a doorknob. The wall curved and curved and curved. Even without sight, he knew he'd just walked in a circle. *I'm in a round room? Without a door or a window?*

He slapped at the wall. "Hey! Let me out!"

Chapter 14

What should have been a stationary yellow-green wall on Winnie's right moved in an odd, fluttery way. Mikey's grip on her hand tightened. She squeezed back, then peered over his head at Kip. The older boy's forehead rippled with uncertainty. She gave him a half nod to communicate that she didn't trust the situation either. When part of the enchanted entrance swelled, it took all her courage to keep from running away.

The shape of a gangly guy with pointed ears passed through the elastic film that covered the entrance. She overheard Kip refer to the humanoid as a goblin.

When he directed his pointy-toothed leer at Mikey, the walls surrounding them sprang to life. Hundreds of butterflies with leaf-like wings swarmed them. She didn't have time to remember anything more than their name. Leaflings. Their yellow-green color matched the shade of the hands in the plant she and Mikey had fed earlier. One must have caught the image in her mind because it hovered inches from her face. The butterfly had a tiny face and body. A fairy! Two other fairies accidentally slammed into the one gaping at Winnie. Her wings lost momentum, and she dropped. To save the fairy from the hard dirt ground, Winnie cupped her hands and caught her. She peered into her hands at the tiny, stunned creature.

"Drop it," the goblin demanded. "It can fly."

Obviously, fairies could fly, but not after a midair collision. Winnie gently slipped the fairy into her sweatshirt pocket so she could recover after the unexpected bump from behind.

"Bah," the goblin spat and turned his attention from Winnie.

Fairies buzzed around him for a few more seconds, then returned to the walls.

A moment later, Eggar and then Kip slipped through the enchanted wall. Now she and Mikey stood alone with the goblin.

He took a menacing step toward Mikey but quickly stopped. Expressions of surprise and fear rolled across his face. "I do beg your pardon. I sense royalty beneath the outer shell of a child." He sniffed the air. "A prince *and* a soldier?"

Mikey stood tall. "I'm General Takka from the realm of Bogen."

The goblin bowed respectfully. "I am unfamiliar with your land as I have been banished to the enchanted wood. You may go."

Even though Mikey didn't move, Winnie still gripped his shoulder. "This is my brother. Where he goes, I go."

The goblin glowered at her. She desperately wanted to look away, but warriors shouldn't show weakness.

Finally, he said, "I am bound by the wishes of the leaflings. They have deemed you fit to enter for reasons that escape me, despite the fact you are who-mon."

Mikey giggled again, probably because the man mispronounced the word "human."

The goblin grunted, apparently offended by Mikey's laughter. He turned and pressed back through the film.

Winnie and Mikey blinked at each other.

She shrugged. "I guess we're allowed in too?"

He skipped toward the film.

"Hang on there, bud. We're going in together."

She clasped his hand. They turned their backs to the elastic wall and leaned into it. At first, it held their weight like a wall of plastic wrap. She pressed harder, and it released them to the other side. She caught herself and Mikey before they fell. Her quick reflexes earned her a round of applause. She spun around, searching for the source of all the clapping. She and her brother stood alone in the forest with no evidence of the tunnel they'd entered, the elastic wall, or the goblin. The vanishing entrance bothered her more than the invisible audience.

"Where's Kip and Eggar?" Mikey asked.

She turned around again in case she'd missed them the first time. "They should be here. We were only a minute behind them."

Another round of applause turned her attention to the bush on the side of the trail.

Mikey let out a squeal of delight. "It's another Handy!"

The green hands stopped clapping and held up their palms.

Mikey wriggled out of the day pack. He pulled out the packaged bread from home and grinned at Winnie. "We can feed them!"

Maybe the boys had each set off to a private bush for a bathroom break. Since she and Mikey had to wait anyway, she grabbed a few slices to share with the bush. "Give them small pieces so we can feed all of them."

The green hands politely waited. The instant one received a bite-sized piece, it disappeared into the greenery, making way for the next hand. Winnie and Mikey had only given out six slices when every hand, even the ones that hadn't been fed, zipped back into the bush with a whoosh.

Mikey shrugged. "I guess they got full."

The birds stopped tweeting, and an eerie stillness settled over the forest.

The words "this is weird" had barely left Winnie's mouth when white smoke billowed toward them. Oddly, no burning smells reached her nose. Whatever it was condensed into a white cylinder that stretched to Winnie's height. The top curved toward her. "What isss thisss?"

She drew back, stunned that smoke could speak.

It pointed its curved end toward Mikey. "Did you just feed the esssa plant?"

The little boy nodded. "That's Handy. He likes bread."

The smoky cylinder bent toward the plant. No hands appeared to confirm or deny Mikey's claim. A rustling in Winnie's sweatshirt turned her attention to the movement. The leafling poked her green head out of the opening.

The cylinder now bent toward Winnie's pocket. "What isss thisss?"

"I think it's a fairy," Winnie replied. "She had a midair collision with two other ones and needed to rest."

The smoky white cylinder rose to meet Winnie's eyes. "Are you not human?"

She knew if Kip were in her place, he'd respectfully answer, even if the request came from smoke that talked. "Yes, um, sir?"

The smoke paused as if in thought. "You

are…mossst unusssual."

"Uh, thank you? We're looking for two boys who came in first. One is a tree sprite named Eggar, and the other is a human like us. His name is Kip."

"The human wasss tainted by a desssceitful wizzzard. The sssprite put him in stasssisss."

"Stasis? Like Princess Gwen?" Her voice went up an octave. "Why?"

"I know nothing of the princesss. Nor do I care. You two, however, have proven worthy. Name your desssire, and I ssshall grant it."

"We were supposed to go to some lady's cottage. Miss Maisie?"

"Mistress Maven," Mikey corrected.

"That's it. Mistress Maven."

The smoke flattened to the ground and coiled around her and Mikey's feet. She protectively gripped her brother's shoulder. The smoke swirled upward past her knees just as the leafling fairy fluttered from her pocket and flew away. The smoke encircled her and Mikey. When it dissipated, they stood at a small stone cottage with a thatched roof.

She hugged her brother, relieved. "Was that weird or what? I never even felt us move."

"Let's do that again!"

The front door banged open, and Eggar burst out. "Winnie! Mikey! I tried to wait for you, but Jajee wouldn't let me."

"Is that the name of the smoke thing? It told us Kip's in stasis."

"What you call a smoke thing is the Myst. Kip is here." Eggar pointed at a tree that stood to the right of the cottage. "And safe. As are you, which is more than a blessing."

"But what happened?"

"With Kip? I'm not sure. I tried to consult the truth stones, but they wouldn't answer. Alil is healing him." He gently stroked the tree's bark. "He'll make a full recovery."

The oddly shaped tree resembled a makeup brush standing upright. "Is it hollow? Is he standing inside there? How can he breathe?"

"He's breathing easily in a dream state."

She frowned down at Mikey. "See? This is why we should never separate."

"You separated from us when you took Stompy to Princess Abbi."

"You just made my point. Kip got you arrested." She turned her frown on Eggar. "I don't like any of this. We came here to help, not to get stuffed inside trees."

"I promise you he'll be out soon. Please come inside and meet my grandmère."

She slipped her hand in Mikey's to assure herself he wouldn't vanish inside a tree and followed Eggar through the front door.

A cozy fire blazed from the fireplace at the back of the main room. A hunched, white-haired woman, whose head reached Winnie's elbow, stepped forward. Her nut-brown face creased into a welcoming smile. "Come in, won't you? Here we are." She spread her arms, indicating a crude wooden table laden with four bowls of steaming soup. "Eggar's truth stones said you'd be hungry."

The smell of freshly baked bread drew Winnie to a seat on the table's long side. "Thank you, um, Mistress Mabel?"

Mikey let out a frustrated breath of air. "Windy, it's Mistress Maven." To the tiny woman, he added, "Thank you, Mistress."

She chuckled and dipped into a short bow. "You are most welcome, General Takka."

"Sorry. I meant to say Mistress Maven. Sometimes I mess up names when I'm worried. Our friend…"

"Will be fit as a fiddle before you know it." Mistress Maven's thin lips curled into a gentle smile. "You must be hungry from your travels to reach us deep in the wood."

The fresh bread, thankfully, had been baked to perfection. In Winnie's opinion, vegetable soup fell at the bottom of her list of appetizing meals. To her surprise, the tomatoes, beans, and leafy green things in the old woman's soup worked well with the delectable broth.

"Not that I'm ungrateful," Eggar said between bites, "but how did the Myst come to bring you here? He doesn't usually help humans."

"I guess partly because Mikey made friends with Handy."

Eggar quirked an eyebrow. "I'm afraid I don't know anyone by that name."

"I think the Myst called it an essa plant," Winnie said.

Eggar directed a startled glance at Mistress Maven.

"We didn't hurt it," Winnie blurted. "We just fed it some of our bread."

The old woman's brow smoothed. "Well done indeed!"

Eggar continued to gape.

Winnie blinked at him. "What?"

"I just...I've never known an essa plant to eat bread. It primarily takes its nourishment from grabbing its victims and eating their meat."

Now it was Winnie's turn to gape. "Are you telling me it could've eaten Mikey?"

Her little brother giggled. "I'm not meat. I'm a person. Besides, Handy is my friend."

She shivered. Her bathroom break could've put him in danger.

"You needn't look so worried," Mistress Maven said kindly. "Essa plants generally feed on squirrels."

"Not just squirrels," Eggar broke in. "I've heard stories of one eating a—"

Mistress Maven cut him off with a quick glare and a subject change. "Tell us more about your encounter with the Myst, dears."

"He liked us," Mikey said, "because of me and Handy and because Windy had a leafling in her pocket."

Eggar paused with his spoon midway to his mouth. "You had a leafling in your pocket?"

Winnie stopped herself from taking the last slice of delectable bread. "When we were in that entranceway with the goblin, or whatever he was, a leafling stopped too quickly. The ones behind her bumped into her. She struggled like she hurt her wing, so I caught her and let her rest in my pocket. I guess she only had a sprain because when the Myst started to wrap around us, she flew away."

Eggar slowly stirred his stew as if in deep contemplation. He lifted his stare from his meal to Winnie. "When we first entered the forest, do you remember what you were thinking when the leafling flew in front of you?"

She replayed the experience in her head. She shrugged. "I might've been thinking their wings were the same shade of green as the essa plant."

Eggar turned toward Mistress Maven. "Even the leaflings were surprised these two befriended a carnivorous plant."

The woman's smile didn't waver. "But we're not surprised, are we? We knew our guests would be quite special. It was foretold."

Winnie might have debated the point, but the earlier excitement and now a full stomach made her drowsy. Even Mikey's eyelids started to droop. Mistress Maven must have noticed too.

"You poor dears are exhausted from your journey."

"Maybe just a little," Mikey said.

The little boy, who usually fought the idea of an afternoon rest, shuffled behind Mistress Maven to a tiny room with just enough space for bunk beds and a bureau.

"This is Eggar's room," Mistress Maven said. "He won't mind taking the top bed during your stay. There's a rollaway cot in my room for you, Warrior Windem."

They thanked the old woman in unison. Winnie had barely tucked the covers up to Mikey's chin when he dozed off. Satisfied, she followed Mistress Maven to the room next door where the cot had already been set up. She stretched out on it and closed her eyes.

"Rest, dear, and gather your strength for tonight."

Winnie yawned. "What's happening tonight?"

"You'll be visiting the glow-stone field, of course."

Winnie's eyes snapped open. "The what?"

But Mistress Maven had already shut the door behind her.

Chapter 15

"Let me out!" Kip banged his fists against the rounded wall in front of him. He yelled until his throat went raw, then slumped against the wall in defeat.

"Who's there?" spoke a familiar female voice in the dark.

He bolted upright. "Princess Abbi?"

"I'm her sister. You're the conjurer who kept me from losing myself. Kip, is it?"

"Princess Stompy?" he guessed.

"I prefer Princess *Gwen*, thank you very much."

He bowed, even though he couldn't see her. "I do beg your pardon, Your Highness. Where are you? And for that matter, where am I?"

"If you can speak with me, you must be in stasis in one of our healing trees. I can guess which one if you describe the tree's shape."

"Describe? I can't see a bloody thing. It's pitch dark in here."

"You only think it is. Try this. Leap upward and let me know what happens."

What an odd request. Had he heard correctly? "Did you say leap?"

Her annoyed huff sounded mere inches away. "Just try."

He didn't like the idea. Still, he flexed his knees and jumped. He shot upward as if propelled by an invisible force. Without sight, he could only guess how high he rose before the tube thinned around him. He arced sharply to the left and lost momentum. "Oi! Now I'm stuck."

"Did you go straight up or to the left or right?"

A ripple of claustrophobia increased his heart rate. To cover his fear, he puffed out an annoyed breath. "Not that it matters, considering I'm wedged in something, but it curved left."

"It's all right," she said in a gentle voice. "Imagine yourself on the ground again, and you'll come back out."

He wanted to call her barking mad but bit his tongue. Even a batty princess deserved respect. He only followed her direction because he thought he could prove her wrong. Instead, he slipped out of the chute and back to the ground. "Oh. Thanks, Princess. Now if you can just tell me where the door is…"

"We're not quite through yet. Take a small step to your right and jump again."

He wished she could see his frown. "I trust there's a point to this?"

"Each jump will give us a better picture of how the limbs are shaped."

It took eight ridiculous leaps into nothingness and getting caught in a tube for him to guess the tree's form. "I'd describe it as an upside-down rake."

"I know exactly who's healing you. Alil."

Having her voice so near bolstered his mood. "Another tree named…Jajee, I believe it was, might have mentioned Alil."

Princess Gwen's disembodied voice let out a trill of laughter. "That sounds like him. Jajee hates it when humans invade his space. He stands right by the gate.

119

Alil is so much friendlier and lives by Mistress Maven's cottage. What happened that you came to need healing? Did Jajee drop a branch on you?"

He hated speaking into the dark. Still, he straightened his shoulders and lifted his chin, or at least where it belonged, if it existed. He still hadn't quite decided whether any of this was real. "The Myst, if you know it, took an instant disliking to me."

A tinkling giggle reached his ears, or at least where his ears were meant to be. "The Myst also hates humans. He isn't too keen on my sister or me either since we have human blood. Although, I must confess, my other form sensed danger in your presence. Yet you helped preserve the memories of my true self. I thank you, as do all the mother trees."

"You're quite welcome, I'm sure. But the Myst didn't just have a problem with me being human. He didn't like that I have magic."

"That's a rule here. We only allow one human conjurer on the island. Right now, that's Argamel. He's permitted to train an apprentice but hasn't chosen one yet. Ooh! I just got a brilliant idea. You can pretend to be his apprentice!"

Kip had no interest in pretending to be anything. He wanted his freedom. "I'm feeling a bit claustrophobic. How do I escape this tree?"

"Escape? You make it sound as if you're being punished. Alil is healing you. What manner of healing tree would he be if he let you out before restoring you to good health?"

Kip struggled to suppress his impatience. "I promise to thank him profusely once the job is done, but in the meantime, I'm jolly well blind. When will my sight come back?"

"It's already back."

He scowled into the dark. "I'm telling you it isn't."

"You just have to believe you can see. You're in what we call a message dream."

"Blimey, message dreams are real? All this time, Win's been nattering on about them, and I just thought she was bonkers."

"If you've never experienced them, I can see where you might question their existence," said the princess. "I'll grant you, Windemere seemed easily distracted when I spoke with her, but I always trusted her soundness. Open your eyes."

He slowly lifted his lids to unexpected yet welcome brightness. A round, inviting sitting room sharpened into focus. A girl resembling Princess Abbi sat at a wooden table.

"It's remarkable how much you look like your sister."

Her leaf-green eyes flashed. "I will have you know my sister looks like *me*. I'm the eldest by a full five minutes and forty-three seconds. By rights, I should become queen, but Papa's crown chose *Abbi*."

Her remark about the king's crown made no sense. Still, he bowed low. "Please forgive me, Your Highness. I never meant to offend."

She folded her arms tightly against her chest, apparently unwilling to let the slight go. "Queens are meant to dress in gowns. *She* only wears them when she pretends to be me."

"Oh." He could think of no better way to respond to her discontent.

Her eyebrows resembled a pair of angry caterpillars

crouched low. "She doesn't even want to be queen. Can you imagine?"

He shook his head. He also couldn't imagine how to steer the conversation toward a safer topic. "You do seem…more…queenly."

Her eyebrows rose to a more sociable height. "Truthfully, I've occasionally asked her to pretend to be me. She doesn't always fool our parents. At the private crowning ceremony, our papa knew."

Kip had never heard of a private crowning ceremony but felt it impolite to ask for details. That didn't stop him from silently wondering, though. He hadn't intended to magically conjure the memory. Still, the tree room dissolved into a cavernous parlor where a single lantern cast a somber glow over the padded chairs and sofas that faced an unlit fireplace. A lone man, no doubt the king, judging by the plain gold circlet around his head at the brow, sat in a cushioned chair. A small silken pillow lay on the round table at his elbow. He removed the crown and laid it on the cushion.

A younger, barefoot version of the princess, dressed in a plain tunic, stood in the open doorway.

"Why would you send Abbi in your place?" the king asked gently.

Kip should have pulled himself from Princess Gwen's memory, but curiosity won over decorum.

Gwen's lower lip pushed out in a pout. "She said the crown made her laugh. It already likes her. If it chose her again, thinking it was me, we could rule together."

"It would have seen through Abbi's deception. Please come forward."

Gwen strode to the table and eagerly reached for the crown.

"Stop!"

She snatched back her hand as if struck.

"Is your mind still?" he asked in a softer tone. "Only then may you slowly take the crown and carefully place it on your head."

She inhaled and let her breath out slowly. Rather than relaxing, her brow wrinkled. "Did it already choose Abbi?"

"It can't choose until you've both worn the crown."

Suddenly, hope glowed from her eyes. "Could it choose both of us?"

"If that is the will of the crown, it will be so."

Gwen nodded and took a second breath. Her leaf-green eyes blazed with desire. She exhaled slowly, raised the crown to her head, and clenched her eyes shut. Barely one second had elapsed when she reopened them. "How long does it take?"

The king shrugged.

"I don't feel anything. Is that good or bad?"

"It's neither good nor bad. It merely is."

"Oh…ow!" She yanked it from her head and threw it at the cushion. "It stung me! It hates me." Gwen dashed from the chamber in tears.

Kip returned with a jolt to the tree and the present princess.

Princess Gwen graciously lifted a china teapot as if Kip hadn't just detoured into her memory. Maybe she didn't know. She poured thick golden-brown liquid into a delicate teacup. "You've no idea how good it feels to entertain a guest in my true form."

"Thank you for your hospitality," he said, even as his cheeks burned with guilt for accidentally spying on her. "How much time do you think has passed since I've been here?"

"There is no time here."

"Does that mean nobody knows I'm missing?"

She passed the cup to him. "I'm sure they know, but what feels like hours to you will only seem like minutes to them. You're inside a vision, remember. This is mine, but you can create your own environment."

He shook his head in amazement. "And I could've created something like this all along?"

She nodded.

"I feel like such an idiot."

"Don't blame yourself. I imagine you don't have healing trees in your world. This tea should speed up your healing." She gave him an encouraging nod.

He took a tentative sip. Sweet thick syrup rolled across his tongue. The liquid's heat changed instantly to a cooling menthol as it coated his throat. "That's quite good."

He set down the cup. The large sitting room had a tree-like quality, but he didn't feel locked inside. He felt cradled. He rose for a better look at the smooth wall. He started to reach for it but stopped himself. "May I touch the wall?"

The princess beamed back. "We appreciate your restraint and request for permission. Not all humans respect mother trees. She says you may."

He gently caressed the soft, smooth wood. "Is this…your mum?"

She giggled. "No, Mama's still living in her first form."

"Oh, right. The tree form happens after…" Kip shrugged, preferring not to mention death while he remained buried inside a tree. "I guess that means one day you'll become a mother tree as well?"

She lowered her gaze. "Nobody knows for sure. Abbi and I are the first to have a tree sprite mother and a human father."

"You and Mikey have something in common. He isn't completely human, either. He's a voga general inside a little kid."

She nodded. "I think that's why we bonded. From the moment he laid eyes on me, he accepted my enchanted state. My own father seemed repulsed by my toad form, which I find troubling. Although, if I'm being honest, Papa always preferred Abbi. Probably because she likes his smelly horse."

"I'm sure your father loves you equally."

She waved the comment away. "My true hero is Takka. If he hadn't found me when he did, I could have lost myself and lived in that other world, perfectly content to be a toad. But I belong here. I'll be forever in his debt. And yours."

Kip forced a smile. He hoped to live up to her high regard, but he had no clue how to restore her.

Chapter 16

Winnie's insides seethed as she scuffed her bare feet across the warm sand. She should have refused this lone nighttime trek to the glow-stone field. She also should have refused to put on the embarrassing outfit she now wore. Mistress Maven had referred to the costume as a tunic and trousers, but Winnie knew better. They were pajamas. According to the old woman, the rocks, or *glow stones*, only received visitors dressed in undyed, lightweight fabric. What a ridiculous notion. Inanimate objects had no opinions on anything. She could've worn a dress (if she'd packed one) or even a bag over her head. How would they know? Could the stones magically sprout eyes?

She knew better than to complain. Kip always accepted alternate world customs without question. She could too and had silently changed into the white tunic and loose-fitting pants. She didn't even object when Mistress Maven asked her to remove her favorite running shoes.

"When entering the glow stones' presence," Mistress Maven instructed earlier, "you must take nothing but a clear mind and a loving heart."

She shuddered at the thought of leaving behind her beloved locket. It held a picture of her mom, who had died five years ago. Without a word, she removed the locket and chain. Next, she lifted her Frama-scope's blue ribbon from around her neck. She hung the chain and ribbon from a hook in the cottage's main room.

Eggar had seen her off by handing her a lantern. She'd accepted it with a nod and exited the cottage. Alone.

Now, at least, the lantern illuminated the sandy trail she'd been told to follow. Thankfully, no pointy stones hid under the warm grit to pierce the bottoms of her feet. No hidden roots tripped her either. According to Mistress Maven's instructions, the soft path would guide her to the glow-stone field and a shelter. After an uneventful five-minute walk, she reached a shadowy structure. The crude building resembled a city bus stop with a sloped roof and three wooden walls. A shaft of light from her lantern fell over a large black lump in the center of a long bench built into the back wall.

Winnie froze, breath held. Wait. Did black feathers cover that lump? She took a tentative step toward it. A long neck stretched from the black form, topped by a familiar head and beak.

"Bird." Her tensed muscles instantly relaxed.

He let out a welcoming honk and waddled two steps to the right to give her room to sit.

She placed the lamp between them and settled onto the bench. "I wondered where you got to after you started that stampede. You scared us practically to death, by the way. I didn't even care that they were small. When those dindal things ran down the hill toward us, I thought they would knock us down and trample us."

Bird shook his head and quacked.

She chuckled, remembering the first time he'd made that noise.

They sat in friendly silence for a few minutes. Pale

moonlight overhead exposed an open field. Tree silhouettes, far in the distance, encircled the vast space.

"Have you noticed any glowing stones out there?"

Bird murmured and tucked his head under his wing.

"I'll take that as a no, but I guess it isn't automatic. According to the keeper of the stone field, if I want to see them glow, I have to sit here until my mind is completely relaxed, and then I'm supposed to douse the lantern's flame and meditate on—"

A snore-like purr came from Bird's side of the bench.

Winnie let out a disappointed sigh. Even though he was just a bird, she needed somebody to tell her troubles to.

She briefly watched him sleep. Why couldn't she find peace as quickly as he did? In his defense, he probably didn't have a jumble of worries churning through his head. Kip's current situation topped her list. Could any human survive inside a tree? What if he never came out? What if she had to go home without him? What would she tell his dad? Why did he end up in that tree in the first place? Without Kip's magic, how could they help Princess Gwen? Would she be trapped as Stompy for the rest of her life? Mikey might not mind. He loved having a toad friend. Mikey. A ripple of ill ease rolled through her. What if he woke and needed her?

She puffed out a frustrated breath of air. How did Mistress Maven expect her to contact magical rocks if she couldn't settle her mind enough to meditate?

An eerie howl sounded in the distance. Bird jumped awake and stretched his neck, swiveling his head side to side.

"What was that?" Winnie whispered.

Another howl answered from her left.

Bird squawked and flapped his wings, knocking over the lantern and killing the flame. He flew away, leaving Winnie in the dark. She pressed her back into the right corner of the shelter, hoping to hide. Why couldn't the hut have a fourth wall? She hugged her arms and waited for her eyes to adjust to the dark. No shadowy creatures prowled through the empty expanse in front of her. For now, at least.

Just when she thought she might breathe normally again, an insect flitted toward her. She sucked in a nervous breath. Did they have poisonous bugs here?

A soft voice whispered from inside her head. *Rescuer. You are safe.*

Could this be the leafling she'd helped?

The internal voice said *yes*.

"Oh yeah, you guys can read minds." Even though the leafling understood Winnie's thoughts, she needed to hear her own voice. "What makes you believe I'm safe?"

The Myst guards you.

She leaned forward and squinted. A low-lying strip of white fog stretched around the open field. She sat back. "If a wolf comes after me, what can fog do?"

The Myst can steal away the breath of an enemy.

Winnie jolted upright. "It can what?" Did the Myst try to steal Kip's breath? She clenched her fists. "Did you?"

She didn't know if he heard her thoughts or her voice, but the white, low-hanging fog floated across the field toward her bench. It gathered into a five-foot-tall column. The top part bent toward her.

"I sssensssed darknesss within the one you call friend. He unlocked a malevolent power."

"Kip would never do that."

"Behold what I unveiled."

A movie played in her mind, showing two tiny guards from her Frama-12 adventure. They stood at attention outside a wooden door until a blast of air sent them hurtling from their post. A second blast shook the door from its hinges, and it fell into the room. Kip stomped over the fallen door and into the queen's meeting chamber, his cape billowing outward. Sparks from his magic wand froze the queen's councilmen.

Now the misunderstanding made sense. After the queen's council had tried to kill her, Kip must have wanted revenge. "He did that for me. And if you play it to the end, you'll see that he never seriously hurt anybody."

"Sssome of thisss darknesss remainzzz."

"Everybody has a little darkness inside. And if you look deeper into what he's done since then, you'll see how much good he does. He helped the princess so she wouldn't lose herself to the toad enchantment."

After a long pause, the Myst said, "I didn't realizzze that."

"You get it now, though, right?"

He said in a soft voice, "I do."

Winnie let out a breath of relief. "Can you please pull him out of the tree?"

"Yesss." The Myst rolled away.

Winnie raced after it along the sandy path to a tree in front of Mistress Maven's cottage. The fog coiled around the trunk and up to its rake-like branches. It swirled beside the tree. When the Myst dissipated, Kip lay on the ground.

She knelt at his side and gripped one of his hands.

Dead cold. *No. Please be alive.*

"Help! Somebody help!"

Eggar burst from the cottage. After a quick examination, he nodded. "He's breathing."

Together, they carried Kip inside and laid him on a cot by the fire. Mistress Maven wrapped him in a blanket. Winnie dashed to the bathroom to change into her jeans, T-shirt, and pink hoodie. She had no idea how Mikey slept through the commotion but appreciated it.

When she returned to the main room, Kip still hadn't revived. She called his name and jostled him. No response. "Why won't he wake up?"

Mistress Maven gently pressed her fingers to his forehead and temples. "His mind appears to be elsewhere."

Winnie knelt beside his cot, determined to bring him back.

When she met the princess in a message dream, the other girl had rejected Winnie's suggestion that a kiss from a prince could undo the enchantment. Now, sitting by an unconscious Kip, she pressed her lips against his cold, unresponsive ones. She held her breath and counted to ten. Nothing. A tear rolled down her cheek and fell on Kip's chin. She turned to Mistress Maven. "Can you bring him back?"

She shook her head. "Only he can do that."

"Then why doesn't he?"

The old woman gently patted Winnie's shoulder. "In good time. In good time. You should rest."

"In a minute," she murmured. Even after Mistress Maven dimmed the lanterns and toddled off to bed, Winnie stayed at Kip's side. She rested her head on the cot's edge, promising to only shut her eyes for a second.

Chapter 17

Now that Kip knew he could create his own environment during stasis, he wanted to give it a go. He gulped the last of his tea, eager to conclude the visit. Besides, he thought it best not to overstay his welcome. He thanked the princess and, with an eye blink, returned to his tree.

"Alil, you don't mind if I do a bit of decorating, do you?"

"Your reverence is noted and will be reciprocated." The tree spoke in a voice so deep the sound rumbled through Kip's chest.

He borrowed from Princess Gwen's round room configuration. The shape called up fond memories of his tower laboratory from Frama-12. A mere thought brought curved shelving into being. He filled the shelves with potions and leatherbound books. Next, he conjured a corner table topped by a skull, used as a candle holder—what self-respecting wizard didn't own one of those? A maroon overstuffed chair faced his newly created unlit fireplace. An office desk took up one side of the curved room, which he covered with important-looking papers.

As an afterthought, he added a door and two round windows. Though neither opened to the outside, just pretending they did helped him breathe easier.

He sat behind his desk and opened a blank journal.

Just maybe, the blank pages would inspire him to find a way to undo the princess's enchantment. A knock sounded at his false door. He lifted his head, startled. "Yes?"

Princess Gwen swept into the room carrying three teacups on a tray.

Kip leaped to his feet. "Princess!" Of course, she would visit. Who else knew how to reach him?

"We've brought more tea. Since you can't do much while you're in here, I thought the sooner you heal, the sooner you'll be released and able to restore me to myself."

Unwilling to admit his lack of confidence in his magical abilities, he directed her attention to the first part of her statement. "We?"

She grinned and stepped aside, revealing Mikey. "Look who's joined us for a visit."

The little boy held up a teapot. "I brought this. I can only stay for a tiny minute."

"Please, come in. Come in." Kip had never felt so happy to see the little chap. A round table materialized with a wave of his hand. "Set your tea things here." As he spoke, three wooden chairs sprouted around the table.

Mikey settled into the chair beside Kip. "I'll try not to wake up."

Kip sat across from the princess. "Where's Winnie?" He glanced at the doorway, hoping she'd join them.

"I think she's too afraid for you to fall asleep," Mikey replied.

"Afraid for me?"

Mikey shrugged. "Well, you won't wake up."

"I feel awake."

The princess only smiled, poured tea into a cup, and handed it to him. "Before we came to you, we started a chat about General Takka." She poured tea into the remaining two cups and slid one toward Mikey. "I wondered what he looked like."

"That's when I said we should come here so I can show both of you my vessel." Mikey lifted his tea, sniffed, grimaced, and set the cup back on the table.

Kip grinned at the boy's failed attempt at diplomacy. So as not to offend the princess and to heal faster, he took a long swallow. After draining the cup, he turned to Mikey. "I've often wondered about your other...vessel."

Mikey grinned eagerly. The instant he sprang to his feet, his little body stretched, transforming into a six-foot-tall beige toad standing upright. His clothes melted into a maroon uniform with gold epaulets.

Kip's mouth fell open. He should have assumed Takka would resemble the toad men Kip had encountered on Frama-12. Still, seeing this creature in Mikey's place took him by surprise.

The princess reacted with a squeal of delight. "When you first saw me, you must have imagined me to look like this." She stood and mutated into a five-foot-six toad dressed in a flowing white gown and a gold ring of a crown on her amphibian-like head. "Your sister told me you were a prince."

General Takka's toad mouth curled upward in a good-natured smile. "Yes," he said in a deep voice, "but I never felt the need to wear a crown."

The oversized toad princess touched her crown. "Should I make mine disappear?"

Takka bowed. "Not at all. It becomes you."

Kip pressed his lips together to avoid gasping over

Mikey's transition from innocent child to flirtatious amphibian. To cover his shock, Kip forced a smile. "What a…what an interesting couple you make."

A giggle emanated from the toad princess. "If I can't change back to myself, I wouldn't mind staying like this as long as I can speak."

General Takka bowed again. "Princess Gwen, you're beautiful as a picture no matter what form you take."

Kip's heart thundered with a sudden fear. If no one could restore Princess Gwen to her original body, would General Takka take her back to Frama-12? Winnie would never forgive Kip if Takka left his human family behind.

"That was fun, guys," Kip said, "but come back to yourselves, all right?"

Thankfully, the pair returned to their normal shapes, or at least normal for Kip.

Mikey smiled wistfully. "It was fun. I have to go now." The little boy's image gradually dissolved.

"Get well soon." The princess also vanished, leaving Kip alone to worry if he'd accidentally given Mikey a reason to abandon his human life.

He'd only paced the room's outer edge once when a second knock sounded at his door. Assuming it was the princess back to retrieve the tea things left behind, he called for her to enter.

The door opened. Thaddeus Krell stepped through the threshold.

Kip gaped at him. "How did you…"

"Get here? Quite simple, dear chap. You summoned me."

"I would never do that."

135

"Understandable. It's human nature to want to be right, even if our minds have to twist themselves into knots to justify our beliefs." He suddenly sobered. "Or perhaps some of us are simply clueless. I was in the midst of delicate negotiations when my house key began to ring like an old telephone. Due to the importance of the meeting, I was unable to respond, but I knew it was you."

"You did respond. Maybe not with words, but I've heard you calling out to me. More than once."

Krell shook his head. "You poor misguided lamb. I've got too much going on now to waste my brainpower thinking about you. If you're hearing things, it's simply an echo from you searching for me."

"Why would I want to have anything to do with you? You're evil."

The man's back stiffened. "I am foremost a scientist. I travel to alternate worlds to observe human nature."

"Observe? You do more than that."

The older wizard smirked. "Well, I may have stirred things up a bit to make them interesting. From an observer's point of view, of course. Now that we've cleared that up, let's move on to the main reason for my visit. What do you know about the glow stones on this island?"

Kip knew ruddy little about them and, at the moment, had no interest in them. He needed all his brain power to guard his thoughts. Thankfully, in his tree-world dream, no enchanted scope hung around his neck. *White bear. White bear.* As long as he didn't think about it—*white bear*—Krell might never discover his secret plan. He hoped.

The wizard snapped his fingers at him. "Glow stones?"

"I would imagine they're stones that glow."

"Don't be cheeky. I find it hard to believe you know nothing about them."

"How would I know anything? I've spent all my time inside a tree since I entered the Oram Forest."

Krell waved a dismissive hand. "I'd been told these stones have magical, and possibly medicinal, qualities. All the more reason to collect some and return to my lab for further study."

"If they're magic, can they even be collected?"

Krell clasped his hands behind his back and began to pace around Kip's center table. "A wizard could collect them."

An unexpected inner pull tugged at him. No voices spoke, but a truth manifested inside Kip's mind. Even though he knew almost nothing about them, he believed with all his being that the glow stones were more than magic. "Had it ever occurred to you that they might not want to be collected?"

"I said they were magic, not sentient. And even if they were, there's a field full of them. There's bound to be an odd few that would like a change of scenery."

Kip frowned. "I doubt they'd willingly go to anyone who planned on cutting them open and studying them."

Krell turned his back on Kip and gazed at the books on the far wall. "The majority glow white, but I understand some reflect a hint of color. Pastel blue, pink, and pale yellow. Since I'm currently on the mainland and you happen to be so near the field, I will promise never to trouble you again if you gather one of each color for me."

Kip clenched his teeth to keep from denying him outright. Could he somehow pretend to go along yet not follow through? That question plagued his mind for so long Krell must have noticed his hesitation.

The wizard pulled a book from the shelf. He turned, facing Kip. "I see what this is. You've come for them for yourself, haven't you?"

If Krell believed that, then he couldn't read Kip's thoughts after all. Or perhaps Kip held the power to keep Krell out of his head. At least in his tree dream, he possessed the power. "If there really are magic stones, I wouldn't keep them for myself. I'd only want to ask them to help me undo a spell you and that other wizard created during a duel."

Krell's left eyebrow rose. "Duel? Oh, right. That happened so long ago I'd almost forgotten. Neither of us made a direct hit."

"Yes, you did. You hit Princess Gwen and turned her into a toad."

Krell let out a boisterous laugh that lasted longer than Kip felt necessary. Once his mirth played out, he wiped his eyes. "Thank you for that. I haven't had a good laugh in years."

Kip recreated a smoky image in miniature of the duel and projected it on the center table. He zoomed in on the area where their wand flashes collided and then ricocheted off a tree, striking the partially hidden princess.

Krell let out an indignant sniff. "That doesn't prove anything. How do I know it didn't just give her a bit of a shock? All the pages in this are blank, by the way." He dropped the book on the table, and the image reverted into haze and drifted away.

Kip clenched his fists. "I know it didn't just *shock* her because she followed you through the portal to Hutra.

She's the toad Mikey found. Remember? He named her Stompy."

Krell snorted. "That figures. So you've brought the creature back to this world."

"What other reason would we have to be here?"

"We? Did you bring that annoying girl, Windy?"

Kip nodded. "And Mikey."

Krell reached him in one long stride and clutched the front of his T-shirt. Desperation blazed from the older man's pale-blue eyes. "When you wake, promise to use the Frama-scope to send Mikey home. It isn't safe here."

Kip tugged out of his grip and smoothed the wrinkled material. "It's never safe anytime you're around."

Krell turned away but quickly turned back. "You don't understand. When that wizard resisted me, I chose another tactic. After my brief detour to Hutra, I returned to this world's mainland and aligned myself with some unsavory characters. They plan to raid this island tomorrow and take the glow stones. Which I've convinced them are rightfully theirs."

"Why would you do that?"

He gave a superior smile. "If everyone's fighting over property rights, they'll be too distracted to stop me from borrowing a few glow stones, won't they?"

"That's a terrible plan!"

Krell stared down his nose at Kip. "If you bring me pink, blue, and yellow stones, I'll call off the invasion."

"How do you expect me to do that? I'm stuck inside a tree!"

"You're not inside a tree, you simpleton. You're only asleep." He swiped his hand through the air, creating a new miniature representation on the table. In it, Kip lay on a cot in front of a glowing fireplace.

He gazed at it in confusion and looked up. "That's not where I am."

Krell pressed the heel of his palm against Kip's forehead and shoved. "Wake up!"

Kip bolted upright with a gasp and found himself sitting in a cot near a fireplace with burning logs inside, just like Krell's image.

Winnie threw her arms around him. "You're back. What happened?"

He held her tight, warmed by her embrace and relieved he'd escaped the confines of a tree. "I think I just had one of those message dreams you've been nattering on about."

Winnie laughed and hugged harder. "Told you I was right!" She let go and sat back. "Did my mom come to you?"

He shook his head. "Krell did."

Chapter 18

Winnie let go of Kip and jumped up. Before she could ask for details, Mikey scampered into the room. He threw himself into Kip's open arms. "Did you remember my message dream?"

Kip clapped him on the back. "I did." To Winnie, he added, "Mikey and Princess Gwen, as a *person*, also visited me while I was in stasis."

"No fair. Why didn't I get to visit?"

Mistress Maven, dressed in a nightgown and robe, stepped out of her room. "Young traveler, I'd hoped when I heard voices you'd returned to us. How wonderful to see you."

"Mistress, that's Kip," Mikey introduced. "Kip, this is Mistress Maven. She's the keeper of the glow stones."

He nodded respectfully. "An honor, Mistress. Thank you for taking us in."

She touched his shoulder. "A pleasure to meet you."

So much had happened Winnie couldn't remember if she'd properly thanked the woman for accepting three otherworlders into her home.

Mikey bounced with excitement. "Can we go see the glow stones now?"

Mistress Maven smiled gently. "When the time is right, you'll meet them."

Eggar shuffled from his room, rubbing his eyes. When his sleepy gaze fell on Kip, he jumped awake.

"You've returned to us!"

Kip smiled shyly. "Back and feeling much better. Thanks for putting me in stasis."

"What was it like?" Winnie and Mikey asked in unison.

He shrugged. "Like a dream when you know you're dreaming."

"We've had quite a bit of excitement for one evening, haven't we?" Mistress Maven turned her attention to Mikey. "Hurry back to bed so morning can come faster."

The little boy raced to Eggar's room. The bedsprings groaned as he leaped into bed. "I'm almost asleep," he called out.

Winnie had so many questions for Kip, but Mistress Maven had a point. "I probably should go too. So you can rest."

Kip reached for her hand. "Not yet. We need to talk about a situation. But not where little ears can hear."

Eggar nodded toward the door. "The front stoop is far enough from Mikey's room and close enough if you need me to consult the truth stones."

Mistress Maven poured water into a kettle. "And I'll make some relaxing tea for when you're through."

Winnie sat on the chilly stone stoop with Kip beside her. She breathed in the pine-scented air, comforted now that Kip and Mikey were safe.

Kip inhaled deeply. "So...I have good news and bad news about Krell."

"This should be interesting. I can't imagine anything good coming from Krell."

"The good news is he still cares about Mikey and wants to protect him."

The last time they encountered Krell, he'd tried to use Mikey to bargain for Winnie's Frama-scope. The plan had failed, but he'd taken such good care of Mikey her brother still fondly referred to Krell as his non-dad.

"I hate to ask, but what's the bad news?"

Kip squeezed her hand. "First, there's regular news. Krell wants us to send Mikey home."

"We're not doing that," she snapped.

"Also, Krell's interested in glow stones. That's what the duel with Argamel was about. Now, for the bad news. He's on the mainland with some men and plans to come here to take the glow stones by force. That might be the war from the prophecy."

She gulped. "We have to fight *Krell*?"

He gripped both her hands. "He made an offer. If I can give him blue, pink, and yellow glow stones, he'll call off the attack."

She pulled back. "What did you say?"

"I woke before I could answer."

"Good." She jumped up and began to pace. "Who says they come in colors?"

He shrugged. "Krell, for one."

"And we know how honest he is." She stopped pacing. "I went to the glow field earlier tonight and didn't see a thing. I'm not even sure they exist."

He snorted. "That would be a laugh, wouldn't it? Krell brings an army out here tomorrow, and there's nothing to steal."

"Tomorrow?" she shrieked.

"Oh yeah, I forgot to tell you that part of the bad news."

"We'll never be ready. We don't even have an army!" She went back to pacing.

Kip hopped up and walked with her. "We won't need one. I just got a brilliant idea. I'll take some plain stones and use magic to make them glow in the colors he wants."

"Oh yeah, that'll work," she retorted. "There's no *way* a wizard would ever figure *that* out." She stepped around him and called to Eggar.

He joined them outside and rattled the stones in his cupped hand. "What should I ask?"

"Are Krell and his men going to attack the island tomorrow?" Winnie asked.

Eggar gasped. "I surely hope not." He rolled the stones onto the stoop, quickly scooped them up, and tried again. And again. He shook his head. "Sorry. I tried four times, and each time the yes and no stones landed the same distance from the indicator."

"Does that mean he lied to me?" Kip asked hopefully.

"Don't ask that," she said. "Ask if Krell will break off his attack if he finds out that Mikey is still here."

Eggar rolled the stones. "Still too close to tell."

She scowled. "Are you kidding me? He's supposed to care about Mikey."

"I'm sure he does, but his men might not," Eggar said. "We don't have a definite answer that he's even coming. What we do know is the princess needs to be restored. I've been rolling for answers to learn if one conjurer's magic alone could restore the princess to her original self."

"And?" Winnie and Kip asked in unison.

"It's not as definite as we'd like, but there's a slim possibility the conjurers could undo the spell together if they recreated their duel."

"If Krell is really planning an invasion," Kip said, "we probably shouldn't ask him to come. It would be like giving him permission to attack."

"Besides," she added, "we'd need Argamel's help, and he's still stuck in a tree."

Eggar turned to Winnie. "Grandmère and I believe you can free him."

She gulped. "Me?"

"Wouldn't me magic work better here?"

Eggar shook his head. "The council of mother trees would never grant you an audience. Your unnatural magic caused the Myst to attack you in the first place."

If the mother tree council was anything like the council Winnie had encountered on Frama-12, she had little faith in her abilities to talk them into anything. "Eggar, you're a tree sprite. Can't you do it?"

"I've already asked the stones. It has to be you. I can show you to the nearest mother tree. Kip, you should rest to gather your strength for later."

"Hate to say it, but I am feeling a bit knackered. Win, will you be all right?"

She nodded despite her doubts. "I'll be in soon."

Eggar guided her through the dark forest to a massive pine tree. "Bow to her first," he murmured. "Then introduce yourself."

She nervously rubbed her arms. "Um. Do I tell her my legal name or my warrior one?"

"Warrior, definitely. She'll know the prophecy."

Winnie shook out her hands to wave away her jitters the way she did before a track meet. She bent at the waist, then slowly straightened. "Greetings, um, Mother Tree. My name is General Windemere, but you might know me as the Warrior Windem."

145

A warm breeze whispered through the pine needles, brushing them together in a way that sounded like a voice. "Yes."

Eggar took a step back. "You'll know what to do."

Did he really believe that? It was too dark to tell if his expression matched his words. She lightly laid her hand on the mother tree's trunk. Rather than rough wood, her fingers brushed over bark soft as crushed velvet.

In an eye blink, she transported from the dark forest to a glowing round room, facing a regal woman with skin the same shade as the gray-brown tree trunks she'd seen in the forest. Winnie knelt. "Your Highness."

"Rise, child. I thank you for the promotion," she said with a smile in her voice, "but my official title is Mother."

Mother. Winnie had heard the tree's title multiple times, but standing in this woman's loving presence conjured memories of her own mom. She choked back a sob, still missing her. One positive from traveling through time tears was her mom, or a guardian who looked like her, always appeared to Winnie and delivered a message to her. This last time, though, Mom hadn't shown up. She took a deep breath and pushed away that thought. She slowly raised her head. "I'm here with a request on behalf of Princess Gwenevieve to try to undo the enchantment that turned her into a toad."

"Sadly, my sisters and I can't nullify that magic. We heal illnesses and broken bones. We also punish the reckless."

"You mean Argamel?"

She gave a regal nod.

"What if he undid the spell? Would you forgive him then?"

A U-shaped table materialized, occupied by at least eighteen tree-women. She tried to count their exact number, but their elaborate hairstyles distracted her. Or did tiny trees actually sprout from their heads? Thin green vines weaved through their hair branches. All wore sleeveless gauzy green gowns exposing glistening arms the color of tree bark. Winnie tried not to gape, but their beauty overwhelmed her.

Two tables appeared on either side of her. The tree mother she'd first met sat at one table beside a wizened little woman with a face so wrinkled Winnie could barely make out her features.

The tree mother directed a gracious nod at Winnie. "You may be seated."

She fumbled into the chair at the other table.

A man in a hooded cloak appeared on her left. He lowered his hood, revealing a mane of wavy brown hair and a trimmed beard. "I know you. Warrior Windem?"

She tugged at her hoodie. "It's the pink 'armor,' isn't it? I'm guessing you're Argamel?"

He nodded once.

"The Warrior Windem," the tree mother announced, "has offered to plead the case of the king's conjurer."

Winnie's mouth dropped open. Had she?

Chapter 19

"You may take a few moments to speak with the accused," said the tree mother.

Winnie turned toward her…client?

The corners of his lips curled upward in a half smile. "This should be easy," he whispered in a sophisticated, arrogant voice. "I haven't been accused of anything, and even if I were, I'm clearly innocent."

"Except for the enchantment," Winnie whispered back.

His brow wrinkled. "What enchantment?"

"Princess Gwen spied on you from behind a tree and got zapped by clashing spells that turned her into a toad."

He grunted. "I should've known my false imprisonment was tree sprite related. That meddlesome princess never could keep her nose out of other people's business. But now that I know what crime I've been accused of, I can defend myself." He cleared his throat. "Honored council of mother trees, there has been a grave misunderstanding."

Even though he didn't speak with an English accent, his condescending tone reminded her of Krell.

"A conjurer from a foreign land arrived with evil intent," he announced. "A magic altercation occurred because I was defending the glow-stone field from a potential thief."

The councilwomen bent their heads toward one

another in animated conversations.

"Sisters." The tree mother's raised voice silenced the others. "This information differs from the warrior's promise." She turned and stared pointedly at Winnie. "You suggested a counter spell from the conjurer would restore our princess."

Her muscles tensed. If Argamel couldn't make things right, would the council put her inside a tree? "I, um, I'm mostly sure he can do it." She silently willed him to agree to make things right or, at the very least, apologize for turning the princess into a toad.

"Honored council," he said, "I've just recently learned the princess followed me to the southern wood. As I know nothing of her enchantment, I can only assume the other conjurer was guilty of putting her in the state she's currently in."

"Sorry, um, honored council," Winnie said, "I saw an image of the battle or duel or whatever it was. A mother tree stands at the edge of the clearing where it took place. Is there any way she can, I don't know, recreate the image here?"

The ladies glanced at their neighbors, then faced forward. The woman seated in the center of the table rose. "I am that mother tree and was witness to the battle. I was not, however, aware of what instigated it. Another foreigner with magic did, indeed, conjure the image with which the warrior speaks. I shall display the image which remains there to this day."

A cloud of gray smoke appeared in the center of the room. It swirled, then slowly took on a faded three-dimensional picture. Winnie could barely make out the wand flashes or the dueling wizards. "I don't understand. We saw it clearly when my friend recreated the image."

"Obviously, your magical friend is a menace," Argamel muttered.

Her muscles tensed at the insult. "If he hadn't shown us what happened, I never would've come to the tree mother and you'd still be stuck in stasis."

He snorted. "We would've figured it out eventually."

During their whispered argument, the mother trees also softly conversed.

Winnie clenched her fists. "We don't have time for this. The princess is a toad!"

A hush fell over the room, making Winnie's last statement sound even louder.

She ducked her head. "Sorry."

The tree women returned to their quiet discussions.

"Your friend opened the image but never closed it," Argamel said in a low voice.

"Can you sharpen the image?"

"They would never permit human magic in here."

Winnie folded her arms, about to give up. "Wait. You said *human* magic. That must mean there's another kind."

The wrinkled little woman seated at the table beside Winnie's must have overheard because she said in a clear voice, "Shalla, kindly recover the scene for us if you would."

The center tree mother dipped her head in a brief bow. Gradually, the image sharpened.

"Thank you, Queen Mother," Argamel said. "Now we can all easily see that my attention is focused exclusively on the intruder. If this display weren't static, we would also see that I successfully defended the isle against this rogue conjurer because he vanished."

The tree mothers mumbled among themselves again.

"What we see," said the wrinkle-faced queen, "is the result of a misguided stream of magic that hit our beloved princess and put her in the unfortunate condition she is in today."

Winnie swallowed hard, reluctant to mention Eggar's suggestion, but maybe he was right. "If we can bring that rogue conjurer to the island, maybe together, he and Argamel can undo the princess's enchantment."

Voices blurted, both in favor and opposed to Winnie's suggestion. The mother tree who had convened the meeting clapped her hands until the room went still. "Sisters, those in favor have the majority. Considering the other sides' concerns, I stipulate that this hostile conjurer be brought here under the condition that he be kept in check."

Winnie's hand shot up before she remembered she wasn't in school. "I know where he is. I think I can bring him here. As long as you guys can keep him…in check."

"As it is claimed, so shall it be done."

Winnie never sensed movement as she reappeared outside the mother tree in the dark. Hardly any time must have elapsed because Eggar still stood nearby.

"I'm back," she whispered to him.

"So am I."

"How long was I in there?"

"Barely five minutes. Time works differently inside. Still, I had time enough to go home and speak briefly with Grandmère. How did the mother trees resolve the issue?"

"They liked your idea to have the two conjurers recreate the fight. Now we just have to find Krell and convince him to come here."

"Thankfully, that can wait until tomorrow. But that means we'll have to speed things up a bit. If you feel up to it, Grandmère would like you to return to the glow-stone field. She still believes the stones can help."

****

Mikey and Kip slept, but Winnie didn't have the luxury. She changed back into her loose-fitting white pajama outfit and kicked off her shoes. She scurried, barefoot, back to the shelter overlooking the empty field. Bird and the leafling didn't accompany her this time.

At least now she carried protection. Mistress Maven had given her a sachet of dried herbs to keep in her pocket. According to the older woman, the herbs, or "deflection moss," would repel anything unsavory that might come her way. Her confidence, though, came more from knowing Kip and Mikey slept safely in the cottage than from a bag that smelled like pine needles and oregano.

She doused the flame from her lantern and took a deep, cleansing breath. According to Mistress Maven, properly connecting with the glow stones required offering them a gift.

"What you give away," Mistress Maven had instructed, "must have great value to you."

Winnie possessed only one cherished object, the locket she'd left at the cottage. But that counted as a material token unacceptable to the glow stones. She pulled up her legs and rested her chin on her knees. What could she possibly give to a bunch of rocks? Nothing. She shook her head. *Positive thoughts, positive thoughts.* Mom used to tell her that whenever her worries threatened to spin out of control. She also sang lullabies to her.

Could a song count as a gift? If not, at least singing would pass the time until a better idea surfaced. She closed her eyes and tentatively hummed the opening bars of her favorite lullaby. As she gained confidence, she increased her volume. Halfway through the song, a soft harmony, almost like an orchestra of tiny violins, played beneath her melody. Only something small, like leaflings, could sing like that. She opened her eyes.

The empty field now glowed with thousands of tiny orbs, pulsing in time to the swelling harmony. They radiated white light as well as pastel blues, pinks, greens, and yellows. They shimmered as a collective with a beauty that brought tears to her eyes. It seemed wrong to take one away. Why would she even want to? They belonged here.

A narrow strip of lights dimmed, revealing a dark path. She slid off the bench, compelled to follow it. The path led her to a giant glowing boulder at the bottom of the field. A gentle female voice spoke in her mind. *We greet you, Warrior Windemere. To reward your selflessness, we will grant you your true desire.*

"Oh." So many emotions flashed through her. Awe, pride, disbelief, uncertainty, excitement, joy. This boulder must be a queen to the smaller stones. Maybe she could help. "I don't know if this counts as a desire, but I'd like to stop a man who wants to invade your island and take your people."

All the glowing stones behind her emitted good-natured laughing sounds.

Winnie peered back at them, confused.

Glow stones choose to reveal themselves only to those who value their well-being. They can neither be stolen nor coerced.

"I don't think the man who wants them understands that."

After a long silence, the boulder's glow dimmed. Guessing that meant their conversation had ended, Winnie turned away. From behind, the boulder flared bright again. *You came to our land with two others.*

Winnie turned back. "Yes."

Bring them to us. We would like to meet them and speak with all of you.

"I'll get them. Thank you," she said and raced back the way she'd come.

Mistress Maven greeted her at the door with a steaming mug of tea. "I suspected you might need this to fortify yourself. I believe you may have spoken with the glow-stone queen?"

Winnie gratefully accepted the mug and took a sip. Hot, but not too hot. Sweet, but not too sweet. And exactly what she needed. "Thank you, and you're right. I met her, and she wants me to go back with Kip and Mikey. Like right now."

"Sit, child, and catch your breath. You'll notice the young wizard is taking a badly needed rest. Spending time in stasis isn't as relaxing as one might think."

Winnie reluctantly sat at the table facing Kip, asleep on the cot by the fire. She took a long swallow of tea. "Think he'll be ready after I finish this?"

Mistress Maven softly chuckled. She poured more tea into Winnie's mug. "As long as you take tiny sips."

Every muscle in her body vibrated with a need to move. She drank, hoping her hostess wouldn't notice that more than a sip glugged down her throat. She stared at Kip, willing him to wake before she finished her tea.

Chapter 20

Kip rolled onto his back to find Winnie and Mikey peering down at him. He propped up on his elbows and gave them a proper scowl. "Can't a bloke sleep?"

Mikey grinned and stepped back to give him room. "You're awake!"

He groaned and sat up all the way. "What bloody time is it?"

"Not quite midnight." Winnie thrust a white shirt and white trousers at him. "Put these on. We're going to meet the queen of the glow stones."

He frowned at the soft material in his hands, then at Winnie and Mikey. Both wore the same all-white costume. "Are you suggesting we wear matching pajamas? To meet a queen?"

Mikey turned to his older sister. "See? I told you they looked like jim-jams." To Kip, he added, "We call 'em jim-jams."

"I call it ruddy bonkers. Why do we need to dress alike? And where's everybody else? Will they be playing dress-up with us?"

"Mistress Maven went to bed after Mikey woke up. Eggar's been asleep the whole time. I wouldn't call it dress-up. It's a custom to wear natural fibers when you visit the glow field. Oh yeah, and we can't wear shoes either. Go change in the bathroom. We'll wait here."

Kip rose, but only because he needed to use the

toilet. "Why must we go to the glow field right now? Can't it keep until morning? You said nothing was out there."

"There wasn't that first time. On my second trip, though, I saw them. Millions of them. And Krell was right. They *do* come in different colors."

Mikey's eyebrows shot upward. "Did you talk to my non-dad?"

"Not exactly, but I'm going to the mainland tomorrow to see him."

Kip stopped outside the bathroom door. "What? That's the first I've heard of it."

"I know. You missed a lot while you slept."

Mikey bounced in front of Winnie. "Can I come too?"

Kip said an emphatic "no." At the same time, Winnie said, "Sure."

As he shut the bathroom door behind him, he distinctly heard Winnie invite Mikey to the mainland. How dare she blatantly disregard his opinion? He angrily jammed one foot, then the other into the loose trousers. He'd calmed by the time he changed into the shirt. He would bring up the Krell topic at another time.

All three, now similarly clad, set out in single file. Barefooted, much to his chagrin. In the past, he'd tread upon many a sharp object, especially in the dark. Soft sand coated the path, much to his relief.

Winnie led the way, carrying a lantern. Mikey followed next with Kip bringing up the rear. For the briefest moment, Kip wished Mikey hadn't been invited. He desperately needed a private talk with Winnie to debate the suitability of allowing a small child to meet with an evil wizard. If anyone should meet with Krell, it should be Kip. Alone. One wizard to another.

The trio hiked to a pasture where short blades of cold, damp grass tickled the bottoms of his feet. Shouldn't a field full of stones feel lumpy underfoot? The clearing, visible even in the dark, went on for hundreds and hundreds of yards. They tramped through the downward-sloping field until they reached the bottom. Winnie's lamp illuminated a row of trees that created a border. An ordinary boulder the size of a minivan stood two feet in front of the trees. She extinguished the light. All three stood quietly in the dark.

After a long moment of stillness, Kip whispered, "Is something supposed to happen?"

"Give it a minute," Winnie whispered back.

He shuffled from one foot to the other, growing uncomfortable on the chilly grass. Why didn't Mikey complain about the cold? Kip couldn't be the only one bothered by the ground's temperature.

A flicker of light bathed the boulder. At first, Kip thought it came from the moon's glow, but dark clouds covered the sky completely. Soft light emanated from the boulder, growing brighter. Maybe glow stones truly glowed after all.

A soothing voice, yet not a voice, spoke inside Kip's head. *Gentle beings, I am Queen Luma. Please introduce yourselves.*

Under the stone's brilliance, Winnie rested a hand on Mikey's shoulder and nodded.

The little lad stepped closer to the stone. He bowed. "Queen Luma, I have two names and two lives. On my first home world, Frama-12, I am called General Takka, son of Queen Bogen. In my second world, Frama-11, known as Earth, my name is Michael Hernandez, son of

Maria. I also live with my sister, Windy, and her dad, Clive."

Even though you can't always remember your first life, you are, and always will be, wise and good. I greet you, General Takka.

Mikey bowed again and stepped back. Winnie hugged him from behind and mumbled something that Kip couldn't hear.

She straightened and strode forward with her head held high. "Your Majesty, I'm Windemere Harris, Winnie, or sometimes Windy. I'm a Frama-traveler and earned a Frama-scope for helping to stop an invasion in Frama-12."

Your valor becomes you, Warrior Windemere. Many, including the Sisters Three, have faith in your creative solutions to challenges. Believe in others as much as they believe in you.

Kip scowled. Why did Winnie gain all the glory? Even back at Frama-12, despite her cheekiness, the queen decreed more authority to her than to him, a wizard. He turned his head, annoyed with himself for his pettiness. He cared about Winnie, so why couldn't he celebrate her rise in status?

Winnie accepted the stone's comments with a gracious bow and backed up to stand at her brother's side. She and Mikey turned as one toward Kip. Each wore an expectant expression.

He tried to shake off the ripple of unease that fluttered through him. No good could come from introducing himself to the queen. He loathed his given name. For the last five years, since the day he turned ten, he'd only answered to the nickname Kip. Even in school. He'd never admitted his proper name to Winnie. What might she think of it?

The queen boulder might not care about his name, but she seemed to know everything. What if she also knew about his magic and attacked him the way the Myst had? Could she shoot lasers at him? Pop out of the ground and roll over him? He let out a sigh.

Winnie hissed for his attention. "It's your turn."

He took a deep breath and stood before the glow-stone queen. He bowed as deeply as the other two. "Queen Luma, you are all-knowing and…forgiving. So you'll forgive me if I—"

Trust. The word floated through his mind. He glanced at Winnie. Had she also heard it in her head? She smiled. He nodded and faced the radiant stone.

Trust. Breathe. Then speak.

He would breathe, and he'd speak if he had to, but trust? She wanted too much.

Winnie let out an exasperated breath of air. "Bro. Did you murder somebody? Just tell her who you are."

"Oh, all right," he muttered. Louder, he said through clenched teeth, "Kenneth Paul Skyler. In my world, called Earth, I'm not a warrior or a general. I'm a magician who performs under the name Kip the Amazing. I became a wizard in Frama-12." He stared hard at Winnie, daring her to mock his given name or his credentials.

Her eyes softened. "Your nickname fits you."

His tensed muscles loosened. He mouthed the words, "Thank you."

You are "the Amazing" in your world and every other world you encounter. Never doubt your worth, Master Wizard. Your magical ability has grown more than you know. So too must you grow to respect this power you wield. See that you never abuse it.

"I never will, Your Majesty." He bowed low, then joined the others. Winnie's hand slid into his. A rush of loving warmth flowed through him.

Now that I have met all of you, I deem each of you worthy to greet the glow stones. Go to the shelter and silently appeal to them. If one chooses you, it will gladly assist you. Only those chosen will see the stone's light. If multiple stones glow, select the one that best "speaks" to you.

"Do we have to think of a gift for them like last time?"

Kip cast a confused frown Winnie's way. Queen Luma, however, appeared to find nothing odd about her request.

Your gift is my endorsement. Go, all of you, with a quiet mind. We wish you well.

The boulder's glow faded, leaving them in darkness. For a moment, no one moved. Kip broke the silence. "Are you able to relight the lantern?"

"No. But we need it to stay dark anyway, or the glow stones won't come out. We'll go to the shelter at the top of this little hill."

Mikey pushed between Winnie and Kip. His cold little hand slid into Kip's. The other probably held Winnie's. They quietly hiked up the hill. A shadowy building on the smallish side loomed in the night. The shelter was little more than a lean-to with a long bench along the back wall. Kip wanted to sit beside Winnie, but Mikey bounced between them once again.

"Okay," Winnie said in her take-charge voice, "all we have to do is close our eyes and clear our minds. When the glow stones are ready, they'll burn so brightly that we'll see the light through our eyelids. The queen said we won't see each other's stones, so if you notice a glow, it's yours."

Kip leaned against the wall. "Seems easy enough."

Easy but mind-numbingly time-consuming. He tried to settle his mind only to become more and more aware of the slow passage of time. A chilly breeze rolled over them. They huddled closer for warmth.

Finally, after what felt like hours, Mikey let out an eager gasp. "I see three! Does that mean we each get one?"

"I don't see them," Winnie said. "Kip, do you?"

He opened his eyes to a dark field. "Nothing."

"They're all yours, bud," Winnie said. "Pick your favorite one and put it in your pocket."

The little boy's shadowy form skipped from the shelter. He bounced from one dark area to another and back again. Did he really see anything? Finally, he bent toward the ground, scooped up something too small to see, and jammed it into his front pants pocket. He pranced back to his place between Kip and Winnie. "I got a blue one."

Winnie hugged him. "Awesome. Let's see who the glow stones call next."

Kip felt nothing and saw nothing. Did his disbelief sabotage his odds? Ten minutes later, Winnie slid off the bench. When Mikey saw his, he'd raced from one option to another. Winnie stopped ten yards from the shelter and faced outward. He wanted to ask what she saw but respected the reverence of the endeavor too much to interrupt her.

She stood in the same place for ages. Mikey leaned against Kip's arm and fell asleep. Finally, Winnie returned, presumably with a glow stone in her pocket.

"That took forever," he complained.

"Sorry. It's not as easy as you'd think to pick one from all those glowing stones."

"How many did you see?"

"I don't know. They lit up the whole place. A thousand?"

He tamped down another bout of jealousy. Why couldn't at least one show itself to him? He let out a sigh. "Let's go back to the cottage. I don't think there's one for me."

"Did you clear your mind?"

"Of course I did."

Mikey yawned. "Didn't any light up?"

"It's black as pitch out there," he grumbled.

"Maybe you don't need one since you have magic," Mikey said in a sleepy voice.

"I…guess that's possible," Winnie said.

"Time to go, then." Kip carried the sleepy little boy to the cottage. Winnie tucked him into bed, then joined Kip in the main room.

Mistress Maven, who must have anticipated they'd need a warm drink, had left a pot of hot water over the low flame in the fireplace. Winnie pulled a pair of mugs from an open shelf and poured steaming tea into each.

They sat across from each other at the table.

"What's your glow stone look like, then?" he asked.

She revealed a rough stone, small enough to fit in her palm. She placed it on the table between them.

He leaned in. The stone had pink, gray, and beige stripes, similar to stones he'd found near a lake he once visited on holiday. "What's it do?"

She shrugged. "No idea."

"Does it feel like a normal rock?"

"Yeah. Go ahead and pick it up."

Kip barely reached for it when a pink spark shot from the stone, shocking his fingers. He snapped his hand back and shook out the sting. "What was that?"

"Sorry. Not sure."

He eyed it warily and took a sip of tea. He returned his mug to the table. "Does that mean it protects the person who owns it?"

"I don't think I own her."

He raised an eyebrow. "It's female?"

"I don't know how I know, but yes. I think so."

"At least it can protect itself from anyone touching it, I mean her. But how safe are you really? Earlier, you mentioned something about going to the mainland to see Krell."

"Oh, right. I never got to tell you about that. Remember that meeting I had with the mother trees? Well, they took that other wizard, Argamel, out of stasis for, I guess you'd call it, a trial. They agreed to let him out again if we can get Krell back here. We think the wizards need their double power to undo the spell."

"We talked about that earlier. What if your visit to see him starts the war?"

"That's why I'm taking Mikey with me. You said he still cares about him."

Kip tapped his thumb on the table. He saw her point, but at the same time, what if Krell took Mikey hostage and attacked the island like he promised? He shook his head. "Too dangerous. I'll go in your place. I've got counter-magic."

"Mikey and I have glow stones. They won't let Krell hurt us."

"What if he finds a way to steal them from you? And what about this?" He pulled out the shoelace that held the enchanted Frama-scope around his neck. "Sister Ava ordered me, not you, to make the switch. I could do that when I meet him on the mainland."

"Now I get why none of the glow stones lit up for you." She tugged the shoelace. "We weren't supposed to take anything with us. That's why I kept my scope and locket here."

He regarded her with a slow eye blink. "If you'll recall, the only thing you told me to do was dress in this ridiculous costume and take off me shoes."

"Sorry. Guess I got too excited to take you guys to the queen that I forgot."

"Or maybe Mikey was right all along that magic means I don't need a glow stone."

She bounced in her chair. "I just got an awesome idea! What if we have Mikey give the scope to Krell?"

"He'd blurt out that it's enchanted. He always gives the game away."

"Not if we don't tell him. Krell knows Mikey always tells the truth. At least the truth the way he understands it. Krell won't even question it if Mikey gives him that scope."

Kip had had too much on his mind to think about how to exchange the enchanted scope for the one Krell now had. He slowly nodded. "That just might work. As long as Krell doesn't suspect anything. He might learn the truth if he rummages around in your mind."

"Not if my glow stone protects me from thought invaders."

He smirked. "What's she going to do? Zap Krell in the head the instant he gets the idea to hypnotize you?

164

How does a stone even know what somebody's thinking?"

The stone expanded from its puny size to the height and width of a loaf of bread. It kept growing until it filled the length of the table and stretched upward, blocking his view of Winnie.

Kip shoved his chair backward and sprang to his feet. "Okay. I get your point."

The stone shrank back to its original size.

Winnie chuckled. "See? I'm totally safe. Remember what the queen said? Trust."

He wanted to, but could he trust Krell not to ruin everything?

Chapter 21

After all she'd done during the day and deep into the night, Winnie expected to fall instantly to sleep. But the moment she lay in bed, her mind cycled from worries about the princess toad's condition to worries about Krell. Would he refuse the enchanted scope even if it came from Mikey? And what if during their conversation she accidentally said something that made him start the war tomorrow?

Mistress Maven's quiet breathing sounded from across the room, slowly in, slowly out. Winnie forced herself to match the older woman's intake and outtake of air. She didn't remember falling asleep.

Far too soon, Mikey shook her shoulder. "We're going on a boat ride!"

She lifted her head, opening her eyes to a dark room. "What time is it?"

"Mistress Maven said it's an hour till dawn. But Kip said two, for too early."

She dropped her head back onto the pillow. "Wake me when it's three. As in three hours *past* dawn."

"I can't. We have to reach the ship before the sun comes up." Mikey jostled her again. "Get dressed, Windy. Breakfast is almost ready."

He padded from the room, leaving the door open. The aroma of frying bacon drifted in. Winnie groaned and climbed out of bed. A cold splash of water and a quick change into her home-world clothes woke her enough to appreciate Mistress Maven's bacon and eggs. Two swallows of bitter tea helped but didn't make her as alert or as energetic as Mikey, seated next to her. He babbled on and on about their upcoming boat ride. A drowsy Kip sat across the table beside an overly alert Eggar.

Mistress Maven at the head of the table beamed at them. "The Myst has kindly offered to convey the two of you to the king's port. You'll be traveling on the ship *Sapphire*."

Kip set down his fork. "Hang about. Did you say the Myst?"

She smiled. "I did, dear."

"Would that be the same Myst that nearly killed me?"

"That was a misunderstanding," Eggar said.

"He likes us," Mikey piped up.

Winnie tousled his hair. "Everybody likes you, bud."

"You needn't worry about those two, Master Kip," said Mistress Maven. "They've each got a glow stone to look after them. We mustn't tarry. The *Sapphire* leaves port within the hour."

After breakfast, Mistress Maven cleared the dishes. Eggar gathered supplies for their day pack. Mikey made one last trip to the bathroom. Amid the flurry of activity, Kip pulled Winnie aside. He slid the enchanted Framascope around her neck and leaned in for a kiss. "Good luck and stay safe."

A flutter rippled through her, but more from her impending meeting with Krell than from the kiss. She tucked the shoelace under her shirt. "Keep your shell phone handy in case we need to call."

He patted his pocket. "Always."

They kissed again. This time it warmed her from the inside out. They might have kissed a third time, but Mikey bounded between them.

"I'm ready!"

Kip rolled his eyes.

Winnie laughed and slid the day pack over one shoulder.

Outside, Mistress Maven delivered last-minute instructions, which Winnie partially heard and promptly forgot. She barely had time to nod to her when a white fog flowed toward them. It enveloped Winnie and Mikey. When it dissolved, they stood on a pier next to a clipper ship.

"Here then, you lot," spoke a bulky human with a shaggy beard. "You the ones wot's headin' fer the mainland?"

She nodded.

"Foller me, then." Without looking back, he plodded up a steep ramp onto the ship.

Winnie and Mikey, holding hands, followed.

The deck bustled with crew members, either stowing crates or coiling ropes. Winnie guessed they were tree sprites by the thin green vines that weaved through their long, braided black hair.

A statuesque man, also a tree sprite, strode up to them. He flashed a smile and bowed. "Greetings, Warrior and young General. I'm Captain Ivers. We're honored to have you sailing with us. As a precaution against rough seas, Eenan will show you to a cabin below."

She had just enough time to thank the captain before

Eenan, the man with the shaggy beard, waved to them. "This way, missy and young gent. Mind yer heads."

They followed him through a narrow opening, down the steep metal stairs, and through the galley and dining area to a small corridor.

"How long will it take to reach the mainland?" Winnie asked.

"Three or four hours, depending on the winds. We got crusty bread and onions fer lunch."

Mikey made a bitter face.

She patted the day pack hanging off her shoulder. "We have our own food in here."

"Sounds like yer all set, then." The man opened a door on their right and nodded for them to enter. "Mind you stay here until we dock. Don't want neither of you falling overboard, do we?" He shut the door, leaving them inside.

Top and bottom bunk beds pressed against the outer wall and practically filled the entire area. A porthole let in enough light to illuminate the cramped room. Less than a foot of walking space lay between the end of the bunks and a table built into the wall. A door on Winnie's left opened into a closet-sized bathroom.

She shrugged and closed the door. "Guess he's right. We have everything we need."

The little boy bounced onto the bottom bunk and crawled across the width to the porthole. He pulled a white, marble-sized object from his pocket and held it to the round window. "This is our view."

Winnie glimpsed from the calm turquoise water outside to the marble in Mikey's hand. "Is that your glow stone?"

He nodded. "He doesn't have a name yet."

She sat on the edge of the bed. "I thought you said he was blue."

"Only when he glows. Right now, he's pretending to be normal. Where's yours?"

She removed her colorful, more rock-shaped stone from her pocket for Mikey's inspection.

He leaned closer. "Is his name Tiger? He has stripes."

"Her. We're still thinking about it," she said, too embarrassed to admit she hadn't even considered asking her stone if she already had a name.

The room gently rocked. Above them, confident voices called directions to each other, and the ship glided from the pier.

"We're moving!" Mikey said eagerly.

Winnie dug through the day pack for the loaf of bread Eggar had packed for them. She'd heard that a little something on the stomach prevented seasickness. She pulled off the end piece and held it out to Mikey. "Eat some of this. It'll settle your stomach."

He shook his head. "My stomach has bacon in it right now."

She should have remembered her little brother hated bread crust anyway. She tore off the next piece. "Just eat the stuff in the middle. It'll keep your bacon company."

He shrugged and picked out the bread, leaving a ring of crust. He looked through the hole as if it were a telescope. Scope! She'd almost forgotten about it.

"Guess what I have?" Without waiting for an answer, she pulled out the Frama-scope hanging around her neck from Kip's long shoelace.

He cocked his head. "What happened to your blue ribbon?"

"I left my scope at the cottage. This one belongs to your non-dad. Remember in Hutra when he said he broke it? Sister Ava fixed it for him."

Mikey let out a whoop and clapped his hands. "The Sisters Three can do anything!"

"That's why we're going to see Krell on the mainland. So I can give it back to him."

She only counted to three when her brother blurted, "Let me do it! I can do it."

"Are you sure? Because I like surprising people with good news."

"I like surprising people. Please? I want to surprise him."

"Well…" She pretended to consider it.

"Please, please?"

"I guess you can give it to him since he is your non-dad." She hung the string around his neck. "You have to take good care of it until we see him."

"I will. I promise." He hid it under his T-shirt.

The boat's gentle rocking motion reminded her of a swinging hammock. Her lack of sleep finally caught up to her. She settled against the pillow. "Promise to stay right here. I want to close my eyes for a few minutes."

"You can take a nap. I'm going over there." He jostled the bed as he crawled across the mattress toward the table. He set his glow stone on the tabletop and softly sang to it. Then he laughed. Maybe his glow stone told him a joke. She smiled at the notion and closed her eyes.

We're coming.

Her eyes snapped open. Did she just imagine those tiny voices? As if in answer, amused titters sounded inside her head. She sat up. "Did you hear anything just then?"

Mikey peered over his shoulder. "You mean the leaflings telling us they're coming?"

She suppressed an annoyed frown. "How do you always know things like that?"

He shrugged. "I listen."

"So do I, but I can't always tell if what I hear is real or if I'm making it up."

"Then you're not really listening."

She harrumphed and flopped onto her back.

****

Winnie woke to a thump and a bed jostle. She lay nearest the porthole and propped up on her elbows to peek out. They'd docked. On her right, Mikey slept with his round glow stone nestled under his chin. She smiled. Her little brother could make friends with anything.

"We're here, bud," she said softly.

He pocketed his glow stone and bounced off the bed, immediately switching from asleep to wide awake. A knock sounded at the door. Mikey opened it to the man with the shaggy beard.

"Here we are, then. We'll be unloading our cargo and reloading supplies for the next two hours. If you're returning to the isle with us, be back here before we lift anchor."

They thanked him and climbed the steep stairs to blazing sunlight and shrieking gulls. Winnie held Mikey's hand at the gangway and walked with him to the dock. They weaved past fishermen tossing foot-long silver fish into barrels and sailors loading wooden crates onto horse-drawn carts. They scuttled out of the way of the busy dock workers and crossed a dusty dirt road. They passed a busy warehouse full of workers hefting crates of smelly fish in and out. The dirt road curved until it straightened and turned into a tree-lined cobblestone street that brought them to the edge of an old-fashioned town with shabby-roofed buildings.

Ladies, dressed in ankle-length willowy skirts and long-sleeved blouses, strolled along the walkway in front of a row of shops. Their long, poofy hair peeked out from under wide-brimmed hats. Some ladies walked together in pairs. Men in striped suits and slicked-back hair accompanied others. Little girls in pigtails and boys in flat caps skipped among the adults.

"This feels like Earth from like a hundred ages ago," Winnie mumbled.

"I don't see any tree sprites," Mikey remarked.

"You won't see anybody dressed like us either. We probably don't want to be seen yet."

She guided him off the road. They headed toward the shopping district, using the trees across the street as cover. So far, none of the old-fashioned people appeared to notice them. They seemed more intent on the window displays. Still, Winnie and Mikey carefully approached, darting along the road from one tree to the next.

Along the way, she silently categorized the row of businesses based on the bins and racks outside. They passed a grocer, then a clothes shop. Next stood a store specializing in hats, beside it, a toy store with toy sailboats in the window. A sign hung in front of a three-story building next in line. The fancy script read *Seaport Inn*.

"I can read that!" She'd never been able to read the writing in any other alternate world.

A restaurant stood beside the inn with four picnic tables shaded by red umbrellas. The name painted on the front window read *Magnificent Millie's*.

Winnie grinned at her newfound ability. That meant she could read their menu. Her stomach grumbled at the prospect.

Mikey tugged the bottom of her hoodie, interrupting. "Windy, where's my non-dad?"

She gulped, her literary achievements forgotten. She'd carefully planned how to switch Frama-scopes with Krell. She'd even imagined their conversation about the toad princess. Why hadn't she also put her brainpower toward a plan to find him once she and Mikey reached the mainland?

Chapter 22

Kip remained outside the cottage long after the Myst whooshed Winnie and Mikey away in a white cloud. Mistress Maven toddled back inside, and Eggar ran errands, leaving Kip to pace and worry alone. If only his hosts owned a crystal ball. At least then he could watch over his friends. A sudden idea sent him skidding to a stop. Magic. Just a little. What negative consequences could come from keeping them safe? He closed his eyes and mumbled a protection incantation for Winnie and Mikey.

When he reopened his eyes, his gaze fell on a tree with garden rake-like limbs growing from a long trunk. "Alil?"

Leaves rustled as if in answer. At least Kip accepted the movement as a yes. He bowed low. "Thank you for caring for me."

The leaves rustled again in the still air. Kip straightened. Branches from the nearby trees swayed as if communicating from one tree to another. As quickly as it started, it stopped. White fog rose up from the ground and grew into a cylindrical shape. The top bent until it faced Kip at eye level. His muscles tightened. *Not again.*

"You have befriended the treezzz. For that, I welcome you."

His muscles relaxed. "Thank you. I never meant

to—"

The Myst evaporated.

"—get on your bad side." He shrugged. He could forget the Myst as quickly as it dismissed him. He had more important things on his mind anyway. With Winnie and Mikey as safe as he could make them, he redirected his attention to ways to restore the princess. He wandered among the trees for hours, sifting through various ideas and scenarios, until they became more implausible. He had one, though, that kept popping into his head. He waited until Eggar had returned and they'd eaten lunch, before inviting him to the table outside to share it out loud.

"The wizards won't have to recreate the duel. They simply need to recall the spells that collided. Then if they cast the opposite of each spell and make them collide again, couldn't that undo the enchantment?"

Eggar scratched his chin thoughtfully. "I'm not sure." He rolled his truth stones onto the table, scooped them up, and rolled two more times. "It looks like it *might* work. Except…"

"Except?"

He repeated the process of gathering, shaking, and shooting so many times Kip lost count. Why couldn't Eggar at least speak his questions out loud?

Finally, he stopped and looked up. "I've asked over and over. Sometimes the spells work, but more often they don't. When I factor in the other conjurer, your suggestion almost never succeeds. We need another idea."

Kip's heart boomed to an eager beat. Part of his magic came from Krell's book. Maybe he could take Krell's place. "What about me? I'm a conjurer. That takes Krell out of the equation."

"By law, only one conjurer may practice magic. The mother trees only made an exception for the other conjurer because he created part of the enchantment."

Kip didn't trust Krell to do anything but make trouble. He knew he could replicate his magic, so why not…then it came to him. "What if I asked to be Argamel's apprentice? Isn't a conjurer legally allowed to have one?"

"That decision must be made by Argamel and agreed to by the mother trees. I'll speak with them on your behalf." Eggar motioned for Kip to follow.

Every tree they passed swooshed its leaves. Eggar stopped in front of an oversized pine. He barely brushed his hand over the bark when he grinned at Kip. "I don't know what you did while I was away, but they're pleased to invite you to the council of mother trees."

The woods transformed into a round chamber with an empty U-shaped table that filled most of the space. Kip stood alone between a pair of square tables that faced the U.

A dark-skinned woman materialized in front of him. The narrow green ivy braided through her long black hair rustled as she regally dipped her head. "Welcome, Wizard Kip. I am Mother. Please take a seat. The other mother trees will convene shortly."

He bowed and slid into the chair she'd indicated. The woman vanished. A moment later, a man with a trimmed beard and shoulder-length brown hair appeared in the seat on Kip's left.

The man glanced around the empty room, then sneered at him. "Who might you be? Another *advocate* to plead my case? If so, I hope you're better than the girl.

I'm still imprisoned."

Kip bobbed his head respectfully. "Sir Argamel, I'm the wizard, Kip. I'm not sure about your case, but I wondered if I could be your apprentice so we can work together."

"Wizard Kip?" Argamel regarded him with a curled lip. "Why would I agree to that? You're careless."

Kip's back stiffened. "You don't even know me."

"I know *of* you. You're the one who never released the image of my confrontation with the rogue conjurer. Because of you, the vision decayed so much that no one could tell what happened."

Kip gasped. "I'm so sorry. I'd no idea there was an off switch to it. It'll never happen again. I promise."

Argamel sniffed and looked away.

"I apologize again. Do you mind if I ask a few questions before the council convenes? They relate to your duel with a wizard named Thaddeus Krell."

Argamel turned his head toward Kip. "Never heard of him."

"That would be the gent you fought, resulting in Princess Gwen's—" He cleared his throat. "—toad enchantment."

"I never knew the gentleman's name. Did the warrior-girl send you?"

"No, but we're both on the same mission. She's gone to the mainland to find Krell and bring him here."

A crease formed above Argamel's eyes. "A fool's errand."

"Quite possibly. That's why I hoped to become your apprentice. If I acted in Krell's place, maybe you and I could combine our magic to reverse Princess Gwen's enchantment. Do you recall the spell you cast that resulted in her unfortunate situation?"

He pushed his angry face inches from Kip's. "Unfortunate? That prying princess should never have been in the wood at that time of night in the first place."

Kip had more important issues than debating the appropriateness of a princess sneaking out of the castle. Especially since the council could show up at any moment. "Please, sir, what spell did you cast?"

Argamel sat back, folding his arms. "I used a number of them, but…I suppose my most frequent one was the freeze spell."

During his visit to Frama-12, Kip had used that same spell but never thought it particularly potent. "Really? A freeze spell?"

Argamel blustered. "Why shouldn't I? I wanted to stop him moving so I could send him into another world, which apparently he did on his own."

"Point taken. He must have lobbed a few spells of his own at you. What counter spells did you use for them?"

"The freeze prevented any of his spells from reaching me."

"Do you happen to remember what those spells were?"

Argamel shrugged.

Kip pulled out his shell phone and spoke into it. "Krell."

"What is that?"

"I use it to speak with people far away." He set the shell on the desk. "I've put it on speaker so you can listen in."

A soft buzz sounded from the shell, causing Argamel's eyes to widen. Did that mean Kip possessed a power that Argamel lacked? He suppressed a superior grin.

After three more purrs from the shell, an exasperated voice came through it. "What?"

"And a jolly good morning to you too, Krell. I'm here with Argamel. You might remember him? He's the wizard you dueled with on Aylen Isle. He claims he sent freeze spells your way during that wand battle. We wondered what spells you shot at him."

After a long pause, Krell spoke. "Not that it should matter to either of you because if I ever meet that conjurer again, I'll use something different. I believe I started with stun, then moved on to a melting spell."

Kip had never heard of that one. "You mean a spell to melt his wand?"

"Don't be daft. A spell to melt *him*."

Kip gulped. Krell had tried to kill Argamel? "I hope Mikey didn't hear you say that."

"Mikey?" Krell cried out from his end.

"He and Winnie took a ship to the mainland to see you."

"The ship hasn't arrived. But why would you allow that? I told you to send him home!"

"You remember Winnie, right? She's his sister, and nobody tells her to do anything."

Krell puffed out a breath loud enough to come through the shell. "I suppose I'll need to find them. I see from my window that a ship from the island just docked."

A disconnecting click sounded from the shell phone. Kip returned it to his pocket. "At least now we know what he used."

Argamel's scowl deepened. "That, my young

wizard, is why he should never return to this island. He's a threat to everyone who lives here. I have no doubt that if he became aware of the mother trees, he'd try to harm them."

"I don't trust him either. And Winnie and Mikey plan to meet with him."

Argamel shook his head. "During my imprisonment, the trees spoke to me. They told me the warrior and her brother each earned a glow stone."

"Trees are a chatty bunch, aren't they? Did they happen to mention what glow stones do, aside from shooting sparks at people?"

"Some stones allow themselves to be used as a form of communication." He took a round white marble from his cloak pocket. "This works the same way your shell does. Some stones heal. And, of course, they all protect their companions."

"So it's possible my friends' glow stones will keep them safe from Krell?"

He slid his communication marble into his cloak. "That sounds likely."

"At least there's that." Kip wanted to believe. He took a deep breath, and a sense of calm rolled over him.

Over a dozen brown-skinned women wearing elaborate hairstyles in the shape of small trees appeared and occupied the U-shaped table. The tree woman Kip had met earlier appeared and sat at the table on his right.

"Sisters," she said. "Shall we begin?"

Thankfully, no one asked Kip to defend Argamel or himself. In fact, no one asked him to speak at all. The brief meeting consisted of Mother requesting a vote on whether or not to temporarily free the king's conjurer to work on restoring the princess. The majority agreed and, with no prompting from Kip, assigned him to Argamel as his apprentice.

In the next instant, Kip and Argamel stood in a vast pasture several hundred yards from a stone mansion. A narrow row of trees bordered the field on three sides.

Argamel let out a contented sigh. "Home at last."

The area offered plenty of space to practice without accidentally hurting anyone. "Shall we see if we can recreate the toad enchantment using freeze and melt spells?"

Argamel turned a harsh stare on him. "I'll have you know when I was your age, I began my apprenticeship with the conjurer Grettan. For the first year, all he taught me was the incantation to boil water so I could make his tea."

"I mean no disrespect, but I already know more than that. And our time is limited."

The king's conjurer heaved a melodramatic sigh. "To perform this experiment, we need a living subject. I doubt anyone would voluntarily allow themselves to be turned into a toad."

"We won't work with a person, certainly," Kip agreed. "We shouldn't test the spells on an animal either. What about a plant?"

"So long as it isn't a tree. Oh. I know just the thing." Argamel produced his white communications stone. "Mittson."

A moment later, a reedy voice spoke from the stone. "Sir? Have you returned?"

"Obviously. I'm just outside my manor. Bring me one of those tomato plants you've been growing."

"Right away, sir."

Soon a lanky gent strode from the corner of an

outbuilding. He carried a barrel with a tomato plant sprouting from the top. Half a dozen fat green tomatoes hung from the branches. After the gentleman set the barrel on the ground, he bowed to Argamel and strutted away. The conjurer pulled a wand from his cloak. He pointed at the plant and mumbled an incantation. A duplicate barrel and tomato plant appeared beside the first one.

"We'll experiment on the copy and save the original."

Kip nodded, impressed. "Could you show me how to do that?"

Argamel smirked. "It's rather a complicated spell. But I'll let you give it a try. Where's your wand?"

"I haven't got one."

Argamel let out a sigh. "How can you expect to become a conjurer without a wand?"

"Well, I did have one. Someone from another world broke it in two."

"Why didn't you simply restore it from the broken pieces?"

"I didn't know I could."

Argamel heaved another great sigh and made a duplicate of his own wand. He handed it to Kip. "It's currently nothing but an empty shell. You'll need to infuse it with your own magic. If you're up to the task, of course." His tone implied he didn't believe Kip was.

Then he'd prove it. He pressed his lips together in determination and directed his will into the conjured wand, filling it with his magic. Argamel grunted at his success and reluctantly shared the incantation used to duplicate objects.

Kip accurately repeated the words and snapped his

arm forward. A blast of light shot from his wand, along with fifteen barrels of tomatoes.

Argamel eyebrows rose but quickly returned to a neutral position. "That gives us more copies for practice, I suppose."

Kip silently gloated over the older man's surprise. Filled with new confidence, he tugged a tomato from one of the duplicate vines and held it in his upturned palm. What if they simply needed an incantation that changed objects into toads and back again? "Once, one of my incantations turned a rabbit into a pillow with ears."

"That's an interesting trick."

"I meant for it to disappear. I can probably transform this if I repeat those words." He closed his eyes and cleared his mind. A memory of the mispronounced incantation swirled into his consciousness. He opened his eyes and spoke them with certainty. The tomato vanished. "What did I just say?"

"I don't know, but don't repeat it. We can't have you vanishing the princess. Clearly, you know a good deal of magic. I'll do the freeze spell. You melt. Simultaneously. Aim for the tomato at the top of the plant straight on. At the count of three. One…two…"

Kip swung his arm upward. A stream of light blasted from his wand, dissolving the entire plant. "Sorry."

On the second try, they fired simultaneously at a duplicate plant. The top half of the tomato froze. The bottom half melted.

"We need a bigger target so we can hit the same spot," Argamel said.

"I can help with that." Kip mumbled an incantation, and a tomato ballooned to the size of a soccer ball.

Argamel shook his head. "That's going too far."

Kip shrugged. "On the plus side, we can easily hit it at ten paces."

"Who trained you?"

"Someone from another world. You wouldn't know him." He preferred not to admit he had learned from Krell's book.

Even when they used oversized tomatoes, it took dozens of tries before their respective spells collided in the same spot. A ball-sized tomato morphed into a green, ball-sized toad. Kip let out a triumphant whoop. Argamel cheered too.

Since they had so many plants, they switched their practice to normal-sized tomatoes. Soon, dozens of green toads hopped through the grass.

"Now," Argamel said with a gleam in his eye, "let's see if we can change one back into a tomato. I'll do melt this time. You do freeze. On my mark."

They moved in perfect synchronization. The targeted "toad" burst apart, sending seeds and tomato bits spewing into the air. Kip stumbled back in horror.

"Focus, focus, focus!" Argamel sputtered. "I can't believe you have so much magic and so little control. Now you see why I was only allowed to heat water as an apprentice."

"I promise I didn't mean for that to happen."

"Since, as you were quick to point out," said the king's conjurer, "time is limited, we'll try again."

They made four more attempts. Each time, the tomato toad exploded.

Kip howled in despair.

Argamel nudged him. "It's all right. We're improving. Only the legs blew off that one."

"We can't keep destroying innocent creatures. It

isn't right."

Argamel puffed out an exasperated breath of air. "We've only blown up an ingredient for a sandwich."

Kip folded his arms and turned away. "I refuse to continue killing them."

Chapter 23

The gravel road led Winnie and Mikey to a collection of buildings on both sides of the street. She hesitated, unsure how to search for Krell without bringing attention to her and Mikey's Earth clothes. Maybe Kip should have joined them after all. He probably knew an incantation that altered appearances.

A blast of air whooshed over her, transforming her jeans and pink hoodie into a long, pale-blue skirt and a long-sleeved white-and-blue-striped top. Did she just think herself into clothes that blended in with the old-fashioned mainlanders?

Her hair, too short for an elaborate style, now lay hidden under a wide-brimmed hat. At least she kept her comfortable running shoes.

Mikey's clothes morphed into a short-sleeved white button-down shirt and short navy pants held up by black suspenders. He laughed and snapped the elastic strips that held up his shorts. "I never wore anything like this. I like it!"

She grinned back. Who would have thought such a normal-looking village possessed so much magic that non-wizards could access it? Especially since the magical beings of Aylen Isle outlawed magic on their island.

Now that they fit in with the people strolling along the sidewalk, Winnie took Mikey's hand and crossed the street. As she guided him toward the shops, she tried to use her newfound magic to locate Krell.

They'd just reached the other side of the road when the hotel's front doors opened. A dark-haired man dressed in a pinstriped suit strode out. Winnie's mouth dropped open. Krell.

Mikey let go of Winnie's hand. "Non-Dad!"

The man bent forward and spread his arms. "Michael!"

The little boy charged into his embrace.

Krell whirled him around and set him back down. He tousled Mikey's hair. "There's a toy shop just there." He pointed to a store three doors down from the hotel. "See what they have in the window. If you're good, I'll let you buy something."

Mikey grinned. "I'm always good. Ask Windy."

"I'll do just that. Go on, then."

Mikey skipped to the toy-store display window. Krell's smile for Mikey hardened into a frown for Winnie. Not even his disapproving stare could dampen her mood. Her phenomenal power had just brought him to her.

"Didn't your *friend* tell you to take Michael home?"

"Wait. See what I just did?"

He cocked his head. "Sorry?"

She confidently waved down at her long skirt. "This. And I made you appear."

He sneered. "Don't be stupid. Kip rang earlier and mentioned you were coming. You didn't transform your clothing, either. I did. I couldn't have the pair of you causing a stir."

She lowered her gaze to the ground, annoyed with herself for believing she had magic. If she had, she never

188

would have created the uncomfortable dress she now wore. She lifted her head. "What happened to our real clothes? I need that pink hoodie."

"I'm sure you're familiar with the fairy tale involving a pumpkin that temporarily becomes a coach. What you're wearing will gradually return to your original outfit."

"You mean we're stuck wearing all this till midnight? It's hot and scratchy."

He shook his head. "It'll change back soon enough. You'll be home by then. There's a time tear behind the greengrocer's building. Just widen it with your Frama-scope, and it'll take you and Michael back to your beach house."

He couldn't get rid of her that easily. Besides, she had an excuse to stay. "I left my scope on the island."

"You should never leave it behind. There might come a time when you need a quick escape. Why are you here?"

"If Kip called you, he must've told you we want to help a princess."

Krell sneered. "She isn't on the mainland."

She gritted her teeth. "I know that. But for some reason, my brother believes you're good. Prove him right and come back to the island with us."

"I can't. I'm currently negotiating a business deal. Kip should have listened to me. It's not safe for Michael to be in this world."

"I found something," Mikey called from the toy store. "Am I good?"

Krell smiled and pulled out his wallet. "You're wonderful. Come take this to pay for it."

Mikey raced to him and accepted the paper

189

currency. Winnie couldn't make out the illustration in the middle, but each corner displayed a number ten in turquoise print.

"Thanks, Non-Dad." Mikey scampered back to the store.

Krell watched him, still smiling. "He reminds me of myself at that age."

"If you were ever like him, you'll stop whatever you're planning."

His smile faded, replaced with a look of regret. "If only I could. There's an expression here. 'You can never shut a door pushed open by the wind.' "

She cocked her head, baffled. "Wind can't stop a wizard. Especially a wizard who cares enough about a little boy to want to keep him out of danger."

Krell jabbed a thumb over his shoulder at the restaurant behind them. "Are you hungry? Millie serves the best fish and chips on the mainland. Not to brag, but I gave her the recipe."

Her stomach, fully recovered from the sea voyage, perked up at the suggestion. Her practical side, however, took over. "We don't have any money."

"It's my treat. Does Michael like fish?"

"At this point, I think he'll eat anything. We only ate a little bread on the ship."

"I'll go see to it." He slid his hands into his pockets and sauntered to the restaurant.

She sat at a picnic table in front of Millie's to wait.

Mikey scampered back, carrying a tiny red wagon, no more than two inches long, in one hand. He held paper money in the other. "Where's Non-Dad? I have his change."

"Went to get us lunch. Let's see the money."

The little boy laid it across her palm and sat opposite her on the picnic bench. Their money matched the size and feel of a dollar bill from their home world. A leaping fish, printed in turquoise ink, decorated the center. The denomination, displayed on all four corners, read two.

"Huh, two-dollar bills. I think we used to have those in our world."

Mikey rolled his new toy across the table. "Now Bunny can go for a ride."

Winnie looked up. "Bunny?"

"My glow stone. I named him when you were sleeping." He slid his hand into his pocket.

She shook her head. "Don't bring him out yet."

"Why not?"

She couldn't admit she worried his "non-dad" might steal it. "Let's eat first, okay?"

He shoved it deeper into his pocket. "Bunny doesn't want to come out yet anyway. I think he wants to take a nap."

She suppressed her own yawn. Even though she'd slept on the ship, she still hadn't caught up on her sleep.

Krell returned, followed by a waiter with a tray. The young man placed three covered plates on the table and three mugs of ice water, napkins, and silverware for each. He removed the covers and strutted back to the restaurant.

She handed Krell the money. "Here's your change. And thanks for lunch."

"My pleasure."

Mikey dug into his fried fish like he hadn't eaten in a month. It only took one bite for Winnie's appetite to appear with a vengeance. Crispy golden-brown batter covered the flakey fish. The fries, thick planks of golden potato, glistened with salt. As much as she hated to admit it, Krell had chosen a winning meal.

He casually peered down at his pocket watch and just as casually put it away. "What brings the both of you to the mainland?"

Winnie wiped her greasy fingers on her napkin. "The princess, remember? We need you to undo a spell you accidentally cast when you dueled with the king's conjurer."

He recoiled. "I never cast accidental spells."

She frowned back. "Are you saying you intentionally turned a princess into a toad?"

"An unfortunate by-product. I would never intentionally turn anyone into a toad."

Mikey pushed his emptied plate aside. "I knew it was an accident, Non-Dad."

"Thank you." The corners of Krell's lips quirked upward. "Non-Son."

Maybe they could trust him. "Come back with us to the island. The other wizard, Argamel, has agreed to work with you to counter the enchantment."

His fatherly expression turned sour. "Argamel is an imbecile. However." He drew out the word. "There might be another way."

Winnie leaned closer, eager to hear it.

"It'll cost you three glow stones. Blue, pink, and yellow."

She sat up. "No deal. They're not objects to trade."

"They're bloody rocks."

"They're special," Mikey announced. He looked to Winnie for permission. She nodded, and he pulled his marble-shaped glow stone into the open.

Krell scrutinized it from his seat. "How interesting.

It's perfectly round."

Mikey gazed back with his big brown eyes. "Bunny isn't just perfectly round. He's perfectly perfect. I'll share him with you. He comes apart."

Winnie stopped eating. "He does?"

"That's why I call him Bunny. When you were asleep on the ship, I pulled a piece off and made bunny ears for him. He even hopped like a bunny." He pulled the rock apart as if it were made of putty. He rolled the pieces into two balls and placed one in front of Krell.

When the wizard reached for it, Winnie expected it to shock him the way Winnie's sent sparks at Kip. Instead, the ball rolled across the level tabletop toward Mikey. Weird.

Her little brother tried again, but the ball rolled back to him a second time. "Sorry. Bunny says I'm not allowed to share." He pressed the two halves together. "But I do have something for you." He pulled out the shoelace and Frama-scope from inside his shirt. "This is for you." He laid it in front of Krell.

"You can keep it, son. I've already got one."

"Technically," Winnie said, "the one you have belongs to the Sisters Three."

"That's impossible. I've never met them."

"Kip accidentally stole all three when we were on Hutra, and you took one of them."

His eyes bulged in panic.

"It's okay," Mikey said calmly. "The one I brought is yours. Sister Ava fixed it, so you can have one that works. We'll give the other one back to the Sisters Three."

Krell pulled a Frama-scope from his inside jacket pocket. He turned it over and hissed a curse under his breath. "This one has writing on it."

"Does it say something about a loft and a lea?" Winnie asked.

"I can't read the language."

A sudden pressure popped Winnie's ears. Mikey jolted in his seat.

Krell must have felt it too. He shot to his feet, wand materializing in his hand. "This was a trap. You brought the conjurer."

A short, rotund woman with iron-gray hair pulled into a tight bun strode to their table with a purpose. Her black cape billowed out behind her. Was she the one who just magically appeared? She had an otherworldly air about her.

The woman stopped two feet from Krell. Her dark eyes blazed up at him from behind round-rimmed glasses. "I do not, good sir, appreciate the unauthorized use of Frama-scopes."

Mikey's eyes widened. "You're a Sisters Three."

The woman turned from Krell to Mikey. Her harsh stare melted. Winnie hadn't recognized the family resemblance to Sister Ava until the woman smiled. "I believe I have the honor of meeting the illustrious General Takka."

Mikey slid off his bench and bowed. "Greetings to you, Sister."

"Sister Bayla, my dear fellow. And..." She directed her gentle smile toward Winnie. "A hearty hello to the young warrior. You must choose your friends more wisely, my dears. You are in the company of a rather objectionable Frama-traveler."

Krell bristled. "Here then. I happen to be a scientist."

Sister Bayla glared at him. "Would a respectable scientist accept stolen property? You have in your possession my Frama-scope. I can prove ownership by the words etched onto it. They read, 'Beware Bayla's Wrath.' "

"Sister Bayla, I assure you I had no idea I'd been given your scope." Krell swept the scope off the table and offered it to her with a bow. "My apologies."

The woman snatched it from his open palm and shoved it into the pouch attached to her belt. "Thank you for keeping it safe," she said in an unthankful tone. "Please be aware that I have no patience for Frama-travelers who interfere with perfectly contented inhabitants of other worlds. Your reputation for stirring up trouble, then leaving precedes you. If I had my way, I'd have you stripped of your Frama-scope. You can thank my overly tolerant sisters for indulging you. And now I shall take my leave. Good day to you, sir." In a kinder voice, she said, "Children," and marched past them to an opening between two buildings.

Krell shook his head. "What an extraordinarily abrasive woman."

"I liked her," Winnie remarked.

"Of course you did. It was fortuitous that you brought my scope with you." He lifted it. "I've always carried it in a pocket, but I see the value in wearing it around one's neck." He snapped his fingers, and the shoelace turned into a gold chain. He slid the chain over his head and tucked the scope under his shirt. "Sadly, I too must be on my way. Sorry I couldn't help with your…toad, but I've got an appointment."

Gunshots sounded from the harbor. Winnie started. "What was that?"

"Fireworks. They're always celebrating something in this world." Krell stepped around the table. He paused just behind Mikey.

Winnie's muscles clenched. "Don't let the name 'Bunny' or his size fool you. If you try anything stupid, like taking Mikey with you, his stone will stop you."

Krell raised his hands as if in surrender. "I only wanted to say goodbye to the boy." He hugged Mikey from behind. "Mind your sister."

"Why can't we come with you?" Mikey asked.

"Stay here."

She rose. "Whatever you're planning, it won't work."

Krell's jaw tightened. "I've heard my entire life that I would never succeed. I've always proven everyone wrong."

She lifted her chin. "You think you can stop me? I prove people wrong all the time too!"

He sneered. "With your pink armor? I've heard the prophecy. You're not wearing it right now anyway." He marched toward the waterfront.

"I will stop you!"

"Non-Dad?"

He hesitated but only for a second and stalked off.

Mikey bowed his head, his lower lip trembling.

Winnie rushed to his side and wrapped her arm around his shoulders. "Don't let him ruin it for other non-dads. They're not all like that. My dad loves you."

He sniffled. "I know."

A pebble at her feet rang like an old-fashioned telephone.

Chapter 24

Kip plopped onto the ground and listlessly picked at blades of grass. He didn't care if Argamel thought him infantile. If the magically formed creatures had thoughts and feelings, they had committed murder with each attempt.

Argamel prodded him from behind with his foot. "Part of sorcery is experimentation. Is this your way of telling me you've decided not to be my apprentice?"

Kip stood with a huff and dusted off the back of his jeans. "There has got to be a better way to undo the enchantment."

Bird soared overhead and shrieked as if in agreement. He spread his massive black wings, nearly blocking the sun. He circled, then hurtled toward the ground, gobbled up two green toads, and swooped upward.

Kip shook his fist at him. "Oi!"

Bird landed and swallowed two more toads before they could jump away. Kip flapped his arms, but the feathered imbecile ignored him and feasted on another. The entire time Kip tried to shoo the bird away, Argamel stood statue still with his hands on his hips.

Kip turned his scowl at his teacher. "Why aren't you helping me?"

"We've got dozens of these blighted things hopping through my field. If that creature wants to eat a few, he's welcome to them."

"But they're alive."

Argamel scowled. "They're not."

"They have eyes!"

Bird stretched his telescoping neck toward what must have been his tenth green toad. He staggered two steps and collapsed.

Kip hurried to his side. "We've poisoned him!"

"For the last time, they're only tomatoes."

"What if they're toxic to him?" Kip hesitantly reached out. Bird blinked. "Are you all right, mate?"

At least the bird remained conscious. His chest rose and fell faster than expected, but the movement proved he hadn't choked. Still, Bird made no attempt to stand. Kip sat back on his heels and examined the bird's feathers. Didn't they used to be completely black? Now a grayish tinge colored the ends. More gray bled farther along his feathers.

Kip lifted his gaze to his teacher. "What's happening?"

"Don't ask me. Ask him."

"How?"

Argamel snorted. "With all your magic, you should be able to do this." He made a slashing motion with his wand. "Now ask him."

"Bird, what's wrong? How can I help?"

"I eat yet grow weaker."

"Maybe you're just not eating the right things."

"Or maybe there are no right things for him here," Argamel remarked. "I've never seen his kind."

"I'm not from your world either, but your food works for me."

"Not that I'm an expert on the matter," Argamel

remarked, "but you possess similarities to my people. I'm sure that's how you can safely eat."

Kip gently stroked the bird's graying feathers. "But he's a bird. You've got birds here."

"Not like him." Argamel bent toward Bird. "Where are you from?"

"We call it Rall, but others have called it Frama-22."

Kip nodded. "Right. Sister Ava mentioned that. We're on Frama-7 at the moment. Since we could pass through more than one Frama on our way here, I'm sure we can find a way to reach your world."

Bird struggled but managed to return to his feet. He shook his feathers. "Thank you, but it's best if you don't accompany me. You might get eaten. Show me to the doorway that leads to my home, and I'll take it."

Kip also rose. "I'm not sure where that doorway is yet. Even if I had a general idea, we'd still need Winnie's Frama-scope to open it for you. Are you able to hold on a bit longer?"

"If I must, but it will be too late when my plumage turns completely gray."

Argamel cleared his throat and cast a meaningful look at Kip, who frowned back questioningly.

The king's conjurer let out an exasperated sigh and pointed at his wand.

Magic, of course. Kip should have thought of it on his own. After all, he'd used magic to prevent the princess from losing herself to her enchantment. He closed his eyes and imagined Bird receiving the necessary sustenance to keep him well. At least until they completed their mission here. When he opened his eyes, most of the bird's gray feathers had darkened to black.

Bird stretched his neck upward, almost matching

Kip's height. "I feel much better now. Thank you." He shot into the air and flew over the treetops.

Kip hoped his magic lasted longer for Bird than it had for the princess.

The man who had brought out the original tomato plant trotted from an outbuilding to where Argamel stood. "Sir, you've been summoned by the mother trees to the western shore. There could be trouble from the sea."

Argamel nodded. He pointed his wand upward and made a circular motion. All the evidence of their experiments vanished. He faced Kip. "Have you learned the teleport spell?"

"Sorry, no."

"Come along, then. Stand by me." Argamel flicked his wand and mumbled an incantation. A cloud encircled them. Kip never sensed movement, but when the cloud dissipated, they stood on a familiar sandy beach.

It had taken nearly two days by horse to reach Oram Forest but less than one eyeblink to return to the same place where the two guards had caught him and Mikey.

Argamel stared out to sea. "That looks like our supply ship."

Kip squinted at little more than a speck on the horizon. He curled the fingers of both hands and held them to his eyes like binoculars. He used his magic to magnify his view. The speck grew into a clipper ship. A group of rough-looking sailors stood on deck. "That might be your ship, but I don't think that crew came from this island."

"That would explain why the mother trees asked us to come here. We need to destroy the invaders before they come ashore."

Kip lowered his hands. He still regretted his overzealous use of magic on the tomato plants. "We have to think this through. There are consequences to our actions."

"Exactly. And the consequence we want is to defeat the enemy."

"Winnie and Mikey might be on there." Even as Kip said it, he knew they weren't. He did, however, catch wind of dark magic. "Krell's on that ship."

"All the more reason to destroy it. He's the enemy."

Kip slowly shook his head. "What if you're wrong? We can't blast him with spells until we know for sure why he's here."

"Please don't tell me you believe he's come to restore the princess."

"Why couldn't he? That's why Winnie and Mikey went to see him."

"Go on, then, contact him on that shell of yours and ask."

Instead, he called for Winnie. He'd barely gotten out his greeting when her voice blurted through the shell, still on speaker, "Krell's on his way to steal glow stones."

"He's here now," Kip said. "I see his ship on the horizon."

"That's impossible. He just left!"

"Magic. But, Win, you were supposed to ask him to help us with the princess."

"I told you he was the enemy," Argamel muttered.

At the same time, Winnie said, "He said something about wind blowing a door open."

Kip squinted, confused. "What?"

"Gotta go." She disconnected.

201

"It's an expression," Argamel said. "It means he started something he can't stop."

Kip put away his shell and reshaped his hands into binoculars. Two more ships glided into view. "Uh-oh. Looks like he brought friends."

"I'd be surprised if they came any closer. If Krell is any kind of strategist, he will have done his research and know the king's guards will be riding by soon. He won't want to be seen. Yet. Look, they're moving away. My guess is he'll wait until nightfall. That's what I'd do."

Kip kept watching through his magical hand binoculars. As the conjurer predicted, the ships slowly vanished from sight. All except one. Instead of retreating, it rotated until it floated parallel to the beach. Kip zoomed in, focusing on the round openings on the ship's side. "Uh-oh."

Argamel swung around, facing the sea. "What is it?"

"Either Krell changed his mind, or one of his ships is going rogue."

Smoke puffed out of the opening. The explosive sound it should have created never reached them. But the black cannonball that blasted high into the air surely would. It reached the apex, then hurtled downward, heading straight toward them. With little time to think, teacher and apprentice moved as one, simultaneously snapping up their wands.

Kip didn't need instruction. They'd both use the melt spell and liquify the iron ball. It would then rain harmlessly into the water.

Electric charges shot from each wand, striking the projectile in the same spot. The object immediately transformed into a black, cannonball-sized toad.

"Kip!" Argamel slashed through the air with his

wand, and the giant toad vanished.

Kip's ears popped. "Where did you send it?"

"Away from here."

"But where did it go? To another world?"

"I'm not bothered by where it went," Argamel snapped. "In the future, always use the freeze spell when faced with a threat. Frozen objects become brittle and burst apart on impact."

Kip tensed over the possibility that another cannonball might come their way. "The ship's still there. Maybe the Myst can go out there and knock everybody out."

"The Myst only protects Oram Forest."

Kip turned to Argamel. "He transported Winnie and Mikey to the harbor to catch a ship."

"He must have put them under his protection. It's rare, but he has been known to protect individuals on the odd occasion. If he finds them worthy."

Kip folded his arms and huffed. Naturally, the Myst found Winnie worthy. The prophecy said so. But why did she always get to be the subject of ruddy prophecies?

"You know," Argamel remarked, "your mention of the Myst gives me an idea. Why don't we create a magical fog that will block their view and interfere with their navigational instruments? Then they'll never find their way here."

Magic. The one gift Winnie didn't possess. His lips curled into an evil grin. "I like it."

No other cannonballs hurtled their way, giving Argamel time to offer Kip quick instruction on how to perform the fog spell. Kip usually learned fast, but this spell required a finesse that eluded him.

Argamel lightly gripped Kip's right forearm. "Relax

the muscles right here. You're moving water, so you must make your motion more fluid."

Kip nodded. He took a deep breath and exhaled, relaxing the tension in his body.

On his third try, white vapor wafted from his wand. Argamel, on his right, produced the same white mist. Their combined fog rolled out to sea. It grew denser and drifted over the calm waves toward the horizon and beyond, leaving a clear sky and no hint of vaper near the shore.

Argamel clapped Kip on the back. "Nicely done."

Kip wished his own father felt the same way about his magic.

A shushing noise from behind caught his full attention. He knew that sound. Two dozen horsemen, dressed in matching red uniforms and silver helmets with dark plumes, strutted along the beach toward them.

"Hoy!" shouted the guard on the lead horse. "What's all this, then?"

Kip's muscles coiled, ready to escape into the woods.

Argamel drew himself up to his full height. "Surely, you recognize me as the king's conjurer." He gently touched Kip's shoulder, preventing him from bolting. "And this is my fine apprentice."

The guard in the lead scowled back. "The king's conjurer is missing. You've magically enhanced your appearance to fool us. The both of you are guilty of trespass. You'll be coming with us, so you will."

Kip let out a puff of air in annoyance. *Not this again. Now would be a good time to teleport out of here.*

As if in answer to his wish, his ears popped. But he and Argamel still stood before the guards.

Chapter 25

Kip's announcement over the pebble phone in Winnie's hand sucked the breath out of her. What kind of magic could propel a ship to the island in minutes?

"I thought he'd never leave," a female voice spoke behind her.

Winnie jumped and twisted around. Sister Bayla returned to the table.

"Gotta go." Winnie dropped the pebble. "You're back." Although she should have guessed the woman had never disappeared. Her ears would have felt the change in pressure if she had. "Sister, we have a serious problem with Krell. He's about to ruin everything."

"No, he isn't," Mikey said in a sulky voice.

Winnie sat beside him and tried to rub his back, but he slid down the bench.

Sister Bayla tutted. "Let's not get ourselves worked up before it's necessary. Don't forget the prophecy of the young female warrior in pink armor."

Winnie, who doubted a warrior could do much good against a wizard, shrugged and looked away.

Sister Bayla chortled. "The pink armor was my sister Kat's idea. I thought it silly at first, but now I rather like it."

She jolted in her seat. "What? Are you telling me the whole prophecy thing was made up by your sister? It's fake?"

"They're all fake," the older woman said amiably. "They only become real when the outcome matches the prediction."

"Oh gee. Is that all?" Winnie retorted. "And by the way, pink is my least favorite color. That hoodie was a gift from my aunt. I didn't even plan on wearing it today."

Sister Bayla smiled benevolently. "We're time guardians, remember? Kat saw you."

"Did she also see me wearing this?" Winnie gestured toward her blouse and long blue skirt. "Nothing pink about any of this."

Sister Bayla pointed her index finger at the sky and waved in a circular motion. Wind whistled past them toward the window shoppers. Everyone on the sidewalk froze. Winnie's mouth dropped open. Mikey laughed and applauded.

Sister Bayla beamed at them. "I'm having a bit of fun with time."

Winnie smiled along with the older woman and her brother. Since it was a fake prophecy anyway, maybe she could beat Krell, especially with a fairy godmother on her side.

"I believe your mother did something similar in the previous world you visited."

Her smile faded as the weight of longing pressed down on her. She'd been nine years old when her mom died. Long-distance running had pulled her out of the deepest part of her grief. And then, on her first trip through a time tear, Winnie had seen her Mom or at least a vision of her. Seeing Mom each time she traveled through time tears gave Winnie the strength to face each alternate world's challenges. Except this last time.

"I…think she's gone." Winnie kept the word *forever* unsaid.

"Ah, yes. The sisters and I temporarily suspended her duties until we looked deeper into her unauthorized use of a time hold. We better understand her motive now and have restored her position. I suspect you'll see her again."

"I will?"

The woman nodded. "Assuredly."

Winnie's eyes watered with tears of gratitude. "Thank you, Sister Bayla."

"The pleasure is mine. I'm so glad I got to meet the two of you. But let's not get overly sentimental. Now that no one can see us, let's put you both back into your traveling togs." With another twirl of her finger, the old-fashioned outfits transformed into their original clothes. "There we are. I'm sure you're much more comfortable now."

"I liked those straps that held up my pants," Mikey remarked.

Winnie chuckled. "They're called suspenders."

"Yup. Suspenders. I need some."

"Of course you do," Winnie said, still grinning.

"Now, let's call up that pink armor, shall we?" Sister Bayla snapped her fingers, and Winnie's hoodie solidified into a shiny pink breastplate and pink hinged sleeves.

Mikey let out a delighted gasp.

Winnie tested her new armor by rapping a fist against her chest. She struck it again, hard enough for her knuckles to sting. The lightweight material absorbed the impact, leaving her chest pain-free.

"Rise, Warrior Windemere, so that I may complete

your transformation."

Winnie eagerly obeyed, hoping for speed and super strength. The air crackled, followed by a pop. A pink leather belt with an attached sheath appeared on the table. *Pink. Why did everything have to be stupid pink?* She frowned from the belt to Bayla.

The older woman nodded. "Go on, then. Put it on."

With a shrug, Winnie slid the leather strap through her belt loops. The sheath rested against her left leg. "Hope you're going to make a sword to go with this."

Bayla chuckled. "In good time. Now, you'll need to pull up your hood for the second part of your armor."

Winnie felt over her shoulder, surprised that a clump of soft material still hung from the back. She lifted the hood, and a helmet molded around her head. She knocked the hardened outside but felt nothing from the helmet's cushiony inside. A pink metal nose piece slid down between her eyes. *Good. Nobody can break my nose.*

Mikey bounced in his seat. "I need a helmet like that! Except make mine green."

Bayla smiled at him. "Your power lies elsewhere."

He slumped in his seat.

Bayla stepped around the table to pat his shoulder. "Mustn't forget you're a general and not a knight, dear Takka."

Voicing his title seemed to appease him.

Winnie slid her hands over the smooth sides of her armor and found no buckles. She slid her thumbs into the ventilation spaces at her armpits and pulled. "Um. How do I get out of this?"

"You don't, dear. The armor will stay with you, or should I say, on you, until you no longer have a use for it."

She almost asked how she could shower, stuck inside the armor. But maybe that just meant she'd have a super-short battle. At least her jeans hadn't transformed. She could still use the bathroom when necessary.

"If you wouldn't mind bringing out your glow stone for a final modification?"

Winnie patted her right hip pocket, locating the rugged outline of her multicolored glow stone. She placed it on the table.

Sister Bayla bent forward and peered at it. "What lovely colors. And an excellent pairing. I even see a hint of pink."

Winnie cringed, embarrassed by her negative thoughts about that color. Would her stone still choose her? The glow stone sent a warmth of acceptance through her. *Thanks for understanding.*

With no help from Sister Bayla, the stone stretched outward into an elongated shape. It grew into a sword. Its dusty pink blade and silver hilt glistened in the sunlight.

Winnie laughed out loud. "No way!" She slid the sword into the sheath.

"Can Bunny turn into a sword too?" He carefully picked his marble-shaped glow stone out of the toy wagon.

Sister Bayla stared kindly at him. "Oh, I'm sure Bunny's quite content to be who he is."

Mikey cocked his head as if listening. "You're right. He is." The little boy returned the stone to his pocket.

"It's time to meet your destiny, Warrior Windemere. You too, General Takka." She held out her hand to Mikey.

He leaped up, grabbed the day pack in one hand, and eagerly slid his other into Sister Bayla's.

"Yours too," she said to Winnie, a girl who hadn't held an adult's hand since crossing the street at age eight.

She clasped the older woman's other hand. Their surroundings immediately shimmered from the quaint shopping district to a row of trees at the edge of a sandy beach. They returned to Aylen Isle and landed behind a gnarled tree, not far from where she, Mikey, and Kip had stood when they first arrived.

The last time she'd been here, an empty stretch of sand lay beside a crystal-blue ocean. Now guards on horseback filled the narrow beach. None looked toward Winnie, Mikey, or Sister Bayla. Probably because the tree hid them. And also because the horsemen faced the king's conjurer and Kip, who stood with their backs to the ocean.

"Can you stop time again so we can rescue them?" Winnie whispered.

"Sorry, dear, I've done more than I should have already." Sister Bayla disappeared with an ear-popping poof.

Dozens of high-pitched voices sang in Winnie's mind. *We're here. We're here!*

Leaflings. They had to be. *Thanks for coming.* Although she had no idea what they could do now that they had arrived.

Mikey smiled up at her. "You heard them, right?" he whispered.

She nodded.

"They're going to help us."

At the moment, though, Kip looked more in need of help than Winnie or Mikey.

"How can it be, as you claim?" Argamel told the leader in a condescending voice. "Your helmets are designed to detect and deflect magic. How could I use it to change my appearance?"

The guards looked from one to the other.

The leader leaned forward in his saddle. "Supposing we believe you are who you claim to be. What are you doing in a restricted zone?"

Argamel pointed out to sea. "Beyond that patch of fog are three hostile ships. One of the ships carries a conjurer with ill intent. Without my—"

Kip bent his head toward Argamel and said, "Our."

"Without *our* magic, they would have already commenced their invasion." Argamel extracted a white marble from inside his cloak. It resembled the one the king had let her use when she met with him. "Allow me to contact the king, and we can sort all of this out."

The guard nodded. "Very well, but no mischief from you. As you so adequately pointed out, our helmets can detect and deflect magic."

Argamel gave an exaggerated bow and murmured into the sphere. Louder, he said, "Your Majesty, I respectfully request that you temporarily lift the ban on magic. Enemy ships have been spotted on the horizon of the western shore. We'll need magic to stop them."

Winnie's internal debate over whether to cower behind a tree or act like a warrior prevented her from overhearing the king's reply. She took a deep breath, thumped her armor plate for good luck, and strode forward. Little footsteps scuffed behind her. She skimmed to a stop and twisted around. "Stay at the tree," she whispered. "It's safer there."

"It's safe here too. We have guards and Kip's magic

and our glow stones."

She groaned inwardly. He probably had a point. "Okay, but keep quiet."

A guard behind the leader spotted her. "Captain! The warrior in pink."

One of the horses sidestepped out of formation, but his rider brought him back in line.

Winnie marched to the head of the regiment. "Yes. I'm the warrior in pink. If we hope to defeat the conjurer on that ship out there…" She squinted toward the foggy area that shrouded the horizon. She turned her frown on Kip. "Are there really ships out there?"

He gawked at her. "Is that…"

"Pink armor? It is. Compliments of one of the Sisters Three."

The leader cleared his throat and nodded a greeting. "Warrior Windem."

She gave him a curt nod. It seemed a warrior thing to do. "Captain, did the king lift the magic ban?"

The leader nodded. "Yes, sir."

"Thanks. Please stand by for further orders. I need to speak with the conjurers." Since Kip couldn't stop gaping, she turned her attention to Argamel. "Is Krell out there?"

The king's conjurer pursed his lips and stared down his nose at her. "He is, but he won't be troubling us. We conjured the haze that surrounds his fleet."

"Can't he counter your magic with his own to make it dissipate?"

"My apprentice and I doubled the potency of the spell," he said in a haughty voice. "The conjurer will be lost in that for at least three days."

She mouthed the word "apprentice" at Kip but he

still seemed to be processing the sudden appearance of her armor. To the leader, she said, "Captain. We're about to enter into a…well, this isn't going to be a typical conflict. I'm pretty sure the person leading the attack will use magic. Which means we'll need to come up with an unconventional counterattack."

The captain inclined his head. "The king's royal guard is at your service."

His acceptance of her authority both surprised and energized her. She stood straighter. "Those low clouds are keeping the enemy from seeing us, so our best defense is to hide the fact we know they're coming. For now, take cover behind the trees and don't come out until you're given the order to advance."

The captain twisted in his saddle, facing his men. "Company. Dismount."

The riders swung their legs over their horses' backs and leaped to the ground in one swift motion. All stood at stiff attention beside their horses.

"Men," the captain announced, "on this day, as it has been foretold, we meet the enemy. And with the warrior's aid, we shall defeat him!"

The guards' deep voices filled the air with their enthusiastic shouts. "To victory!"

The captain called to three of his guards. "Take the horses back to the castle. The rest, take your positions in the woods."

Winnie had never led an army so strong and capable. She hoped they'd follow her orders when it mattered. Now that magic was legal, maybe Kip's convincement spell could help.

The guards marched into the woods. She said to Argamel, "Excuse me while I meet with my…advisers."

She nodded to Kip and Mikey to follow her out of the conjurer's hearing. "I'm worried Krell's coming sooner than Argamel believes."

Kip nodded. "Agreed."

Mikey stepped between them. "Nuh-uh. My non-dad would never attack us."

"Remember, bud, he has men who might not feel the same way."

Kip grinned. "I know two pieces of information that will help us. First, what does Krell love the most?"

Winnie said, "Power."

At the same time, Mikey blurted, "Me."

Kip pointed at her little brother. "Got it in one, mate. Second, Argamel taught me a duplication spell."

She shrugged, finding no connection between the two. "And?"

"Isn't it obvious? I'll duplicate an army of Mikeys. Krell wouldn't dare let anyone harm them because he won't know which one is the real one."

Mikey clapped and chanted, "I'm an army. I'm an army."

Winnie rested her hands on her hips and waited for the little boy to settle down. "First of all. No. It's my job to take care of him. We're not putting him in danger."

"But he wouldn't be."

"I said it's not happening."

Mikey patted her armor. "Please? I want to be an army."

She glared at Kip. "Now see what you did?"

Argamel stepped up to them. "All right. You've had your fun, but this is no game." He pointed at Kip. "You're only an apprentice." He cast a harsh stare at Mikey. "You are a small child. And you," he said, glaring at Winnie, "are only a slightly larger child."

She opened her mouth to protest.

Argamel raised his hand, palm outward. "I don't want to hear about that ridiculous prophecy. You're not a female warrior. You're a *girl*."

"Would a girl have this?" She yanked her pink sword from its sheath and held it high.

"Put that toy away."

"This *toy* was forged from a glow stone. You might not believe the prophecy, but the king does. I want to see him. Now."

The king materialized in front of her. They gaped at each other, then his crown and her sword glowed white. Just as quickly as he'd appeared, he disappeared again.

Winnie looked from Kip to Argamel. "What just happened?"

The king's conjurer glowered. "You must never use magic to summon the king!"

"I didn't know I had any," she sputtered.

Argamel clapped a hand on her shoulder. The two materialized in the king's office. Eight startled humans and tree sprites leaped from their chairs. They yelled as one, demanding that a sword must always be sheathed in the presence of a king.

The king, appearing unconcerned, remained seated behind his desk.

Abbi, standing at his side, let out an eager squeal. "Winnie, you have real armor now!"

Argamel still hadn't let her go. "Your Majesty," he said, "please forgive our unexpected intrusion. And also forgive this child for unintentionally pulling you from this room."

Winnie shrugged out of the conjurer's grip, insulted

by his "child" reference. Although she agreed, she owed him an apology. "Yeah, sorry about that, Your Majesty. I think it was the sword." She quickly sheathed it. "It's made from a glow stone."

The men, probably the king's advisers, shouted over each other. Some insisted that no warrior, female or otherwise, needed a magic sword. Others yelled for her arrest for the unauthorized use of magic.

King Steffin rose. He swiped his hand through the air, silencing the room.

Winnie stiffened. "Isn't it true, Your Majesty, that you lifted the ban on magic?"

"I did."

"But only for the king's conjurer and his apprentice," said a human adviser with a neatly trimmed black beard and blazing dark eyes.

The tan-skinned tree sprite on the man's left straightened to his full height, which Winnie guessed to be over six feet. "We've already unconditionally agreed that even with the lifted ban, they may only detect and deflect magic."

Winnie pressed her lips together to keep from howling in frustration. Didn't they realize their lifted ban still limited the good guys? She took a deep breath and forced an even tone to her voice. "You do realize there's a wiz—conjurer on a ship, waiting to attack the island."

The man with the trimmed beard faced the king. "All the more reason, Your Majesty, to deploy the royal navy. They can sink the conjurer's ship before it comes ashore."

"Wait," Winnie blurted. Krell had never killed anyone. At least she didn't think he had. But if a fleet of ships shot at him, he'd defend himself with magic. And what if that meant destroying the king's navy? "Normal weapons can't defeat sorcery."

As the king returned to his seat, his gold crown began to glow white. He turned toward his conjurer. "The crown wishes to speak with you."

Argamel bobbed his head once, then closed his eyes. The king did the same. In the time it took the advisers to settle back into their seats, both men reopened their eyes. The crown dimmed to its original gold color. *What just happened?*

Abbi's eyes glistened eagerly. "Did he give you news about my sister?"

A surge of guilt pulsed through Winnie. She should have done more to help the toad princess. In her defense, though, Krell's looming invasion required her full attention.

The king scowled. "Abbidrelle, you were invited to this meeting under the condition that you would remain silent."

The girl bowed her head. "Sorry, Papa."

"Arrigo," the king addressed the man with the black beard. "We shall have the conjurer assess the rogue sorcerer's abilities. In the meantime, put our navy on standby."

Arrigo clicked his bootheels together. "As you command, Your Majesty, so shall it be." He strode from the room.

The king's crown glowed white again. "Warrior Windemere, the crown wishes to speak with you."

She cringed. *This can't be good.*

Chapter 26

Kip stared at the empty sand where Argamel and Winnie had stood just moments ago. An unexpected sense of abandonment rolled over him. He frowned at himself for feeling alone. Mikey stood at his side, and a regiment of guards hid among the trees less than ten yards away. Maybe he just needed to hydrate. He reached for the day pack Mikey had dropped in the sand and pulled out the canteen. After a long swallow, he offered the water to Mikey.

The little boy took a drink. "Windy is right most of the time, but not always."

Kip raised an eyebrow. "Is that so?"

Mikey bobbed his head up and down and handed the canteen back. "Like your idea to make an army of me's? She didn't like it, but I do. My non-dad would never attack the island if he saw a bunch of me's on the beach."

He capped the canteen and returned it to the pack. "Your non-dad isn't alone. He's got two other ships with him. Before you came, one of those ships shot a cannonball at Argamel and me."

Mikey's eyes widened, but not from fear. "Can I see it? Where is it?"

"Argamel made it disappear." He kept it to himself that he and the conjurer had accidentally turned the cannonball into a toad first.

"What would happen if a cannonball hit the fake

me's?"

Kip didn't dare mention the explosion of bits and seeds when he and Argamel failed to turn their fake toads back into green tomatoes. "I wouldn't want to chance it."

Mikey gripped his arm and peered up with his big brown eyes. "Please? Just make two."

The odds of a cannonball striking two little duplicate boys had to be slim. "Okay. But just two. Stand still whilst I recite the incantation."

Mikey grinned and stood as still as any little boy bursting with energy could.

Kip mumbled the words Argamel had taught him. Fifteen duplicate Mikeys shot from the end. "Oh, bugger." He'd only meant to create two.

Mikey's eyes glistened in wonder. "Bunny has to see this!" He pulled a white marble out of his pocket and promptly dropped it. As he bent to collect it, his replicas repeated his motion. They even straightened when he did. Unlike Mikey, they kept bending toward the ground and straightening again. "They're doing what I did!"

And they kept it up like a collection of windup toys. Down and up, down and up.

Kip rubbed a hand down the back of his head. "I'm not sure we want them to do that, mate. Maybe I should send these away and try again."

"No. We have to keep them. I like it."

Secretly, Kip didn't dare vanish them anyway. They might end up in an alternate world, and who knew what might happen to them there? He warmed to the idea that a variety of movements would make the real Mikey harder to spot.

"Stand back, mate. I'll make some more. Do something different this time."

A second batch of Mikeys spewed from Kip's wand. Mikey didn't move fast enough, and the new group just stood there.

At least fifty frozen clones dotted the beach before Mikey got the timing right. The latest set of duplicate Mikeys skipped five steps down the beach, turned around, and skipped back. Kip shot more Mikeys from his wand.

"Wait!" the original wailed. "I wasn't ready."

The latest copies moved their right hands toward their noses.

"Were you picking your nose just then?"

Mikey shook his head. "I was scratching it."

Kip sighed. "Okay. Do something normal this time." Of course, the instant he suggested it, he knew he should have given more detailed instructions.

Mikey's "normal" involved running in a tight circle, flapping his arms, and shouting, "I'm an airplane!"

Thankfully, the clones imitated his motions in silence.

"Right. Now wave at the sea like you're greeting your non-dad."

Mikey eagerly obeyed.

More and more of Kip's creations filled the beach, becoming a symphony of motion. Unlike an orchestra where identical instruments grouped together, Kip moved individual clones so there wouldn't be great clumps doing the same thing. He found them surprisingly light and hefted one under each arm to rearrange them. Even Mikey could pick them up one at a time and reposition them.

Kip stood back and admired the multiples of bending, skipping, and waving clones. "That's probably enough, don't you think?"

Mikey spread his arms. "I never saw so many me's. I bet there's a million. I'm going to count them."

Kip laughed. "Knock yourself out."

With Mikey occupied, Kip turned his attention to the fog on the horizon. He pocketed his wand and made magical binoculars of his curled fingers.

"Hoy there, apprentice!" the captain called from behind.

Kip faced him. "Sir?"

"We've just been ordered by the king's high commander to return to the castle."

His brows rose in horror. "You were? Why?"

"We never question Commander Arrigo's orders. Likewise, as you are the king's conjurer's apprentice, we won't question why the beach is now filled with children." The captain pivoted on his heel and marched with his men to the sandy path that cut through the woods. After the last man strode from view, Kip sighed and sat on the sand. Had the fog thinned, or did he imagine it? To be safe, he mumbled the vapor incantation and pointed his wand toward the horizon. More Mikey clones spilled from the end and landed on the shoreline.

Oops. He'd forgotten to undo the duplication spell. He spoke it under his breath and waved his wand to test it. A dozen more infernal Mikeys gushed out.

He hissed a curse and tried again, but no matter what incantation he recited, each time he waved his wand, more and more duplicate Mikeys appeared. In frustration, he hurled his wand. Thankfully, when it hit the ground, nothing spilled out. He hoped that ended the spell. The beach literally jumped with hundreds of silent Mikeys.

Winnie is going to kill me.

"Oi, Mikey! Stop counting and come back. We need a plan to appease your sister."

No response.

"Mikey?"

He retrieved his wand but hesitated, afraid to attempt the location spell. *Please, please, please work.* He spoke the location spell through clenched teeth, cringed, and pointed.

Another batch of Mikeys spurted from his wand.

He howled in desperation and slumped onto the sand in defeat.

Chapter 27

Winnie bowed her head and closed her eyes the way Argamel had when the king announced the crown wished to speak with him. Since both king and conjurer remained in the room, she didn't think she'd leave either. She reopened her eyes. At least, she thought she did. Had the lights gone out in the king's office?

No. She sensed a vast space connected to the blackness that surrounded her. She also felt a soft cushion under her bottom but didn't remember sitting. The crown, it had to be the crown, had sent her to another place. To a cave? Outer space? Transporting happened a lot in this world. But at least the trip included a comfy chair.

A dim light from the crown gradually brightened, illuminating the king seated nearby. A white satin pillow, similar to what a ringbearer might carry, lay on a small table between them.

"Excuse me, Your Majesty, but where are we?"

"I think of it as a non-place. You could say we're outside of time. It's the crown's doing, of course." He lifted the crown with both hands and placed it gently on the shiny cushion.

Sudden light shone from the sheath on Winnie's side. She blinked at the king in surprise. "I didn't tell it to do that."

"It's all right. Bring it out."

She carefully unsheathed her sword, about to lay it across her lap, but it tugged her hand toward the table. Winnie fought the magnetic draw, but the sword forced her to place it beside the crown.

She winced. Had she just broken royal protocol by placing her weapon beside the crown? "Um. Sorry, Your Majesty."

He shook his head. "You needn't be. They're probably communing."

She strained to hear. "Can you tell what they're saying?"

"It's not for us to know. Like so many things." He sighed. "It's a burden sometimes. Being king. But I suppose it's just as much of a burden to be chosen by a prophecy."

"Yeah. I never asked, you know, to be…" She pointed at her armored chest. "This."

He smiled. "You fulfilled the first part of the prophecy when you put on the crown and survived."

A nervous pulse thrummed in her temples. Should she confess that a time guardian made up the prophecy on a whim? At least it seemed like a whim to her.

"When I was born," the king said in a quiet voice, "sixteen brothers and cousins, ranging in age from twenty-three to eight, stood in line for succession before me."

Winnie raised her head.

"On the second week after my birth, my uncle, the king, held a private ceremony. Only the king's heirs attended. He blessed me with a long life, wisdom, and compassion. He also proclaimed to all the heirs that I could never be king."

She leaned forward, elbows on knees, eager to hear

his story even though she knew how it ended.

He gave her a sad smile. "I don't know if he chose to protect me from the others' competitiveness or if he truly believed he'd die before I came of age. He was nearly seventy at my birth and in poor health. As a result of his declaration, all sixteen princes treated me with patience and great kindness. One cousin taught me to ride. Another hand-to-hand combat. My brothers taught me swordplay and how to read and write. A cousin even taught me how to play the lute. They all accepted me because…"

"You would never become king."

He nodded. "Regrettably, they weren't as tolerant amongst themselves. One by one, they fell. In battle, failed quests, duels, or outright murder of each other."

Winnie bolted upright. "That doesn't sound very kingly of them."

"Just so. On my twentieth birthday, the king lay ill in his bed. By then, there were only four in line for the crown. Excluding me, of course. Uncle called us, one by one, to his bedchamber. Eldest to the youngest. Each cousin entered, then exited the chamber. I guessed by their grim faces that Uncle was failing quickly. In fact, I expected I'd find a corpse by the time my turn came."

The non-place dissolved into a dark bedroom. A single lit candle stood on the table beside a curtained four-poster bed. Winnie stepped deeper into the room. On her right, heavy curtains shut out any light, making it hard to determine the time of day. A white-haired man lay in the bed, mouth partially open, but he breathed. A familiar crown shaped like a plain gold ring encircled his head.

The man didn't acknowledge her sudden

appearance, but she didn't expect him to. The crown must have sent her into a memory just like last time.

It also didn't surprise her when a younger version of King Steffin tiptoed into the room. "Uncle?" he said in a soft voice.

The old man struggled to lift his arm. "My boy," he said, barely above a whisper.

He rushed to his side and took the old man's hand. "Uncle. Dearest Uncle."

The elderly king struggled to sit up but failed.

"Can I get you anything? Water? The nurse?"

The man let out a weak cough. "I've but one small request. Please remove my crown and set it just there." He nodded toward the bedside table.

"Of course."

"At the time," the current king said.

Winnie jumped, surprised that King Steffin stood beside her. She believed she'd entered the memory alone.

"I knew nothing of the crown's discerning properties. I lifted it." As he spoke, his younger self moved in synch with his description. "Without a thought, I placed it on the table."

The elderly king's eyes remained closed, but he smiled. "Thank you. I can rest now." His body went slack, and he started to snore.

Winnie sucked in a breath of air and turned to the current king. "Did he die that night?"

"No, he lived eight years after that."

The bedroom melted away. She and the king sat together in the non-place again.

"When I left my uncle, my cousins gathered around me, wanting to know if the king had asked me a question." He shrugged. "I was too embarrassed to admit he hadn't. So I told them I didn't know the answer. They embraced me, assuring me I was perfect just the way I was."

She sat forward again, wanting more. "What do you think he asked everybody else?"

He snorted. "Even though he didn't use the words, I believe he asked, 'Can you touch the crown and not be harmed by it?' "

"Whoa," she said in an awed whisper. "And then I showed up and put it on my head."

"That's how I knew you were the warrior in pink."

"Did any of your cousins survive after you...I guess...won the crown?"

"Three. Cousin Arrigo is the commander I sent to alert the navy. The other two, Hesh and Hogart, live on the mainland. There's always been talk of their plots to take the crown, but nothing can come of it. The crown would never allow it."

"I'd be wary this time," spoke a female voice. "The trees hear things."

Winnie sprang to her feet. She'd never heard the leaf-green-eyed queen arrive. Her deep-brown skin glistened in the low light. Winnie, overwhelmed by the tree sprite queen's poise and beauty, tried to bow and curtsey at the same time. She almost fell over.

The queen let out a joyful laugh. "Warrior Windemere. I had hoped to meet you."

"Your Majesty." She tried the curtsey thing again and failed miserably.

By then, the queen turned her attention to the glowing objects on the table.

Winnie gulped, afraid the queen would confiscate

her sword. "Uh, my sword is talking to your husband's crown."

"Glow stones call to glow stones," the queen replied. "I must admit, this is the first time I've seen a sword made of one."

"Uh, yeah. It kind of stretched into that shape because of the whole..." Winnie shrugged. "Female warrior thing."

The queen flashed a dazzling smile. "We have every confidence in you."

The king's office rematerialized around her. She stood facing the seated king, still wearing his crown, as if they'd never left. Well, he did say they'd entered a non-place outside of time. She didn't remember sheathing her sword but felt the weight of it at her side.

The king turned to his advisers. "Gentlemen, please leave us."

The men filed out without a backward glance.

"Abbidrelle, take the warrior to the stables and find her a suitable mount. She must return to the western shore immediately."

"Yes, Papa."

Why? Had something happened? They'd never discussed anything about the western shore during their meeting.

"Conjurer, we've much to discuss."

Winnie hesitated at the door. Shouldn't she be part of that discussion? Especially if it related to the invasion.

King Steffin impatiently waved her away. "Go on, then."

Abbi clasped Winnie's hand and pulled her into the hallway. They marched down a marble staircase toward the exit.

"You don't take direction very well, do you? I like that about you."

"It isn't about directions," Winnie replied. "We're almost at war. I have a right to know what everybody's planning. We should coordinate magic and, you know, war stuff."

"According to the prophecy, the female warrior already knows what to do."

Winnie wished she could admit the Sisters Three had made the whole thing up. But nobody would believe her. Especially now that she wore actual pink armor.

She pretended to know what to do by decisively requesting Ollie as her mount. She didn't trust any of the other horses. Abbi approved of her choice and tacked the pony for her. Soon, pony and rider charged along the sandy trail at an exhilarating trot.

A break in the woods revealed a crowded beach. Winnie's confused frown turned to an annoyed scowl. She slowed Ollie to a stop and dismounted, allowing him to munch on the bushes at the wood's edge. She weaved around her brother's duplicates and strode to Kip, who sat in the sand at the edge of the tidal line.

"Kip! I told you not to do this. Sister Ava warned you about consequences, and you promised not to do magic unless we agreed."

He let out a dejected sigh. "Got caught up in the mo."

"Why'd you make so many?" she demanded.

"Me wand malfunctioned."

Her body sizzled with a fury she could barely contain. She clenched her teeth to keep from yelling at him. The silent Mikeys waved and bounced around like little idiots. "Did your defective wand make them move like that?"

"They mimicked Mikey's actions," he said in a dull voice.

Winnie pointed at a synchronized group that moved from a handstand to a tumble. "What's that action supposed to be?"

He glanced over his shoulder. "Tried to do a cartwheel."

She huffed. "And that bunch?"

"Said his nose itched."

She exhaled another annoyed breath and plopped onto the sand beside him. "Where are the guards? Or did they leave because all your copies crowded them out?"

"They did leave. But not because of that. The captain and his men got called back by some commander named Arrigo." He peered at her out of the corners of his eyes. "I think we're on our own."

"They would never do that. Where's the real Mikey?"

"Went off to count all his clones. Should be a while, I'd expect."

"Did you tell him to do that?"

Kip shook his head.

"Then why is he counting them?"

"I don't know," he said irritably. "Because he's Mikey."

Winnie rose and angrily brushed the sand off her jeans. "Okay. You proved you can do this. Now use an incantation to shove them back into your wand."

"I don't know how," he snapped back. "Where's Argamel? He can fix this."

"Still with the king. Quit sulking and tell Mikey to stop counting."

"Well. Um…"

She swung her arms toward the crowd. "Did you lose him in all this?"

No reply.

"You had one job while I was away. To not lose Mikey. One job!"

"He's here. Somewhere. I promise he's fine."

She pivoted on her heel and shouted for her brother. All the Mikey replicas kept up their odd little dances as if she'd never spoken. She frowned over her shoulder. "This is seriously creepy, Kip."

He finally stood. "True. But what invading army would attack with all that going on?"

"I hope you're right. Help me look." She didn't wait for him to follow, just balled her fists, and stormed through the crowd, calling her brother's name. She passed what felt like the ninetieth Mikey when her sword trembled. She pulled it from its sheath. To add to her frustration, the sword's tip blinked white. Her throat ached to scream *why are you doing that?*

If only she could communicate with her stone the way Mikey could with his. Communicate. Didn't the queen say glow stones called to glow stones?

"Um. Can you find Bunny?"

The tiny light winked faster.

"I'll take that as a yes."

She used the sword's beacon as a Mikey detector. When it blinked fast, she moved forward. When the light dimmed, she changed direction until it brightened up again. The sword led her to the same gnarled tree they'd hidden behind when Sister Bayla returned them to the island. "Mikey?"

No answer.

"Hey, Kip!"

He rushed to her side.

"Could Mikey be inside this tree?" she asked.

"I don't see how that's possible."

"You were inside one."

"Yeah, but I was in stasis." He laid a gentle hand on the bark.

Winnie steadied her breathing in an attempt to quiet her thoughts. *Stone? Uh, Pinky?* In that instant, she knew her glow stone accepted that name. *Can you contact Mikey?*

"What's happening?" Kip whispered.

She hissed for silence. No phone rang, at least none she heard, but she sensed the call connected. *Hello? Mikey, can you hear me?*

A deep voice in her mind said *Windy?* He had used Mikey's nickname for her, but the voice sounded too low to belong to her brother.

Mikey?

Actually, spoke the voice in her head, *it's General Takka. When I'm here, I can take my true form. Princess Gwen is with me. We're at a ball.*

Winnie squinted at the tree. *A ball, like a dance? Just the two of you?*

Tree sprites are here too. We've got quite the gathering.

We're about to go to war, and you're…dancing?

You have to agree it's the safest place for us.

She reluctantly had to admit the truth in his statement. One less worry. Except Mikey described himself as General Takka. What if he decided to keep that form and refused to leave the tree?

Chapter 28

Winnie stepped from the tree, dazed. She absently slid her sword into the sheath.

Kip pushed his face close to hers. "What happened? It was like you went into a trance."

"I...guess I did. Mikey really is in there." She pointed at the tree.

"How'd he get inside, then?"

"I don't know. He's with Princess Gwen. He also said he's in his General Takka form."

"Oh yeah."

She raised an eyebrow. "What do you mean, oh yeah?"

"Remember I told you he did a dream visit when I was in stasis? He showed the princess and me what he looked like as General Takka. Then the princess transformed into a human-sized toad dressed as a princess."

"What?" Winnie shrieked. "And you never thought to tell me that?"

"If I'm honest, I forgot all about it till now." He grinned. "They made a cute couple in an amphibian kind of way."

"Mikey's only six!"

"Maybe so, but General Takka is considerably older."

During her Frama-12 visit, she'd seen the adult

General Takka. The oracle's sister had frozen him in a block of ice to preserve his body until he returned to it. That's where things got complicated. The way she understood it, Mikey and Takka shared one soul. If he decided to go back to his Takka form, Mikey's soulless body would die. She shuddered at the thought.

"Win?"

She faced him with jaw jutted out. "This is all your fault! None of this would have happened if you'd kept him with you."

"What happened? I mean, well, he's in a tree, obviously, but isn't that a good thing? He's safe from Krell's attack. As long as nobody tries to burn down the forest, at least."

"Never mind." She stomped along the sandy path between the back row of Mikeys and the tree line.

"Win!"

She walked faster. With each angry step, her frustration turned inward. She shouldn't have left Mikey behind. If she'd taken him with her when Argamel teleported her to the king, he never would have ended up inside a tree.

But he's safe there.

Winnie scuffed to a stop. She hadn't generated that thought. Well, she'd had one similar to it, but not now. *Pinky?*

Nothing.

She clenched her teeth. Why did mental communications with other entities come so hard to her? The helmet! Maybe it blocked messages. She shoved it over the back of her head with an angry thrust. It thumped into the armor between her shoulders with a painless twang. She reached over her shoulder. Her fingers brushed across the helmet, still attached to the armor at the back of her neck. She lifted the helmet over her head and then pushed it off again. "Okay. I get it," she said even though she stood alone. "It's like a helmet hoodie."

Leaves rustled behind her. A familiar yellow-green tint mingled with the deep-green leaves. Now she understood what the leaflings meant when they said they were here. If Krell's men tried to storm the beach, maybe they could fly into their faces like they had the goblin at the Oram Forest gate.

The leaflings flitted their wings. *We are at your command.*

She raised her eyebrows. "You are? Thanks." She imagined a million green fairies attacking the invaders. The vision sent her into a fit of laughter, but a sudden mental picture of men squishing the leaflings in their fists cut off her glee. "They can't hurt you can they?"

The fairies giggled.

"If you're sure, then okay. But wait for my signal."

The tiny voices in her head giggled again and called her "Commander."

Their offer to help lightened her mood enough to forgive Kip.

He walked in the opposite direction with his shell held to his ear.

Who are you calling?

As if in answer, static hissed from her sword. Could that be Mikey or Takka trying to contact her? She unsheathed it and held it to her ear. Through interference, Kip's faint voice said, "Argamel." After a long pause, he repeated the name. He tried three times. With each attempt, his voice grew louder.

"What is it?" the conjurer's voice blasted through Winnie's sword, making her jump. "I happen to be in the middle of an important meeting if you don't mind."

"Sorry." Kip's voice also came through the sword. "It's just...I'm worried about the fog rolling away and the men on the ships seeing us. I wondered if you could come back and help me thicken it again."

"I agree," Winnie said. "Twice as much magic will hold the fog twice as long."

"It doesn't matter right now," Argamel said in an annoyed tone.

She clenched her fist around the hilt. "What do you mean it doesn't matter?"

Argamel spoke over her. "Hide in the woods. If the men on board can see through the haze, they'll only find a deserted beach."

"Can you guys hear me?"

"Well, the beach isn't exactly deserted," Kip replied through the sword.

"It is if you don't count your battalion of Mikeys," Winnie teased.

Kip didn't acknowledge her. "I've been having a bit of a bother with me wand. It keeps shooting out duplicates."

Maybe she and her sword stood too far away for a back-and-forth conversation.

Argamel harrumphed. "Why would you make more tomato plants?"

Tomato plants?

"Actually, I created a few copies of that little boy, Mikey, whilst you were away. And now I can't make the wand do anything else."

"You're reminding me why I never wanted an

236

apprentice in the first place." Argamel breathed out an overly dramatic sigh. "Did you forget already that you must put your thumb over one end of the wand as you speak the incantation?"

"Right. That's the step I missed. Got it. Ta."

"There's one problem solved," Winnie mumbled, returning her sword to its sheath.

A screech blasted through the air. She started. Even the leaflings briefly fluttered from the trees.

"Bird! You almost gave me a heart attack."

He circled overhead and landed at her feet. He honked a greeting.

"Glad to see you too." She bent to pet him, but her hand froze inches from his graying feathers. She straightened. "You're running out of time."

He waddled toward a Mikey clone that waved at the ocean.

"Ignore them. They're not real. But what about you? How do you feel?"

He gently batted the waving duplicate with the side of his beak. The clone tipped over. As it lay in the sand, it continued to wave. Winnie righted it, surprised by its insubstantial weight. A strong breeze could knock them over like bowling pins. What would Krell's men think if they saw half of Kip's army writhing on the ground?

She peered over the heads of the short Mikeys at Kip, who focused on the ocean through his cupped hands. "Is anything coming?" she shouted.

"Not yet," he called back. "Fog's not as thick, though."

Bird upended three more clones.

"Hey, Bird." She forced an enthusiastic tone. "You like fish. Why don't you go get some? Maybe they'll keep up your strength until we find a time tear to take you home."

The bird flapped his massive wings, knocking over half a dozen more Mikeys. He glided to the ocean, allowing Winnie to set them up again. Bird floated on the calm water. He ducked his head under and popped up with a silver fish in his beak.

Please let the fish be nourishing for him.

With Bird occupied, she raced along the back row of clones to Kip. "Can you—"

"What happened to your helmet?"

"Works like a hoodie." She demonstrated by pushing it on and off.

"That's brill!"

"Yeah. Now let's focus. Can you make your clones sturdier?"

He blinked at her. "Didn't you tell me a bit ago to watch out for consequences?"

"I also said we should agree on the magic you use. I agree you should magically make them stronger. We can use them as our actual army."

He raised an eyebrow at her. "You realize they're just for appearances. To slow Krell down long enough for us to…well, I'm not sure exactly what we'll do yet."

"Obviously, as an army, they can't fight. *But* if you make them hard and heavy on the inside, swords will bounce right off if anybody attacks them."

The corners of his lips slowly curled upward. "Now that me wand is back to normal, I know just the spell." He closed his eyes, pressing his lips into a thin line.

Winnie grinned at how cute he looked when he concentrated.

He waved his wand toward the Mikeys and

murmured several unintelligible words. He flicked his wrist once and opened his eyes. "Give one a tap."

She whacked one of the still ones with the back of her hand. A burst of pain shot up her arm. "Yow!" She gripped her throbbing hand and stepped back.

Kip chuckled. "Didn't mean for you to hit it that hard." He pushed at one, but it remained upright. He laughed. "It's a ruddy statue!"

Despite the pain, she grinned along with him. "We're going to win this war."

"Last time we had an invasion, I was jealous. Me in the dungeon and you leading an army and getting all the glory." He rested his hands on her shoulders and gazed into her eyes. "But you make a good general. And I'll be—"

"My magical sidekick," she teased.

He shoved her playfully, then pulled her close. Winnie shut her eyes just as his soft lips pressed against hers. She wrapped her arms around his shoulders, insides tingling, and returned his kiss.

The sword at her side vibrated. She opened her eyes and stepped back. "Sorry. We should probably strategize."

He let go with a disappointed sigh. "Yeah. We've got a war to fight." He cupped his fingers around his eyes and stared out to sea.

"I hate to tell you this, but you don't have binoculars."

He continued to stare through his curled fingers. "These are magic ones. Nobody's coming yet, and the vaper is still holding. Thankfully."

Winnie's naked eyes could only make out white fog on the horizon. "Can you turn my hands into binoculars too?"

He swung toward her with an impish grin. "Of course." He held out his hands, palms up. She placed her hands across his. When he bent his head toward hers as if for another kiss, she laughed and shoved him away.

"You can't make magic binoculars."

A high-pitched titter sounded from her sword.

"Oi. Did your sword just laugh?"

She still hadn't figured out the whole glow-stone thing yet. "Probably."

"Can I have a look at it?"

She slid it from the sheath. Silver flecks on the pink blade sparkled in the sunlight.

Kip reached out. "May I?"

She held it away from him. "It shocked you last time, remember?"

"She didn't know me then."

"Who says she knows you now?"

"Let's see how close I can get before I'm repelled."

Winnie shrugged. "Give it a try."

He stretched his index finger closer, inch by inch, and lightly poked the grip. The sword remained still, but he jumped back anyway.

"Did she shock you?"

He shook out his hands. "No. I just thought she might. Should I try again?"

"She isn't giving me any kind of message that you shouldn't."

On his slow second attempt, Winnie slid her hand out of the way, allowing him to wrap his fingers around the grip. She let go, amazed that Pinky had changed her mind about Kip. "I guess she likes you now," she whispered. "Her name is Pinky."

"I'm pleased to meet you, Pinky," he said in a soft, reverent tone. He gripped the sword in both hands and swung it gently through the air. He turned a worried stare toward Winnie. "She's vibrating a bit. Is that normal, or is she about to blow me up?"

She smiled. "You're fine. She might be trying to communicate through her thoughts. I don't always hear them, but maybe you will."

A crackling hiss emanated from the sword. Murmured voices sounded through the static.

He directed a worried stare toward Winnie. "What's that?"

"A different kind of message. Glow stones call out to glow stones. Somebody must be talking through a communicator stone. Pinky can pick those up." She didn't add that she'd overheard his conversation with Argamel. "If you move her, you might get better reception."

He raised the sword to the sky.

Winnie strained to listen. The hiss diminished slightly. She could only make out one or two words, but the voice belonged to Krell. Kip must have reached the same conclusion. He aimed the sword at the ocean.

"And I'm telling you to wait." Krell's distinctive British voice blasted through the reduced interference.

Winnie and Kip blinked at each other. He recovered first. "We knew he was out there," he whispered.

"We can hear him, but he can't hear us. Now we'll know what—" She cut herself off.

"Who got you these ships?" a gruff voice spoke through the sword. "Who found men sympathetic to your cause? Prove you're as magical as you claim to be and rid us of this fog."

"My magic is shrouding us until the time is right," Krell said.

"That's a lie," Kip muttered. "Argamel and I did that."

"...king's army will have collected on the beach, waiting," Krell said. "When the fog dissipates, they won't see three ships sailing toward the island. They'll see hundreds of them and quake with fear."

"*Hundreds*?" she squeaked.

"I only saw three. My guess is he'll use the duplication spell like I did."

Winnie blew out a relieved breath. "Good. When they see all your jumping Mikeys waiting on the beach instead of the king's army, they're going to quake from laughing."

He grinned back. "Well, it's a battle strategy."

Their conversation overshadowed the one transmitting from the sword. "...won't let us shoot at them again," came the other man's reply.

"Crap, we missed it," she grumbled. She wanted to hear Krell's response, so she mouthed the words, "They shot at you?"

He nodded. "Argamel and I turned their cannonball into a toad."

She burst into laughter and missed the words Krell barked back.

"Sorry, *conjurer*," the gruff voice said in an unapologetic voice, "you're no longer in charge. I will commence the invasion without your magic."

"How do you expect to navigate through the shroud?" Krell demanded.

"By sending rowboats in all directions. The ones that see the island will let me know, and I'll send more men that way."

"When the king's army shoots arrows at you, you won't have my magic to repel them."

The last whisper of static vanished, and Winnie took back her sword. "They hung up."

"And it sounds like Krell's got a mutiny on his hands."

Her sword crackled again.

Kip rubbed his hands together. "Ooh. Another call. I like this sword."

"Good news, Hesh," an enthusiastic voice blasted from the blade. "I've convinced the king to withdraw his men from the beach. My men will meet you when you land."

"Well done, Arrigo. Victory is ours. I've discovered the conjurer's—"

"Arrigo!" Winnie jammed her sword into the sheath, severing the connection. "That's the king's commander. We have to warn the castle. Can I borrow your shell phone?"

He slipped it out of his pocket and pinched it. "Now it's on speaker."

Her call immediately went through.

"What an uncanny coincidence," the king said. "I was about to contact you."

"Your Majesty, we have an emergency," she said in one breath. "I just found out your high commander is part of Krell's invasion."

"That makes no sense," the king grumbled. "What would he hope to achieve?"

"He wants to steal glow stones."

"You must have misunderstood," he blustered. "Arrigo knows as well as anyone that glow stones won't allow it."

"Just because they won't allow it doesn't mean—"

The king cut her off. "The queen, my conjurer, and Abbi are with me. We've decided—"

"I didn't," Abbi's voice blurted through the shell.

Muffled conversation sounded from his end. A moment later, his voice came back on. "*We've* decided that you shall take full control of the situation. The prophecy states that the female warrior in pink alone will protect us in our time of need."

She sucked in a deep breath and let it out slowly, hoping to breathe away her frustration. "Your Majesty," she said in a forced civil tone. "Are you telling me you won't send any of your men to stop your cousin from trying to take over?"

"The crown would never allow him to. But if he poses a threat, we'll deal with it at the castle. According to prophecy, the main conflict is magical in nature. Only magical beings should fight it. You might not be magical yourself, Warrior Windemere, but your armor and weapon certainly are. If needed, my conjurer's apprentice may assist you."

Kip spoke into the shell. "Your Majesty, forgive me. This is your conjurer's apprentice. Will your conjurer be joining me?"

Argamel's voice came through next. "If, as the warrior says, a revolution is about to occur, I must protect the castle and the royal family. As a last line of defense."

Winnie stared at Kip in disbelief.

"Your Majesty," he said, "you understand I'm just an apprentice."

Argamel's voice broke through again. "His Majesty

has every confidence in you, as do I. I've informed the king that you've duplicated a magical army to fight the other conjurer."

"Listen," Winnie cut in. "That so-called army—"

Kip disconnected the call.

"Why did you do that?" she demanded.

"Because the prophecy doesn't say the king's army wins this war. It says the female warrior in pink armor does."

"It isn't real!" she cried out.

He cocked his head. "What isn't?"

"That stupid prophecy. The Sisters Three made it up."

His mouth dropped open. "Why?"

"I don't know why. They just did, and now we're stuck with it, and I *hate* it."

He gently bumped against her. "You didn't quit when you had to fight a war on Frama-12, and I was in the dungeon at the time. We've got this."

She scowled even harder. How could they, with their supposed army making all those weird movements? Unless… She shook off her despair and focused on a solution. "If that's our army, it has to look like one. Can you make them stop bouncing and flapping and whatever else they're doing? An army is supposed to stand at attention in straight rows."

"Now that they don't have to distract Krell from the real Mikey, I can do that."

He mumbled words Winnie didn't understand and waved his wand. Immediately, the tiny soldiers snapped to attention.

"That's a thousand times better. Thanks."

Bird, who had been floating nearby, shrieked. He

flapped from the water and soared past them, disappearing through the trees.

"What do you think that was about?" she asked.

Kip trained his magic binoculars on the horizon. "Uh-oh. They're coming."

Chapter 29

One rowboat, then a second, cut through the haze into the clear sea. Kip's hand binoculars zoomed in on each boat. He counted the shiny silver helmets covering the rowers' heads. Six men per boat. Another rowboat appeared farther along the wall of fog. "Bloody."

"How many?" Winnie whispered.

"Three rowboats so far, but I expect more to follow."

"I have an idea. If Pinky agrees. Let me ask." She closed her eyes.

He left her to her silent communication and peered through his binoculars again. The bobbing boats, far out to sea, inched forward. He and Winnie had time. For what, he hadn't a clue. He hoped Pinky agreed to her plan, whatever it was.

She reopened her eyes and withdrew her sword. The tip glowed orange-pink, and she pulled at it. The piece stretched as if made of taffy. After returning her sword to the sheath, she rolled the broken bit into a marble-sized ball. She cradled it in her palm. "Think you can duplicate enough of these to fit in each of the Mikeys' right hands? They can throw them."

"I suppose so, but that's a bit feeble, don't you think? I mean, at best, the Mikeys might bung a few pebbles into their eyes. That'll just infuriate them."

"Not if the Mikeys aim for the boats and the men's

arms. They aren't pebbles. They're glow stones."

"When you say arms, do you mean their weapons?"

She shook her head. "Their actual arms. So they can't row or fight."

He supposed her idea might work. She had taken a piece of her magic sword, after all. Under his wand's direction, each of the Mikeys raised his right hand, palm upward. With a mumbled incantation and a flick of his wand, duplicates of Winnie's magical ball sprouted onto the boys' open hands.

She pulled out her sword again and pressed the ball into the tip. It melted into the blade. "Pinky says this will work. As soon as a Mikey throws a ball, a new one will take its place."

He mumbled another incantation. "Right. I've programmed the army to throw continuously, but they can only throw straight ahead. That's good for a frontal attack. We'll have to deal with any boats that figure that out and paddle on either side of the Mikeys. I've got this end with me magic."

"I'll take the other side with my magic sword."

Did he note a hint of doubt in her voice?

They waited for the invaders to glide into range. Their army of Mikeys stood at the ready, straight as statues. Every right hand gripped a ball weapon. The boats paddled closer. Kip's heart thundered. Closer. "Wait for it. Wait for it. And...*now*."

"Company," Winnie commanded. "Aim for arms and boats. Fire!"

All the Mikeys simultaneously hurled their glow stones at the advancing rowboats. Some stones cascaded over the men's heads, but others hit their mark in a stream of sparks. Men who were hit shrieked in pain and stopped rowing. A few flying stones pierced the hull of one boat, causing it to slowly sink.

"Jolly oh!" Kip cried out. "Uh-oh. We've got more coming through the fog. It's only a matter of time before one heads toward the open beach on your end. Are you ready to fight?"

She took a ragged breath. "Think so. I took fencing in gym class, plus, well…magic sword."

He pulled her helmet over her head and gave her a quick kiss. "Stay safe."

She turned and sprinted past the rows of Mikeys toward the end of their battalion.

Kip dashed to the tree line and ducked behind a tree, using it as a shield.

A man in the nearest boat aimed a bow and arrow at the regiment of clones. Kip stepped out of hiding long enough to send a freeze spell at the archer. The spell diffused and spread to two more men, also freezing them.

Kip cackled. "You'll think twice before firing again."

The other three in the boat paddled hard but moved in a circle. They shouted curses at each other until they finally synchronized their strokes. The boat retreated toward the horizon, passing five more headed to shore.

The Mikeys' well-aimed stones prevented most from coming closer. So far, only one stayed out of the Mikeys' firing range. It landed just beyond the last column of clones. A stocky man with a broken nose and a thick black beard marched onto the beach, followed by his five men. He sneered at the Mikeys. "Hoy! Since when does the king send children to fight his battles?"

The Mikeys, unable to acknowledge the men at their flank, kept firing straight ahead.

"This is rather unexpected, my lord," one of his men remarked.

"Hoy! Stop throwing stones at my men." The stocky lord raised his sword over his head and charged.

"Lord Hesh!" the second man cried out. "They're but children."

The stocky lord slammed his sword over a clone's shoulder with a clang. The force sent the sword flying from his hands. He snatched it up.

Kip stepped into the open, his wand raised. "I don't recommend trying that again."

"Men," Lord Hesh commanded, "attack him."

Two charged, but Kip froze them mid-stride. The other three dropped their swords, raised their hands in surrender, and backed away.

Hesh held his sword at his side and gave a half smile. "Well, well, well. And I thought my brother made it up."

Kip only partially lowered his wand. "Made what up?"

"That our conjurer back there," he said, jabbing a thumb over his shoulder toward the horizon, "has an apprentice."

Kip stared haughtily back. "I believe you've got your conjurers mixed up. I'm actually Argamel's apprentice."

The man bared his teeth in a false smile. "Argamel's abilities are far too lacking to teach an apprentice anything. Accept the other conjurer as your teacher and align with us. We can reward you with power and wealth beyond your dreams."

"That's kind of you to offer." Kip forced a friendly tone. "But I'm not interested."

Hesh briefly pointed his gaze over Kip's shoulder

and sneered. "You might want to rethink that."

Bird's alarmed squawk sounded from behind. Kip spun and cast a freeze spell at a man creeping from the woods. The invader solidified into a frosty white image of himself. An icy backsplash from the spell caught Bird, and his body dropped at the frozen man's feet.

Kip gasped in horror. Muffled footsteps charged from the shoreline. He slung his wand over his shoulder and shot, then pivoted to face two immobile, frost-covered men. Lord Hesh, unaffected, mumbled into a white communications pebble.

Kip aimed his wand at the lord. "Who are you speaking to?"

Hesh simply grinned and returned the pebble to his pocket.

"Tell me now." Kip waved his wand menacingly. "Or I'll freeze you like I did the others."

"Your magic can't harm me." Hesh thumped the side of his dome-shaped helmet.

"Didn't seem to help that lot." Kip nodded toward the frozen men, also clad in helmets.

"Mine is of higher quality."

"If you'd rather not test it, tell me who you contacted."

"I contacted the one who believes he's in charge," Hesh replied.

The lord might be telling the truth, but he had a dishonest look about him. Besides, bragging about his helmet's quality spurred Kip to test the claim. He hurled a freeze spell at the arrogant lord. The helmet turned to ice just as quickly as the lord wearing it.

"I'm *not* Krell's apprentice."

He understood why Argamel had used the freeze

spell during his duel with Krell. If one had to go on the offensive, nothing beat the ease and effectiveness of that particular spell. Now, he shot ice at anything that moved on the ocean until he remembered Bird.

He let out an anguished wail and bounded to the motionless creature. Kip knelt beside him and gently stroked his icy feathers. "I am so sorry. I never meant for this to happen."

Sister Ava's voice whispered in his head. *Consequences.*

He clenched his teeth and pushed the thought away. He knew he'd made a mistake. Now, he'd correct it. He used a levitation spell to transport Bird to the same mother tree that housed Mikey. He lowered Bird beside an exposed root. "Is anyone there who can help my friend?"

Bird melted into the root. Kip gazed at the ground where Bird had lain, praying his time in stasis would heal him.

Chapter 30

On the way to her position beside the Mikey regiment, she bowed to the leaflings that covered the trees. *I'll call if I need help. Please promise to be careful.*

Tinkling laughter sounded in her head. Did that mean they liked battles? As if in answer, they giggled again. Winnie shrugged. "Okay. I guess."

Over a dozen rowboats paddled toward shore. The army of Mikeys tossed glow stones at them. Some magic missiles hit the men's rowing arms, and others hit their boats, slowing or stopping their progress altogether. Kip, on the other side of their army, helped by freezing the boats the clones missed. She hooted with glee.

Only one rowboat, with six men aboard, rowed toward her side of the beach. She tracked the boat's progress, gradually coming closer. A stick snapped behind her. In one motion, she drew her sword and spun toward the noise.

An ogre of a man crashed through the brush, his sword raised.

She deflected the first strike, but the clash sent a sharp tingle up her arm. She stumbled backward with a grunt. Why hadn't her sword used its magic?

Her attacker bared his crooked teeth. "Yield, little one. Yer no match fer me."

She roared and hurled herself at him. Nobody called her little. Their swords clanged, then pulled apart. She whipped her sword back and forth, matching him, blow for blow. He cut through her defenses once, but her armor took the brunt. *Pinky, anytime now.*

She swirled and feinted, then danced just out of reach. If she couldn't beat him, maybe she could wear him out.

A splash and a thud sounded on the shoreline. From the corner of her eye, she spotted the oarsmen as they scrambled from their vessel. They let out a mighty roar and attacked the first row of Mikeys. No matter how many times the men struck them, the clones remained upright.

"Not the brightest, are they?" her opponent teased, then swung his sword at her.

Winnie deflected just as five men surged from the woods with their swords held high. No way could she defend against them.

Leaflings, attack now!

A yellow-green swarm rose from the trees and soared toward the invaders. A small group of leaflings buzzed at her opponent's face. He swiped at them with his free hand but never caught one. Winnie lowered her own sword and watched in amazement. Men dropped their weapons and batted at the cloud of fluttering wings. The leaflings flitted toward the men's eyes and mouths but never touched them.

Arrigo stormed onto the beach from the tree line, sword in hand. "What is going on?"

"Make your men stand down," Winnie commanded. "If they do as you say, I'll ask my green army to withdraw."

He glared at her. "You have nothing to do with that."

Leaflings, please show him.

The swarm flew to Winnie, hovering at her sides.

Arrigo held on to the scowl, but only for a moment. "Company, attention!"

Everyone, including the man who'd fought Winnie, stood still.

"Those of you who came by sea, push off," Arrigo ordered. "My men, you're dismissed. I'll handle this."

His men marched in quick time back into the woods. The others, as ordered, shoved their boat off the sand, climbed in, and paddled away. Winnie nodded to the hovering leaflings, and they flew back to the treetops. *Thanks.*

Arrigo sheathed his sword. "Let's talk." He stared pointedly at hers until she reluctantly did the same.

She waited for him to start the conversation since he suggested it. But he just stood there with his back straight and jaw tight. During the silence that stretched between them, her mind wandered to the king's memory from when he entered his sick uncle's bedchamber. As one of the king's cousins, Arrigo must have tried and failed to touch the crown. Could he have wanted it as badly as she wanted her mom to live?

"I know how it feels to desperately want something and have it snatched away."

He lifted his chin in defiance. "What does that have to do with anything?"

"When the last king was sick, he asked you to take the crown off his head. You couldn't do it. The crown chose your cousin."

He clenched both fists. "Steffin was never meant to be king!"

"And my mom was never meant to die," Winnie snapped. "I wished for her to live. I prayed for it. But no matter how badly I wanted it…" She looked away to hide how close to tears she came. She took a deep breath and faced him again. "Mom never quit. All the way till the end. Even with all her pain, she still smiled at me. And it wasn't fake. I saw it in her eyes. I saw love, and I saw the strength of a warrior. So I do know how it feels to want something you can't have."

He didn't respond for a long moment. Finally, he directed his remark to the sea. "Steffin fell off his pony into a water trough when he was five. He thrashed so frantically that I worried for his life. My older brothers laughed and said leave him to learn from it." Now he turned his gaze on Winnie. "I saw a little boy drowning in two feet of water, so I grabbed him by the collar and yanked him out."

A warm glow waved over her. Maybe Arrigo wasn't so terrible after all.

"He stood panting and dripping, then looked up at me with such adoration and gratitude in his eyes that I vowed I would never allow harm to come to him." He snorted. "But then he stole the crown. That blighted crown."

She shifted her weight, gathering the courage to tell him to give up that fight the same way she had given up the fight for her mom's recovery.

"Last year, I gave Steffin a drink laced with poison."

He spoke so casually her mouth dropped open in disbelief. She tried to ask how he could do such a thing, but her mouth had only started to form the word "how" when he continued.

"Easy. I'm his favorite cousin. The last person he'd ever suspect. He'd barely taken a sip when the crown started to glow. I believe it neutralized the poison.

Although Steffin did set down his cup immediately. I remember he looked at me and said, 'Does this taste off to you?' "

"That's horrible! Why would you try to assassinate the person you vowed to protect?"

He snorted. "Nobody takes the vow of a thirteen-year-old seriously. Besides, Steffin is just as much to blame for my actions. He was never supposed to be king."

Arrigo deserved a kick in the shins for his stupid logic, but there was probably a rule about not riling a rabid dog. Crazy or not, she had to know one thing. "Why now?"

"Oh, that. The plan started to come together after my brother Hesh met a foreign sorcerer on the mainland. The sorcerer had come to recruit men to help him steal glow stones."

Winnie shook her head. "I don't see the connection."

"That's the beauty of it. Hesh lied to that conjurer. We don't want to steal glow stones. We want to destroy them."

Her temples pulsed at the horror of it. Even her sword quivered in distress. *It's okay, Pinky. You guys are indestructible.* "You're insane!"

Arrigo beamed as if she'd just complimented him.

She put her hands on her hips. "Explain to me how you can lie to a wizard like Krell. He can read thoughts."

He pointed at his leather helmet. "We keep these on. They detect and deflect magic."

"Okay, so he doesn't know your plan, but come on. I'm new here, and even I know you can't destroy glow stones."

"What a naïve little poppet you are. Of course, you can. It just takes a double amount of magical power. Why did you think magic was illegal here? It's to protect the glow stones, of which the crown is one." He grinned at his brilliance. "You see, the king's conjurer doesn't have nearly the power necessary to do the job. But the foreign conjurer, combined with the magic from the young man across the way, has more than enough power to accomplish our goal."

She glanced over the heads of the Mikey army. "Kip?" She turned a frown on Arrigo. "He would never agree to that."

He laughed. "You'd be surprised what people can do when properly motivated. By this time tomorrow, the glow-stone queen will be destroyed. The light in every glow stone will fade, along with their power. When that happens, the crown will be nothing but a plain gold circlet and unable to protect Steffin when my brothers and I take the castle."

Is that possible? Her sword quivered again, which she took as a yes. She pressed her lips in determination. She and Pinky could never let Arrigo win. A new thought gave her hope. "Krell wants to study glow stones. He'd never let you destroy them."

"He will because we found his weakness."

"Except for arrogance, he doesn't have a weakness," she said confidently.

Arrigo's thin lips curled into an evil grin. "Do you see these little boys hurling rocks at the ocean? The original holds a special place for Krell. He'll do anything to keep the boy safe."

Oh crap, he's right. But with Mikey hidden inside a mother tree, nobody could hurt him. *Right, Pinky?* Her

258

glow stone sword pulsated in agreement. With Krell's threat out of the way, they only had to neutralize the one they had for Kip.

"What weakness did you find for the young man across the way?"

His eyes focused sharply on hers. "According to Krell…you."

She was Kip's weakness? Love flutters rippled through her. She fought to not grin, since that sounded kind of romantic. *Get back in the game.* She forced a stern stare. "Krell totally lied to you. Kip and I can't stand each other."

She knew, by the gleam in Arrigo's eyes, that he didn't believe her.

"Okay," she amended, "we might not *hate* each other, but Kip would never go against his principles for me."

In a lightning motion, Arrigo pulled out his sword and slashed at her, cutting deeply into her leg. She cried out and collapsed, clutching her throbbing thigh.

"Don't be such a baby. I barely nicked you."

She panted in shock and pain. More than a nick sent sticky blood gushing through the tear in her jeans and between her fingers. She fell into darkness.

Chapter 31

Kip, the only mobile person on his section of beach, smiled in satisfaction. Over a dozen sword-bearing men, encrusted in a layer of frost, stood like statues throughout the immediate area. Thanks to his freeze spell, ice-covered boats, with their equally frozen oarsmen, drifted on the tide. The only movement came from the sea as the invaders, who had avoided the Mikeys' magical stones, retreated, steering their boats toward the dissipating fog.

The next moment, his ears popped, and Krell appeared before him. He jumped to a defensive stance, wand at the ready. The older wizard murmured an incantation that froze his arm mid-swing. Kip gnashed his teeth and fought to escape the hold.

"Unlike my defiant marauders," Krell said, releasing him, "I'm not here to attack you. I've come to talk." He nodded toward the army of Mikeys, still throwing stones even though all the targets had retreated. "Duplication spell. Impressive."

Had Krell just offered a compliment, or was he up to something?

The older wizard turned his attention from the frozen rowboats to the various combative poses of the incapacitated men on the beach. "They're all wearing deflection helmets. How did your freeze spell get through?"

Did Kip perceive a note of admiration? "That one,"

he said, pointing, "Lord Hesh. He said my magic wouldn't work." He shrugged. "Thought he was lying, so I shot him."

Krell threw back his head and laughed. "Well done, you cheeky monkey. I guess if I'd been more skeptical, I might have had more success with my own spells."

Now it was Kip's turn to bark out a laugh. "Maybe you should become my apprentice."

Krell's lips formed a grim line. "I have limited tolerance for your mischief."

He stopped grinning. "Right. So, uh, sorry about disarming your men, but they came at me first."

Krell sniffed indifferently. "They rarely did what I asked of them anyway, so I'd say they got what they deserved." With an angry wave of his wand, every frozen man, including the ones on the water, vanished.

Kip gulped in alarm. "Did you just send the lot of them to another world?"

"Don't be stupid. I transported them back to their ship. One was starting to thaw, and I'd rather keep them out of this."

Kip secretly agreed. If he had to fight Krell, the fewer the distractions, the better. Men with swords sneaking up on him definitely counted as a distraction. Then again, how much of a threat did Krell hold? After all, Kip had accidentally received an extra dose of magic from the Sisters Three.

"Which one is the original?" Krell asked, indicating the stone-throwing Mikeys with a nod in their direction.

Buoyed by his new confidence in his extra magic, and the fact that the real Mikey safely bounced about inside a tree, Kip sneered. "Try finding him yourself, mate."

"I could wring the answer out of you, but I'm not in the mood." He circled his wand through the air, then flicked his wrist. The dozen that vanished did little to deplete the legion of Mikeys. He turned a confused frown on Kip.

The boy flashed a sheepish grin and shrugged. "I might have made more than one batch."

Krell shook his head with a sigh. "Only you."

He repeated the process, diminishing the duplicates in groups of fifteen or twenty, with many more to go. The more he huffed and puffed in annoyance, the more Kip delighted in Krell's angry attempts to rid the beach of all the clones.

After multiple swishes of his wand, a clear beach finally stretched before them. "The real Mikey isn't here."

Kip started to joke about it, but his newly unobstructed view exposed Winnie on the ground with a man standing over her. "Win!" He charged across the sand and crashed to his knees beside her. So much blood had seeped into the ground by hcr right leg. He glared up at the stranger with her. "What did you do?"

"I-I only meant to graze her."

"You did more than that, you fiend!" Kip clutched Winnie's cold hand.

By then, Krell reached the group and faced her attacker. "If you move or speak, our combined magic will blast you out of existence."

Did he just defend Winnie? Kip gaped at Krell, stunned by his warning.

"And," Krell continued, "don't think for a moment that helmet will protect you. The lad with me froze every man who attempted to reach the island on that side."

Kip, surprised and confused, almost missed it when Winnie blinked up at him. She winked and closed her eyes again. Or had he imagined it? He squeezed her hand. *Please be all right. Please be all right.*

A voice in his head whispered *she's healing.*

Pinky? Was that you? Who else would speak inside his head? *Will she be all right?* A comforting sensation rolled over him. He also understood the game Pinky wanted him to play. He sprang to his feet, fists clenched. "You tried to kill her!"

The stranger gasped. "Surely not. Bind the wound for now. There's a doctor on my brother's ship. We'll help you. Provided you honor one request."

Krell nudged Kip. "Listen to this prisoner, trying to bargain with a pair of wizards who can heal the girl without a doctor's help."

Kip hadn't considered healing her through magic, a testament to how rattled he'd become. Of course, he'd just been assured Pinky had the matter in hand.

"Don't look so smug, conjurer," the man said in a lofty tone. "We've captured your little one and won't let him go unless you *and* your magical colleague obey us."

"What?" Krell cried out.

"I don't think so," Kip said with a head shake. "My superior wizardry tells me you're lying." He wanted to call him a meager human but decided that might be going too far.

"What?" Krell said again.

Looking pale but very alive, Winnie propped herself on her elbows. "You don't know the half of it. Arrigo here and his brothers have been playing you."

The older wizard recoiled.

"Why are you even awake?" Arrigo demanded.

"Because I'm the warrior in pink. The prophecy never mentioned anything about me passing out and staying that way."

A rush of relief flowed over Kip. Pinky's healing worked. He reached out his hand to Winnie, but Krell clutched him by the shoulder, stopping him.

"What did you mean just now that they were playing me?"

Winnie slowly pushed herself to her feet, testing her leg.

Kip pulled from Krell and gently wrapped an arm around her. "You all right?"

She gave him a weak smile and nodded. "Give me a minute, and I'll be fine."

"Obviously, since everyone's fine," Arrigo said, "I'll just be on my way."

"You're not moving," Krell ordered. To Winnie, he said, "You were saying?"

"Yeah. They weren't going to help you collect glow stones."

"Let it go," Arrigo said through clenched teeth.

His command didn't stop her. "They wanted to pressure you into destroying them."

"That's ruddy bonkers," Kip blurted. "Nobody would agree to that."

"Where's Michael?" Krell demanded. "Who has him?"

"You wouldn't believe us if we told you," Winnie said, sounding stronger.

"But he's safe," Kip added.

"Well then, why is this menace still standing here? Kip. You know what must be done."

He reluctantly left Winnie to stand beside the

wizard. "I do." He raised his wand and pointed it at Arrigo. Krell did the same.

The man raised his hands. "It was my brothers, not me, that started this. Attack them."

Krell nodded to Kip. A stream of sparks simultaneously shot from their wands. With a sizzle and a pop, Arrigo shrank into a toad.

"You imbecile!" Krell cried out. "We were only going to freeze him! You had no trouble freezing every other invader in sight. Why not him?"

"A double freeze would've killed him," Kip argued.

"Really?" Krell shouted. "And enchanting this poor bloke is better?"

"He tried to kill my girlfriend. If anybody deserves to be enchanted, it's him."

Winnie's lips curled into a silly grin. "I'm your girlfriend?"

"Did I say that out loud?" he teased.

She laughed and embraced him. He'd just called her his girlfriend, and she hadn't punched him in the neck.

He kissed her temple. "You're truly all right? Pinky said she'd heal you."

She nodded. "I guess that makes her a healing stone because she was crap when it came to dueling."

Kip, relieved to find her well, laughed.

"This is all so touching," Krell retorted, "but where is your brother?"

"I'm ready to see him too." She scooped up Arrigo, who hadn't moved since his transition. "Follow us."

A short hike brought them to the same gnarled healing tree that housed Mikey and had later accepted Bird. Maybe it would also receive the enchanted Arrigo. Kip eased the toad out of Winnie's hands and set him on the exposed root. Ten seconds elapsed, then twenty.

Krell folded his arms. "Is something supposed to happen?"

The toad gazed back with his pop-eyed stare.

"That's odd," Kip remarked. "He should've disappeared inside by now."

"None of this explains where Michael is," Krell said impatiently.

Kip and Winnie exchanged glances. With a shrug, Kip gently rapped on the trunk. "Oi, Mikey. It's safe to come out now."

The little boy tumbled from the tree and rolled to a stand. "Non-Dad!"

"Michael!" Beaming like a proud father, Krell scooped him into an embrace, then set him back down.

Kip cheered and clapped the little boy on the back.

Winnie pushed between him and Krell to give her brother a hug of her own. "Buddy!"

Mikey giggled and squirmed in her arms.

She let go and sat back on her heels. "How'd you get inside that tree in the first place?"

"Bunny heard somebody calling. When I touched the bark, I fell right inside. The princess met us there. She changed into a voga, and I changed into Takka, and we danced."

Kip nodded. "That's one of the advantages the princess has in stasis. She can look like herself, or she can morph into one of Takka's people."

"What should we do about the princess?" Winnie asked. "Should we call Argamel?"

"Where's my army?"

She clutched Mikey in another hug. "They did such an amazing job they got to go back home. Now we have to help the—"

"Back inside Kip's wand?"

"Inside mine," Krell clarified.

Mikey jumped to the man's side. "Thanks! Save them in case we need them for later."

Krell smiled at the little boy and gently stroked his hair.

Kip puzzled over the man's transformation from arrogant adversary to caring father figure. How could he possess both qualities?

Winnie stood. "Excuse me, but Princess Gwen…"

Almost as if the tree had heard, the trunk stretched outward, releasing a girl dressed in a white gown. Winnie squealed in delight. "Princess Gwenevieve, you're back!"

"The tree cured you!" Kip whooped. Since he couldn't very well grab hold of a princess, he clasped Winnie's arms and twirled her in a celebratory circle.

Mikey tugged the back of Kip's T-shirt, ending the dance. "The tree didn't do it."

Kip stopped reveling and sent a questioning stare the princess's way.

She smiled as she examined her human hands and outstretched arms. She raised her head. "I'm myself again." At the sight of Krell, she scowled and clenched her fists. "You! You're the brute who put me in that sorry state."

"Many apologies, Your Highness," Krell said with a deep bow.

Kip shook his head in bewilderment at this respectful version of the wizard.

"I never intended for you to be affected by a spell I'd aimed at another."

"My father's conjurer. Where is he? I thought I heard his voice earlier."

"He teleported back to the king," Winnie replied. "We can call him back with Kip's shell phone. Right, Kip?"

He scratched the back of his head, not just confused by Krell's behavior. He still hadn't fully processed how the princess had transformed. "We're beyond relieved to have you back, Your Highness. Did the healing tree do this?" Mikey had to be wrong about it.

The princess shook her head. "Healing trees can prevent a permanent change but can't reverse enchantments."

"I kissed her," Mikey announced casually. "Well, Takka did. While we were dancing."

"What?" Kip and Winnie said and burst into laughter.

Kip patted the boy on the back. "Well done, mate."

"Not to brag or anything," Winnie said, "but I said that was how to undo the enchantment from the beginning."

"Not completely," the princess replied. "You wanted your brother to kiss Stompy. For it to work, Prince Takka had to kiss Princess Gwenevieve."

"Or at least a person-sized toad version of her," Kip said.

"You were going to contact Argamel," the princess reminded.

"Of course, Your Highness." Kip placed the call. Summarizing all their successes would've taken too long, so he simply announced, "Princess Gwen is with us on the western beach. And she's been restored."

In an instant, Argamel appeared. He bowed low.

"Your Majesty. Welcome back." He straightened and pointed between Kip and Krell. "Did you two…"

Krell took a giant step, blocking Kip's view of the king's conjurer. "Yes, we did. And as payment, we would like three glow stones. One yellow, one blue, and one pink."

Kip jumped to the front. "We didn't break the enchantment. A prince did it."

Krell let out an annoyed snort.

Argamel moved to shield Princess Gwen from Krell. "Any reward shall go to the prince when we see him. The uprising you'd warned the king about never came to be. And from the looks of things here, the western beach was never attacked either."

"Are you kidding me?" Winnie cried out. "Look at the tear in my jeans and the dried blood. We countered their attack and sent them home."

"And for that," Krell said, stepping forward again, "we require the payment of three—"

"Give it a rest, mate," Kip broke in. "They're not giving you ruddy glow stones."

"Argamel," the princess said in a dignified tone, "that is the female warrior in pink. The prophecy stated that she would save us. The absence of invaders proves that she did."

Winnie bowed. "Thank you, Your Majesty."

"Then I thank you," he said in a thankless tone. He lightly touched the girl's arm, and both disappeared.

Chapter 32

Argamel and Princess Gwen vanished, but Winnie's ears didn't pop. "That's weird. I didn't feel anything that time."

"He used a de-vacuum spell. Show off," Krell muttered.

"What ruddy cheek!" Kip cried out. "Telling us we didn't do anything."

"Ya know what's really weird?" Mikey said. "Bird's still in the tree."

Winnie sucked in a quick breath. She'd forgotten all about him. "How'd he get in there?"

"I bunged him in for healing." Kip sounded way too casual.

"Is he okay?" she asked. "What happened?"

Kip grimaced. "I might've...accidentally frozen him."

"Kip!"

He frowned at her. "I said it was an accident."

Mikey bent toward the tree and clapped. "Bird. Come on out."

The trunk bowed outward the way it had for the princess. Bird plopped onto the sand. He ruffled his graying feathers and squawked.

Kip turned to Winnie. "See? Unfrozen. Although I had hoped the healing tree would've helped get more of the gray out."

She gently stroked Bird's neck. "We have to find a way to send him home. Now."

"Hey!" Mikey bent over the enchanted Arrigo. "Here's another Stompy."

"You might want to leave that one be," said Krell.

In typical stubborn-child fashion, Mikey sat in front of the toad and spoke gently to him.

Winnie's sword shimmied with such urgency it made a buzzing sound.

"Is another communication coming through?" Kip asked.

Krell grunted. "That thing can pick those up? I thought you said it healed."

She unsheathed her sword. "Pinky is multitalented."

"That's what you named it?" Krell sighed. "Lord help us."

She ignored him and pointed her sword toward the ocean. Maybe they'd hear what the defeated invaders had to say about their loss. The sword trembled and tugged from the water as if another hand gripped it. She clutched the handle in both hands and struggled against the opposing force. "This doesn't make sense."

Kip joined her. "Don't fight it. See where she points."

Bird quacked and waddled between them.

She couldn't hold off the force anyway, so she relaxed her muscles. The sword repositioned itself, parallel to the water, and pointed toward the long stretch of beach. A beam of light flared from the tip, creating a swirling opening that telescoped into the distance. A jungle of black-and-gold spiked trees with yellow, barbed undergrowth lay at the other end.

"Does everybody see this?" she murmured.

"Yeah," Kip said in a respectful tone.

"Glow stones can open time tears?" Even Krell spoke in an awed whisper.

Bird squawked and flew through the opening. He landed in the jungle, turned toward them, and honked.

Winnie, Kip, and Mikey had just enough time to wave and call out their final goodbyes before the swirling tunnel snapped shut.

"Pinky! Why didn't you tell me you could do that?"

You never asked.

Kip elbowed her. "What did she say?"

"Never mind." She jammed her sword into the sheath with more force than necessary to let Pinky know she hated secrets. Of course, without Pinky's help, they might never have found a doorway to Bird's world. At least, not in time. *Thanks.*

With Pinky's help, they'd accomplished all their tasks. Winnie counted them off in her head. *Replace Krell's Frama-scope with one that would prevent him from traveling to alternate worlds. Check. Fulfill a fake prophecy by stopping an invasion. Check. Undo the princess's enchantment. Check. Return Bird to his home world. Check.*

She tugged at her armor. "This was supposed to turn back into a hoodie after I won the war, restored the princess, and sent Bird home."

Krell smirked. "Did you actually do any of that? The way I see it, your sword showed the bird the way home. Michael restored the princess, and your friend Kip and his army of duplicates sent the invaders away. With my assistance, of course."

Winnie's shoulders slumped. As much as she hated to admit it, Krell had a point. Except for his claim that he assisted.

Kip nudged her. "It was a group effort."

"Which probably means it's time for the group to go home." Krell pulled the gold chain hidden inside his shirt, revealing his Frama-scope. He peered through it.

Winnie cast an uneasy glance at Kip. He responded with a slight head shake. *White bear. I'm thinking of a white bear.*

"Just as I suspected," Krell said.

She gulped.

"There's a time bubble less than a meter behind you. Too bad you didn't bring your scope." He tucked his back inside his shirt. "Now that you know the way home, maybe you'll be good enough to acknowledge my hand in protecting the glow-stone queen from destruction. I'm not asking too much if I request three glow stones as payment for services rendered."

She rolled her eyes. "How many times do we have to tell you that's *not* how it works? You have to go to the glow field, and we're never taking you there."

"Although," Kip said thoughtfully, "I might've seen a few out this way."

"You what?" Winnie cried out.

"Krell once suggested to me that there might be the odd few interested in a change in scenery, and I found them. So…if you promise not to harm them, I might have just the ones you're looking for."

Krell bowed. "You have my word."

"I still don't trust you," Winnie muttered.

Kip strode past her and into the woods.

She chewed her lower lip and hoped he'd just implemented his plan to give Krell fake stones. If not, she'd totally punch him in the neck.

"Haven't I proven myself trustworthy?"

She frowned at Krell.

He stared placidly back. "Look at how well I've always treated Michael."

"No offense to Mikey, who I love to pieces, but he makes friends with toads and plants."

Mikey set the enchanted Arrigo onto his shoulder and rose. "I make friends with lots of things. But toads are my favorite. This one's a prince."

"If he is," she said, "he's a bad one."

"Not anymore. He's sorry."

She might have argued, but Kip returned, his right hand clutched in a fist. He opened his hand, displaying three pebbles. One pebble glowed blue, another pink, and the third yellow.

She never should have doubted him. The proof lay in his palm. Real glow stones only shone at night.

Krell accepted them into his open hand. After a brief examination, he turned a questioning stare toward Mikey. The little boy looked to Winnie. *Tell him they're real.*

Mikey returned his attention to Krell. "Glow stones don't do that in the day."

"So much for telepathy," she muttered to herself.

Kip clapped himself on the forehead. "Mikey, you did it again!"

Krell slammed the stones on the ground. "I should have known better than to trust you. Go home, you little blighter." He snapped up his wand and pointed it at Kip.

Winnie jumped in front of her friend, catching the wand's blast in the chest. The stream bounced off her armor and hit Krell. He vanished with a pop.

Kip scooped her into a bear hug. "That was brill!

274

You saved me!"

"Well, you know…warrior in pink," she teased.

"Non-Dad!" Mikey cried out.

She reached for her brother at the same moment her armor melted back into a pink hoodie.

The little boy's lower lip trembled. "Where did he go?"

She rubbed his back. "It's okay, bud. He went home."

"But I didn't get to say goodbye."

"Sometimes goodbyes just aren't meant to be." She felt the sting of not saying goodbye to Princess Abbi.

"It's probably time we headed home ourselves," Kip remarked. "Can Pinky make another one of those openings for us?"

Winnie silently asked but received no answer. "Looks like that's a no." She didn't want to go home from the beach anyway. "I guess you'll have to ask Argamel to teleport us back to Oram Forest so we can pick up the Frama-scope and my locket."

"I'm not too keen on speaking with him after he insulted us." Still, he reached for the shell in his pocket just as it began to ring. "Wonder who this is." He pressed it to answer.

"Michael!" Krell's enraged voice boomed from the shell. "You lied to me!"

"What?" Kip asked.

The other wizard disconnected.

Mikey's little face creased in bewilderment. "I didn't lie, but he's mad at me." Tears glistened in his eyes.

Winnie hugged him, careful not to bump the toad perched on his shoulder. She sat in the sand and pulled her little brother into her lap. "It's okay, bud."

Kip knelt beside them. "Not your fault, mate. Sister Ava modified the Frama-scope you gave him. He can't travel to alternate worlds anymore."

"Why would she do that?" he wailed. "I'll never see him again."

Winnie held him tighter. "You still have my dad, right? I'm happy to share."

He crawled away from her and cradled the toad in his arms. "You're my friend," he murmured to it.

"Now I feel like the worst sister in the world," she mumbled to Kip.

He kissed her cheek. "Nah, I'm the bounder. It should've been me giving Krell the—" His shell rang again. He made a bitter face. "Ooh. I'm almost afraid to answer." It rang again. He cleared his throat. "Kip here."

"You and the warrior in pink did it!" Eggar's excited voice sounded from the shell. "Is she with you?"

Winnie and Kip shared smiles. "She's right here."

"Everyone in Oram Forest thanks you. You stopped the invasion, just as it was foretold! Gran and I followed your progress with my truth stones."

She grinned and spoke toward the shell. "Just doing our jobs."

"We also have one more bit of news for you. Gran says there's a time tear starting to rise just behind our cottage. We hate to see you go, but if you must, the time tear will only be at the proper height for three hours before it rises out of reach."

Home! "Thanks, Eggar. We're on the way." Winnie pinched the shell. "Time to give Argamel that call."

Kip reluctantly contacted the king's conjurer. Instead of the man's distinctive baritone on the other end, two eager high-pitched voices, speaking in stereo, squealed through the shell. "General Windemere, we're planning a banquet in your honor."

Her honor? Her cheeks blazed with heat. "It was a group effort, Your Majesties," she said, borrowing Kip's phrase.

"Of course, our invitation extends to the conjurer's apprentice," spoke one princess.

"And General Takka," said the other.

"Thank you, Your Majesties," Kip said. "As much as we appreciate the gesture, we have to return to our world."

"Yeah, thanks," Winnie cut in. "Sorry we couldn't see you one more time."

"The reason I rang," Kip added, "was to see if Argamel could teleport us to Mistress Maven's cottage."

Kip hadn't even ended the call when Argamel appeared on the beach. He spread his arms. "Friends, the king and queen extend their deepest gratitude. Now, if you'll gather round, I will gladly return you to Mistress Maven." He rested one hand on Winnie's shoulder and the other on Mikey's back. Kip clasped hold of the man's sleeve on Winnie's side. "We'll take a bit of a detour first, but I promise the delay won't take long."

In an instant, all four stood in a row in a dimly lit room. Mikey on her left, Kip on her right, and Argamel at the end. They faced a dais with four thrones occupied by the royal family.

Chapter 33

The transition from sunny beach to dark chamber came as more of a shock to Kip than the instantaneous trip to reach the castle. When his eyes finally adjusted, he and the others stood in the company of the royal family. The regal king, wearing a plain gold circlet for a crown, sat on a throne to the right of the poised queen. Her gold crown resembled the king's except for the thin green vine intertwined with the gold. The identical princesses, seated on either side of their parents like a pair of bookends, also wore crowns. Theirs were made of delicate green vines braided into a circle.

"Visitors from a foreign world," the king said. "In two days, we intend to recognize and celebrate your heroism with a banquet and a parade."

Kip enjoyed banquets and parades as much as the next bloke, but time prevented them from participating. Rejecting a king, however, required diplomacy and tact, two qualities Winnie lacked. To prevent her from accidentally insulting the royal family, Kip bowed low. "Your Majesties, it is with utmost respect and gratitude that we thank you for this honor. It is with greater regret that we must humbly request your leave. We're scheduled to return to our home world within the next few hours."

The queen gracefully inclined her head. "We anticipated such a request from you and grant it. For that reason, we've invited you for a brief, private ceremony to receive the medals of honor each of you have earned."

Kip straightened to attention, hoping to cover his excitement with decorum.

The queen nodded to the princess on her right.

The girl, face aglow, stepped off the dais. An attendant followed, carrying a polished wooden box that he opened.

Princess Gwen, Kip presumed. The princesses looked so much alike he wasn't sure which was which until she stopped at Mikey.

"General Takka, I bestow upon you this small token." She removed a medal, attached to a red-and-white ribbon, from the box. She draped the ribbon over Mikey's head and kissed his cheek. "For returning me to my homeland." She placed a second medal around his neck and kissed his other cheek. "This is for restoring me."

She and the attendant moved toward Kip. His heart thudded hopefully. Had he earned an award as well?

"Apprentice Kip. I bestow upon you this small token." She slid the ribbon with a medal around his neck. "For preventing me from losing myself so I could safely enter stasis."

He bowed again.

By the ceremony's conclusion, two more ribbons hung from his neck. One from the queen for earning the trees' respect and one from the king for helping to prevent division between the island and mainland. Winnie also wore three ribbons. One from Princess Abbi for returning her sister to her, one from the king for winning the crown's respect, and another for fulfilling the prophecy. The royal family thanked them again, and after wishing them safe travels, Argamel transported them with their clinking medals to the bottom of the glow field.

"You were meant to take us to Mistress Maven," Kip reminded.

Argamel merely bowed and vanished.

Winnie nudged him to turn around. They'd been brought to Queen Luma, the ruler of the glow stones. Contrary to his initial understanding that they only lit up at night, the boulder glowed with dazzling brilliance.

Gentle beings. A soothing voice spoke inside his head. He supposed Winnie and Mikey also heard her. *It is with high regard that I welcome you one final time to this sacred space.*

Without prompting, Kip bowed to the glow-stone queen along with the others.

General Takka.

The little boy, with the enchanted toad still gripping his right shoulder, straightened his posture and stepped forward.

You have proven your greatness despite your small stature. We thank you.

He bowed and took a backward step to his proud sister's side. She bent and kissed his cheek. He grinned and wiped his face with the back of his hand.

Warrior Windemere.

To Kip's surprise her confidence seemed to wane. Then, acting more like the Winnie he knew, she stepped forward, shoulders back, head high.

You hold within yourself a fear that you didn't live up to the prophecy. Please release it. Your willingness to allow others to assist you brought you greater success than if you had fought alone. We thank you.

Had she worried about that? Kip never would have guessed.

One more thing, Windemere.

She froze mid-bow.

Now that your time of conflict has ended, your sword will resume its original shape. You may remove your warrior's belt.

"Thank you, Your Majesty." She bowed and stepped back. When she unsheathed her sword, it shrank to the size of a stone. She slid it into her pocket, unfastened the belt, and laid it on the ground. The leather strap dissolved into the grass.

Master Wizard.

Kip's Adam's apple bobbed, and his insides shook. He took a hesitant step forward.

Your increased magical ability nearly foiled you.

He ducked his head.

But you proved that you are a magical protector. For this, we thank you.

He lifted his head and, with a bright smile and a bow, joined Winnie and Mikey.

Gentle beings. We wish you continued success in your further travels. The white glow dimmed until the queen resembled a typical boulder.

A brisk hike through the glow-stone field and a trail brought them back to Mistress Maven's cottage.

Eggar burst onto the porch. "You restored the princess, and you protected the glow stones!"

He hugged Winnie, then Kip, clapping them on the backs.

"And we brought you this." Mikey held up the toad.

Eggar examined it. "Is this another enchantment?"

Kip grinned. "It's all right. He deserved it."

Winnie chuckled. "When you get a chance, tell the king that his traitorous high commander eats bugs now."

Eggar placed the toad-man next to a shrub beside the house. "We have plenty of bugs here. Please come in. Grandmère is waiting."

They filed into the cottage for another round of hugs from Mistress Maven. Kip and Mikey showed off their medals, allowing Winnie time to dash to the peg on the wall for her locket and Frama-scope. She added them to the collection of ribbons that hung around her neck.

"You'll find an opening to your world behind the cottage," Mistress Maven announced. "We wish you safe travels."

A tug of sorrow gripped his chest. Leaving new friends never got easier. They hugged one final time, then trooped outside.

He stood by as Winnie used her Frama-scope to locate the promised time tear. "Got it. It has those ridges like the opening had for Bird. I guess those are the Framas we'll pass through on the way home. Ready, guys? The tear's big enough for us to go in together, but stick close."

Kip lightly gripped her upper arm, allowing her to hold the scope to her right eye. Mikey clasped her left hand.

"Nobody let go," Kip said.

The time tear's invisible web wrapped around him with breath-stealing pressure. He closed his eyes, muscles tensed. Air whooshed around him, and the pressure released. He stumbled forward and landed on his knees in the damp sand facing his ocean. Home!

Mikey bumped into him from behind. Kip steadied him, then glanced left to right. "Where's Winnie?"

Chapter 34

Winnie opened her eyes to billowing fog. A female figure dressed in white stepped through the smokey atmosphere. As she drew closer, the woman's blond ponytail, sunny smile, and vibrant green eyes came into view.

Winnie squealed and galloped into the woman's open arms. "Mom!"

They hugged for a long moment. Mom held her at arm's length. "My sweet, sweet Windy." She kissed both her cheeks and her forehead.

Winnie laughed through her tears. "I thought I'd never see you again."

Mom grinned lovingly. "Not a chance. I saw what you did on Frama-7. You and Kip are quite the power duo. And look at all these medals!" She tugged at one.

Winnie laughed. "I have a million things to tell you!"

"I wish we could talk, but it'll worry the boys if you're gone too long. I brought you here for a quick hello." She kissed Winnie's cheek one last time. "And to tell you I love you."

"I love you too." She held tight, not wanting to let go.

"We'll meet again," Mom promised.

Winnie lurched from the time tear and onto the beach. Kip and Mikey sat on the sand, watching the tide roll in. Both twisted their necks toward her. Mikey sprang to his feet first, but Kip's longer legs reached her ahead of him.

"Why do we always lose you like that?"

She threw her arms around him, still grinning over her reunion with Mom. "It's good. We're home!"

Mikey tugged the back of her hoodie. "Bunny wants to see Frama-12. Can we take him there? Please?"

"Frama-12," Kip said playfully. "That takes me back."

Winnie gave him an annoyed side glance. She liked him a lot, but he could be so clueless when it came to Mikey's complicated citizenship between two worlds. "Let me think for a sec."

She scuffed through the sand to the shoreline. Gray waves splashed foam over her sneakers, but she barely noticed. If she said yes to a Frama-12 visit, her little brother might give up being Mikey forever. He'd already gotten a taste of his former self in stasis. But if she said no, wouldn't that make him want to go even more? He might even take her Frama-scope and go by himself. He'd borrowed it once before without permission.

How could she choose when both answers seemed wrong? She sucked in the sea air and let out a ragged breath. She breathed in again, slower this time. And out. On the third deliberate exhale, she marched back to Kip and Mikey, decision made.

She breathed in again for courage and stroked the back of Mikey's head. "Okay, bud, if we find a time bubble that opens to Frama-12, we'll go. But only for a visit. We can't stay."

Mikey pulled out his glow stone. He bounced up and down, singing to it. "We get to go. We get to go." He skipped a few yards away, still singing.

Winnie's ears popped just as Sister Ava appeared at her side. "I see by our dear general's celebration that you've agreed to return to Frama-12."

"Well, you know, he's my brother."

"Yes. And as it happens, we have a task for you while you're there."

"You do?" Winnie and Kip said in unison.

Sister Ava's smile wavered. "In our eagerness to prevent Thaddeus Krell from traveling to alternate worlds, my sisters and I forgot that he created a working time tear in his laboratory in this world. Thankfully, it only opens into Frama-12. I know you just got back, but we need you to go after him again."

"Blimey," Kip murmured. "He stole his original scope from the oracle on Frama-12. Do you think he'll try stealing another one?"

"He won't if you stop him. The time tear you need is by the gate to your backyard, Kip."

Mikey skipped back to them. "Sister Ava!"

"Hello, dear. And goodbye. Travel well." She vanished with a pop.

Kip took Winnie's hand. "Ready to give Frama-12 another go?"

She forced a smile. "Do we have a choice?"

Mikey clasped her other hand. "Yay! We're going home!"

A word about the author…

Aud Supplee, a reformed reluctant reader, started writing at a young age because she believed if she couldn't find the right book to read, she'd create her own. It wasn't until a college juvenile literature class that she realized she hadn't looked hard enough to find great fiction. She gained an ear for dialog early in life by listening to her mother and grandmother tell stories around the kitchen table. Her love of fantasy and alternate worlds came from reading The Hobbit as an adult and playing Dungeons and Dragons. She resides in Southeastern Pennsylvania with her husband, where they are currently raising three house plants. But it doesn't look good. Some of the leaves are turning yellow. You can visit her online at www.AudSupplee.com, where she blogs on the categories Live, Read, Write, which sum up her creative process.

~*~

Find Aud Supplee online at:
http://www.AudSupplee.com